GILLIAN POUCHER

AFTER

the

FUNERAL

RedDoor

Published by RedDoor
www.reddoorpublishing.com

ISBN 978-1-910453-76-6

A CIP catalogue record for this book is available from
the British Library

Cover design: Rawshock Design

Typesetting: Westchester Publishing Services

Printed and bound in Denmark by Nørhaven

To Neil and Alice with love

– CHAPTER 1 –

Julia stared down at the flowers. Among them lay a bouquet of mixed yellow and russet chrysanthemums which her mother would have hated. She had always said they were flowers for the dead. As of course they were today. Julia bent to look at the tribute card and read: 'To Emily. Love always. Linda.'

Julia hunched her shoulders inside her black trench coat against the biting January wind. The grief of the last nine days had numbed all other feelings and the sudden spark of curiosity triggered by the card was welcome. Who on earth was Linda? She had never heard her mother mention her.

She turned. The other mourners were standing a little apart from her, giving her space. The respectful murmurs were giving way to a rising volume of chat, sombre tones yielding to short bursts of laughter.

Julia spotted her half-brother, James, standing just outside the crematorium exit, waylaid by some family friends. She took a step in their direction, walking straight into the open arms of Edith, her mother's neighbour. The scent of camphor rose from the old woman's outdated double-breasted black fur coat as Julia submitted to the embrace. Unbidden the thought came that the coat must have had many outings: the focus of Edith's life in recent years had been funerals not only of those she knew well but also of passing acquaintances. The coat should be well-aired. It was the kind of mischievous remark her mother might have made, and Julia felt tears pricking at the back of her eyes even as a smile tugged her lips. 'Let it out, dear, just let it out,' the old woman encouraged, further threatening Julia's already shaky composure.

Over Edith's knobbly shoulder, Julia spotted someone she didn't recognise standing to the left of James, scanning the small groups. The woman was in late middle age with curly dyed chestnut hair straggling down the back of her purple coat. She had rouged cheeks and scarlet lips. Heavy use of eyeliner and old-fashioned green eye shadow drew attention to her large eyes which settled on Julia. She began to pick her way carefully over the icy paving stones in her high-heeled knee-length boots.

'You won't know me, but I feel I know you,' the woman began when she reached Julia's side. 'I got in touch with your mum through Genes Reunited. I found out I was her second cousin. Both our grandmothers were Thurstons, you see. We chatted on the phone, and I visited a few times. I was going to see her just before Christmas, but didn't get an answer when I rang. Then I saw the death notice in *The Herald* so I thought I'd come along today.' She smiled brightly, as though they had met at a party. 'My name's Linda.'

Julia stared at her speechlessly.

'I know it seems an odd place to meet for the first time,' the woman babbled on, 'but I'm sure you'll appreciate support from your family at a time like this, even if we don't know one another.' Her smile faded as Julia continued to gaze at her blankly. 'But with your mum telling me so much about you, I feel I know you already. She didn't mention me to you?' She didn't wait for a reply, forcing another smile. 'Of course she wouldn't have, why would she? But I'm so pleased to meet you, even under these sad circumstances.'

She placed a bony hand on Julia's arm and the younger woman resisted the temptation to shake it off. Each finger-nail was painted a different colour: red, purple, green, orange, black.

'I'm so sorry for your loss. I know you'll have so many people to speak to,' Linda continued, 'but I just wanted to introduce myself before you go to the reception. I won't go on there, as I don't know anyone. Well, except you now! I'm so pleased we've met. I'll be in touch soon, when things have settled down. Bye.'

'Who was that?' asked James, having detached him-self from the family friends, and looking towards Linda as she tottered away.

'Mother's second cousin apparently. She sent the chry-sants.' Julia pointed at the despised flowers. Her hand was shaking. 'She's called Linda. I've never heard of her. Have you?'

'No. You OK?'

'I think so. Just a bit much, the funeral and then this woman turning up. She said she found Mother through Genes Reunited.'

'Probably just lonely. Greg didn't show then, did he?'

She shook her head. Suddenly the tears spilled down her cheeks.

'Hey. It'll be OK.' James enveloped her in a brief hug.

'I just thought, whatever else has happened, today he would. . .' Julia swallowed and composed herself.

'I know, I know. And speaking of unwanted relations, here's Aunt Ada. Dying for years, but always manages to get herself wheeled out for a family funeral. Literally.'

'James!' In spite of everything, a bubble of laughter escaped Julia as she bent forward to take the hand Aunt Ada extended regally from her wheelchair.

'Always said Emily wasn't strong,' said the old woman. 'Still, I didn't expect to outlive her. I'm nearly four years older, you know.'

'Yes,' said Julia. 'I know.'

'Heart failure in the end, wasn't it? Not that she bothered to tell me. Hadn't heard from her for a while apart from her Christmas card.'

Julia bit her lip, but James couldn't resist. 'Had you tried to get in contact with Mother recently yourself, Aunt Ada?'

Ada flicked her heavy-lidded grey eyes towards him. 'I sent her a Christmas card myself.' She shifted her shrunken frame in the wheelchair, wincing. Julia grimaced in sympathy. 'I've not clapped eyes on either of you two since your party the summer before last.' She nodded in her niece's direction and licked her lips. Taking in the gesture, the hooded eyes and the wrinkled skin, Julia reflected that Aunt Ada looked more lizard-like than ever. She braced herself for the barb she knew would follow as a corner of the old woman's thin mouth rose in a sneer. 'For your engagement, wasn't it? Though I gather we shouldn't be expecting a wedding now, should we?'

James stepped in quickly as his blonde petite wife,

4

Clare, arrived at his side. 'Things don't always work out, do they, Aunt Ada? At least Julia hadn't actually got married before Greg left her for someone else.'

Clare broke in as Ada took one sharp intake of breath, then another. 'James, I think it's time we headed off to The Wingate, don't you? We're due at two.' Turning to Julia, she went on, 'Don't let her get to you, Jules. No wonder her husband left her all those years ago! Come on.' She placed a gloved hand on Julia's arm and steered her towards the car park.

Julia didn't know how she got through the reception. By turns it consisted of feigning interest in the progress of children she had never met, and fending off enquiries about Greg from distant relations who recalled his name from Christmas cards. In the frequent lulls in conversation with her relatives, she overheard snatches of discussion among her mother's friends. They seemed to be enjoying themselves, exchanging news of medical complaints, hospital appointments and funerals of their contemporaries. She deliberately avoided catching James's eye, knowing there was a risk that she might descend into hysteria on a day of such heightened emotion, even as tears threatened whenever she thought how much her mother would have taken quiet enjoyment from seeing all her family and friends together.

But it was difficult not to smile when Edith expressed her approval of the buffet. 'Very nice, very nice indeed. I always say The Wingate does the best buffet in town. Although I must say The Bird and Feathers has improved. I was there last month for Elsie Baxter. Or was it Doreen Platt?'

Aunt Ada, however, wasn't so impressed, complaining

that sausage rolls would have been preferable to vegetable samosas. 'You know what you're getting with a sausage roll. That's what you want, not this fancy food. Careful, girl! That's my bad foot you nearly knocked against the table!' The young Jewish carer from the residential home muttered an apology. She swerved the wheelchair round so quickly that the other foot was millimetres from colliding with the table leg, leading to further protests from the old woman.

As the last of the light faded from the grey January sky, Julia was relieved when James and Clare offered to see off the final guests so that she could return home. But as she parked her Mondeo on the street outside the two-bedroomed cottage which had been her home for six years, she wished she had stayed on at the hotel to the end.

Ignoring the chill which pervaded the car as soon as she switched off the engine, she contemplated the outline of the quaint cottage against the night sky. She had fallen in love with it on her first viewing and hadn't been put off by an adverse survey report. Soon after completing the purchase she had met Greg and he had moved in a year later. She still hadn't got used to coming home to an empty house since he had left five months ago. A familiar shroud of despair settled on her. This time she gave way to her tears, leaning her head against the steering-wheel, her slim body shaking.

She was roused by the faint sound of the phone ringing inside the cottage. Perhaps it was Greg after all, ringing to ask how the funeral had gone. By the time she had unlocked the front door and flicked the hall light on, the answerphone had clicked in. Whoever it was didn't leave a message. The flashing red light indicated there had been four previous calls. Julia pressed the button to retrieve any messages, but was greeted by silence followed by the buzz of a terminated call each time. No doubt whoever it was would call back.

She went through to the kitchen and listlessly ran water into the kettle. It was coming up to boil when the phone rang again. She took a steadying breath as she went out to the hall and picked up.

'Hello?'

There was a pause before a young-sounding female voice said, 'Hello. Is that – is that Julia Butler?'

'Yes. Julia Butler speaking.'

'Julia Butler, the counsellor?'

'That's right.'

'Oh.'

There was an interval before Julia spoke again, guessing from experience that the woman was a potential client. 'Can I help you?'

'I'm sorry. It's just I called earlier, and there was no reply, so I didn't expect you to answer. Sorry, I know that doesn't make sense.'

'It's OK,' said Julia gently. She took another breath, switching into professional gear. 'I know how difficult it can be to make that first phone call.'

'You do? Yes. Yes, it is.'

There was another silence before the woman spoke again. 'My name is Grace, Grace Hutton. My father died recently and, well, I've been struggling. Not that we were particularly close. My GP suggested counselling might help. So I wondered, if it might be possible – I've never been for counselling before – do you offer one-off appointments, just so I could see. . . ?'

Grace swallowed, and Julia sensed the effort it had taken for her to make contact.

'Yes, I do offer an initial appointment. That would give both of us the opportunity to see if we feel we could work together. I wonder if you think that might help, Grace? May I call you Grace?'

'Yes, of course. That would be good, an initial appointment. Thank you.'

Julia turned to her diary which she kept alongside the phone on the walnut bookcase. She had given herself a few more days off for compassionate leave. Her supervisor, Louise, had encouraged her to take more time when Julia rang to postpone her monthly appointment after her mother's death. But Julia felt that work would help her to cope with her present difficulties. She had always found it relatively easy to detach from her clients' issues. There was another consideration too: her financial situation meant she could ill afford to take extended leave. Not that Louise would view that as a reason to return to work if she wasn't fit.

Julia arranged a first meeting with Grace for the following Wednesday morning. After giving directions to her counselling office, she rang off and returned to the kitchen. She disliked the metallic taste of re-boiled water so she emptied the kettle and re-filled it, opting for fresh green leaves over tea bags. She wasn't sure how much longer she could justify the luxury of the expensive Chinese tea, but she found the ritual of preparing the brew soothing. And if ever she needed soothing, Julia thought, kicking off her black court shoes and going into the sitting room: it was tonight.

She set a match to the log fire she had laid that

morning and settled into her favourite brown leather arm-chair. She was watching the leaves of the tea unfurl into their flower in the glass teapot when the phone rang again. Thinking it might be Grace calling back, Julia stiffened when she heard the breathless voice at the other end.

'Hello. I hope I'm not disturbing you, Julia. It's Linda again. I just wanted to know how everything went at the reception. I thought I'd ring to let you know I was thinking about you.'

Julia searched for the words to end the call quickly without being rude. She wanted to ask, 'Who are you, and what do you want?' But it was hardly tactful, and she was always tactful.

'Julia?'

'I'm sorry. It's been a difficult day. The reception went as well as could be expected, thank you.'

'I am glad! These events can be so distressing. And I know you don't have much family, apart from your brother, and what with your partner leaving so recently, with what a terrible time you've been having, I rang to tell you you're not on your own. You aren't without support, Julia, that's what I wanted to say.'

Linda's knowledge of her split from Greg shocked Julia. Clearly she and her mother had grown close. How strange that her mother had never mentioned Linda. Perhaps she'd felt that the news of the new family member was insignificant as she provided a listening ear to her daughter struggling after her break up. It was soon after that Emily's heart failure had been diagnosed. She had begun to look increasingly frail and tired during the autumn. Christmas had been overshadowed with the unspoken thought that it would be her last.

Now Julia closed her eyes, inhaling deeply. Why on earth would this woman think she would look to her for support? 'Thank you, Linda. It's kind of you, but. . .'

'Not at all. Family is so important at times like this. . .'

But I didn't know you existed before today! thought Julia.

'. . . and so I wondered whether, to take your mind off things, you might like to join me next Wednesday when my exhibition opens in town? It would mean so much to me to have you there.'

'I'm not sure. . .' Julia stalled, but her curiosity was piqued. 'Your exhibition?'

'Yes. Just a few paintings. That's what I do. I'm an artist, not very well-known; you won't have heard of me. It would be so lovely if you could be there. I've never had family at an exhibition before.'

Julia hesitated a moment. She wasn't sure whether it was the easiest way of ending the conversation or whether her sympathetic nature responded to the longing in the other woman's voice, but she found herself accepting the invitation. She had promised herself that she would fill her leisure time as much as possible, fearful that if she spent too much time alone she would sink into despair. And whilst she wasn't drawn to Linda, in fact rather the opposite, she had never received a personal invitation from an artist to an exhibition before.

'Yes, I should be able to make that.'

'Oh, how wonderful! It's at seven o'clock at the gallery on Steep Hill. I could meet you before, if you like, or. . . ?'

'It might be a bit of a rush,' Julia responded quickly. 'What with work, and everything. I'll see you there. Seven on Wednesday. Bye for now.'

'Bye. Take care, Julia, and if you need a chat any time. . .'

'Thanks. I really must go now, Linda. Bye.' Julia hung up before returning to the sitting room and her cold green tea. She stood before the fire, looking at the sepia photograph on the mantelpiece of her mother as a young woman. 'Why didn't you tell me about Linda, Mum?' she asked. 'Who is she?' She jumped when a log shifted and cracked in a sudden burst of flames in the fireplace, and went across to flick on the TV. She never watched soap operas, but this evening she was grateful to immerse herself in the problems of fictional characters and escape her own.

***

An hour later, Julia started in her chair. From a distance she could hear someone calling. Then she realised it was her own voice, but the words were indistinct; mere sounds between gasping breaths.

She shivered as she surfaced into consciousness. The sitting room was cold, the fire burned to ashes. Fire. She had been trying to save someone from a fire. She sensed it would be better if she didn't recover the dream, if she pushed it away into the recesses of her mind, but the images and sounds crowded in. Her familiar sitting room seemed to be full of unwelcome and sinister visitors.

On the internal screen of her mind, more vivid than the burbling TV, Julia saw a woman framed at the upstairs window of an unfamiliar stone house. Flames leaped behind her. Somewhere a baby was screaming. Julia knew with the certainty that comes with dreams that the woman was the baby's mother. But the woman didn't move from the window. She stared out at the night from the burning house. There was a terrible vacancy in her expression. She seemed oblivious to the mortal danger threatening her and her child. Julia was shouting to her, trying to rouse her, to urge her to save herself and the baby.

Julia shook her head, trying to dispel the disturbing dream. The events of the day rushed back into her mind as she tried to focus her attention on the cookery programme that had followed the soap opera. She shuddered when the chef set light to his banana flambé and reached for the remote to turn off the TV. It was only nine o'clock but a hot bath and an early night beckoned after her traumatic day.

– CHAPTER 2 –

When Julia returned to work the following Wednesday, the board in the lobby indicated that only two of the other three tenants were in. She unlocked her mailbox. Most of the post that had accumulated during her three weeks' absence was junk mail. Two envelopes carried the logo of professional organisations, and she recognised the landlord's sprawling handwriting on a brown envelope.

Her footsteps echoed in the tiled passage as she made her way to her office. It was difficult to imagine that the Victorian building, a former school, had once been filled with children's voices. One of the fluorescent strip lights was unlit. Judging from the dust and muddy footprints along the floor, the cleaners hadn't been in since Christmas. The dimly lit corridor did nothing to lift her spirits.

Pete, the reflexologist, popped his shaved blonde head out of his door. 'Hi, Julia, how are you?'

'OK thanks.' She smiled at Pete and suppressed a yawn. The two of them were the only remaining original tenants. They were on friendly terms, but Julia wouldn't be confiding in him about her broken nights of sleep and the bouts of crying which seemed to come from nowhere.

'Glad you're back, it's been as quiet as the grave. I'm so sorry!' He clapped a hand to his mouth.

'Don't worry about it.' She forced another smile and changed the subject quickly. 'Any new tenants yet?'

'No. That's one of the things I wanted to mention. You'll have a letter there,' Pete nodded towards Julia's mail. 'Not good news. The landlord's decided he can't afford to keep the place on with those four offices empty for the last six months. He's planning to move in himself, convert to residential use. We'll have to find new offices. Hey, you sure you're OK?'

'Yes,' Julia gulped and wiped her right eye. 'New contact lenses,' she lied. She turned her head away.

There was a pause before Pete spoke again, weighing his words carefully. 'We've always got on well, you and me, haven't we Jules? Maybe we could look for somewhere together, set up a kind of complementary therapy centre?'

'Maybe. Sorry, Pete. Must go and sort out this lens. We'll talk again.' She hurried along to her room three doors along. Pete might be hurt by her non-committal response to his suggestion that they share premises, but her first priority was to compose herself before her new client arrived. Plus his casual abbreviation of her name always irritated her. She didn't mind close friends and family calling her 'Jules', but she didn't count Pete in that circle.

The office was cold after her time away. She turned on the electric fire and opened the blind. The bottom slat had been hanging at an angle since the summer and she hadn't attempted to repair it. Looking round the room after her break it struck Julia how dingy it looked. She hadn't redecorated since moving in. The arms of the beech Ikea chairs were scuffed and their beige cushions sagged. The edges of the cork noticeboard were thick with dust and she was shocked to see how out-of-date some of the publicity was. When had she last refreshed it? The smoking cessation classes had long since moved venue, the leisure centre timetable was from two years ago, and the drug addiction advisory service had closed down due to lack of funds. The poinsettia which a grateful client had given her before Christmas had shed its shrivelled leaves on the window sill.

Fingering the bereft leggy stem of the neglected poinsettia, recalling its vibrant red and green colouring, it occurred to Julia that the plant was a metaphor for how her life had been when she set up as a counsellor five years ago, compared to the present. After long years of training through evening classes and weekend courses, she had made the career change from teaching the year after she had bought the cottage, soon after Greg moved in. It had been a time of new beginnings. What a contrast to now! Tears pricked her eyes again. She took a tissue from the box placed strategically on the side table by the client's chair and wiped her eyes.

Pushing aside the question of whether she was fit to be counselling today, Julia went across to the filing cabinet to extract her form for new clients. The blind rattled as the wind whistled around the window, carrying the faint sound of the cathedral clock striking ten miles away across the city. On cue, the intercom buzzed. The new client spoke quietly.

'Hello. It's Grace, Grace Hutton. I have an appointment.'

'Hello, Grace. I'll buzz you through and meet you outside my office. Turn to the right through the lobby.'

As her client came into view, Julia saw that she was

older than she had expected from her rather high-pitched voice; somewhere in her early thirties. She was very slim with large blue eyes beneath finely arched brows. She glanced at Julia shyly as she advanced towards her, adjusting her heavy strawberry blonde plait over her right shoulder.

Julia greeted Grace with the reassuring smile which Greg used to call her 'counselling smile.' In the early days of their relationship he had teased her about it. But in an argument shortly before they separated he had said, 'Don't try your patronising smile on me, Julia. I'm not one of your clients who needs fixing.' The words had stung at the time, and as the recollection came to her now her smile faded. She hoped Grace didn't notice. Even here, after only half an hour back at work, she felt haunted by memories just as she had been during her leave. Greg and her mother flashed through her waking mind frequently. Both inhabited her dreams. She had found herself dwelling too on the encounter at the funeral with Linda. There was something unsettling about the woman, and she wasn't sure she had made the right decision in agreeing to attend her exhibition later that evening.

Ushering Grace into her office, Julia closed her eyes briefly, telling herself to focus on setting aside her own difficulties and put her new client at ease. She invited Grace to sit down and began to take the standard personal details.

The younger woman provided concise responses to the preliminary questions, rarely lifting her gaze from the clipboard on which Julia was writing. She remained perched on the edge of her seat, making no move to unbutton her grey and white checked tweed coat, although the heat from the radiator had permeated through the chill of the room. Having completed her form, Julia placed the clipboard on the table and invited Grace to say more about what had led her to contact her.

'Well. . .' Grace coiled the end of her plait around her long fingers.

'You mentioned on the phone that you lost your father recently?' Julia prompted gently.

'Yes. That's right.' Grace took a breath. She crossed her legs, their length accentuated by her skinny jeans, and tapped her left foot on the floor. She fixed her eyes on the worn grey carpet beneath Julia's chair.

Julia waited, knowing it was important for Grace to tell her story at her own pace.

The younger woman didn't look up. 'I'm sorry. I don't know if I can do this,' she said eventually. 'I'm not sure why I'm here, except that the doctor thought it might be a good idea.'

'You wouldn't have thought of coming yourself?'

'No. Counselling isn't something my family believe in.'

'So you feel you're letting your family down by being here? Perhaps your father in particular?' Julia hazarded.

Grace looked at her directly for the first time since entering the room. 'I suppose so. Yes, that's exactly what it feels like. I can't help thinking that Dad would have dis-approved. The rest of the family, well. . .' she shrugged, suggesting to Julia that their opinion didn't matter.

'His good opinion meant a lot to you, then?' Julia glanced at the form she had completed, and calculated that Grace was thirty-three. Age, she knew, didn't neces-sarily lessen parental influence.

'Yes.' Grace bowed her head. She uncrossed her legs

and traced a circle with the pointed toe of her right boot on the carpet. 'You see, it was just me and him for a while, when I was a little girl. And after what had happened, with my mother –' She broke off, before rushing on, 'It was seven years later that he met Frances, my step-mother. They married quickly, and then Suzanne was born.' She paused again.

'A lot of change for a little girl.'

'You could say that.' The right corner of Grace's full mouth curled.

'It must have been difficult for you to suddenly find yourself with a new mother and baby sister after so long alone with your father.'

'It was very difficult.' Grace spoke so softly that Julia barely heard her. There was another interval. Again Julia waited.

'Frances never liked me,' the younger woman burst out suddenly. 'Sometimes I think she hated me, she still does. She tried to turn my father against me. It was even worse after Suzanne was born. Frances made sure that they took all his attention, and she wouldn't even let me play with the baby, with Suzanne. It was like –' Grace broke off, searching for the right phrase. 'Like I might contaminate her.'

'Contaminate her?'

'Yes.' Grace stifled a sob and reached for a tissue from the box on the side table. 'As I grew older, I began to wonder if Frances was worried I might turn out like my mother.'

'You mentioned your mother before without telling me what happened to her,' Julia prompted.

'She nearly killed me,' Grace said bluntly. 'When I was

a baby, just a few months old. She set fire to our house one night when Dad was out. He came back just in time. My mother was certified and taken into psychiatric care. My father divorced her. We left Norfolk and came here to Lincolnshire. He changed our names. I never saw my mother again.' Her eyes were haunted as she concluded in a whisper, 'I don't know whether she's dead or alive.'

Julia exhaled slowly. She realised she had been holding her breath since Grace mentioned the fire. She had almost forgotten the nightmare from the evening of her mother's funeral. Now it flooded her mind. She saw again the woman at the first floor window, the flames leaping into the night sky, she heard the baby screaming in the background. No more than a strange coincidence she told herself, shuddering all the same. She struggled to find an adequate response. When she murmured, 'How terrible for you, Grace,' the words sounded hollow.

She tried to recover the thread of her client's earlier narrative. 'So when you say you wondered if Frances was worried you might turn out like your mother, you mean your step-mother was anxious in case you manifested symptoms of mental illness, might even harm the baby?'

'Yes.' Grace sat back in her chair, unbuttoning her coat, relaxing now she had told Julia the tragedy of her early life. 'I don't think Frances understood that my mother's condition might have been triggered by my birth. From the little Dad told me, I think she might have been suffering from postpartum psychosis. But Frances is a born-again Christian, and she's always been reluctant to accept psychiatric explanations. Dad converted as well when he met Frances. I mean, he'd been a Catholic before, but he became quite fundamentalist when he met Frances.'

She smiled briefly, a wry smile which didn't reach her cornflower eyes. 'Frances is much more likely to attribute psychiatric illnesses to demons,' she went on. 'And although Dad didn't agree with her on that, he did believe that any problems can be sorted out by prayer, that it's a kind of weakness to look for help away from God.'

'I see.' Julia recalled Grace's earlier words, '*Counselling isn't something my family believe in*,' and her sense that her step-mother feared that she might 'contaminate' her half-sister. 'So am I right in thinking that your hesitation about counselling has come from growing up in this atmosphere? I'm wondering whether, as an impressionable young girl when your father remarried, you might have absorbed some of these beliefs? Maybe it seems a weakness to you to be here?'

There was a long pause as Grace considered Julia's suggestion. 'I think so, yes.' She balled up the tissue in her hand. 'I know how strange it sounds,' she went on, 'but when you've grown up like that, thinking you're somehow. . .' she groped for the word, '*tainted*, because of your mother's illness, because of something she couldn't help, you begin to believe it might be true. And with Dad becoming so absorbed with Frances and Suzanne, I suppose I felt. . .'

'You did feel "tainted"?' Julia asked as Grace wiped the tears from her cheeks.

Grace swallowed and nodded. 'Yes, I suppose so. And I always hoped that when I grew up, Dad and I would be close again, like when I was little. But it didn't happen. He didn't seem interested in me, didn't even bother to come to my Masters graduation last year. I thought he might be interested in what I was studying, the psychohistory of the Reformation. That's what I'm researching now, in more depth, for my PhD. It related to his faith journey in some ways, from Catholic to Protestant. But no, it was all Suzanne this, Suzanne that.' She took a deep breath, looking up at Julia with a half-smile. 'I'm sorry. I sound like a jealous child, don't I?'

Julia allowed a beat to pass. Then she suggested softly, 'Or perhaps a girl who misses her father very much, and has missed him for a long time?'

Grace gazed at Julia in silence, her lips slightly parted. She seemed to be drinking in Julia's words, like parched land soaking up the first raindrops after a drought. She bent her head as a ray of weak January sunlight filtered through the blind, setting her strawberry blonde hair alight. Julia shivered, the image of the burning house with the woman framed at the window reignited in her mind.

After a few moments Grace looked up. Her eyes were bright with unshed tears, but there was a new calmness about her. Julia glanced up at the clock on the wall behind her head. It was nearly time to end the session, but her client's reference to her research had attracted her attention. James was a history lecturer at the university and she should make an effort to avoid any potential conflict of interest in accordance with professional guidelines.

'You mentioned earlier that you were still studying after finishing your Masters last year. Are you working towards your PhD now?'

'Yes.' Grace's lip curled into her ironic half-smile again. 'You might think my background has contributed to the topic for my thesis. I'm still pursuing a psychohistorical study during the Reformation, but this time I'm concentrating on the relationship between Mary Tudor and Elizabeth I. Half-sisters, as you probably know.'

'I can see how you might find that interesting.' Julia smiled back. 'I'm guessing it might be tricky to supervise, since it crosses disciplines?' she asked.

'Yes.' Grace laughed, her face shining with enthusiasm. 'The university couldn't decide whether to appoint a psychology or history lecturer as lead supervisor to begin with, but eventually they settled on Professor Evershed from the Psychology Department. He's done a little psychohistorical work around the First World War. I'll have a few tutorials with the Tudor History lecturer as well, but Professor Evershed will supervise. And of course at PhD level, most of the research is self-directed.'

'I see.' James was a mediaeval specialist. He often described himself as knowing nothing after the battle of Bosworth Field in 1485 when Henry Tudor had killed Richard III.

Buoyed by the inner glow which came when she sensed an instant connection with a new client, Julia decided not to pursue the question of a potential conflict of interest further. 'We're nearly out of time today, Grace,' she said gently. 'How would you feel about coming back again at the same time next week?'

Her client didn't hesitate before replying. 'Yes, please,' she said. 'I'd like that very much.'

– CHAPTER 3 –

The cathedral clock was striking seven when Julia arrived at Linda's exhibition that evening. The whitewashed gallery was located in the renovated crypt of a disused church on the hill which linked the cathedral quarter with the city's main shopping area. She had passed it many times without venturing inside. Now she picked her way carefully down the uneven stone steps from the pavement, shaking the rain from her black umbrella before pushing open the heavy oak door.

Glancing around as she unbuttoned her coat, Julia estimated that there were around thirty people in the gallery. She spotted Linda chatting with a middle-aged couple to her right. The artist was wearing a purple and green striped dress, a lilac wrap around her shoulders. Her back was turned to Julia who sighed with relief, registering how little she had been looking forward to seeing the new family member again.

Taking a glass of white wine from a tray by the door, Julia slipped through an archway opposite the entrance. She decided to spend a few minutes in the quiet inner area before saying a few words to Linda and making her escape. She would then have fulfilled her rash commitment to her newly-discovered relative. Commitment. Duty. Obligation.

Principles she lived her life by, as Greg had pointed out during one of the arguments which she later identified as marking the beginning of the end of their relationship.

Julia glanced unseeingly at the pictures in the inner gallery, trying to dispel the image which rose before her. Greg had been chopping vegetables for ratatouille, spitting the words at her: 'Commitment. Duty. Obligation. Those are your rules. Your code, not mine. I'm not going to James and Clare's for dinner, whatever you agreed, because I can't stand another bloody night listening to her going on and on about IVF and you doing your counsellor thing with her. I'm staying here and watching the football. End of.'

She had stood there stunned into speechlessness. He was dicing red pepper at furious speed, and she felt as though each slice was a stab at her and their relationship. Eventually she said, 'I didn't know you felt like that about Clare talking about her IVF.'

Greg stopped cutting and laid the knife down by the wooden chopping board. He didn't raise his eyes as he said slowly and deliberately, as if interpreting a foreign language, 'You don't know what I feel about a lot of things because you never ask, do you? You're too busy sorting out other people's lives to think about what *I* want.'

The silence stretched between them, taut as an elastic band pulled to its limit.

'What do you mean? What is it you want?' Julia asked finally, stooping to pick up some onion peel from the floor.

'Nothing. Forget it. Leave that, I can tidy up. You'll be late for James and Clare.' He picked up the knife again and set about the courgette, dissecting it with a calm precision which made her shiver. She left without saying anything further.

When she returned after 11 p.m., Greg seemed in a better frame of mind. Exhausted by a day's work, the earlier argument, and comforting Clare who had been very tearful after a second failed IVF attempt, Julia hadn't pursued his comments that night. Greg didn't raise the matter again. But even though Julia knew that it was futile to speculate, she had wondered many times since if she should have asked him what he meant, if somehow that might have salvaged their relationship.

Now she shook her head, trying to erase the memory. She sipped her wine and focused on the large painting opposite the archway which drew her eye. A grey farmhouse stood under a leaden sky. The building looked vaguely familiar, but Julia couldn't place it. Behind the farmhouse, obscured by slanting white rain, was the shadowy outline of a ruined abbey. Four other people who had followed her into the inner area of the gallery stopped in front of it.

'That's reminiscent of her early work,' remarked a burly ruddy-cheeked man in an olive green Barbour jacket.

'Very much so,' agreed the woman alongside him, elegant in a grey dress and matching coat which complemented her carefully coiffed silver hair. 'That Gothic atmosphere.' The woman turned to the other couple, and they began a discussion of the change in Linda's style over the years. With a start, Julia realised that Linda must be a well-established artist, however modest she had sounded in their phone conversation. *I'm an artist, not very well-known; you won't have heard of me.* Her curiosity about her recently discovered relative grew, despite her misgivings.

Other people were moving into the inner area as she stepped to the left of the group. A series of four small oils in black frames hung here, showing a heavy white wooden door surrounded by a trellis of roses. Julia stopped suddenly in front of them, spilling wine over the edge of her glass. In the first picture the door was closed, before being progressively opened in the following paintings. The fourth picture revealed a white-haired old woman dozing in a rocking chair. She was in shadow, so it was impossible to identify her. But Julia didn't need Linda to tell her who it was when the older woman materialised at her side in a waft of jasmine. Julia closed her eyes. Jasmine. Her mother's perfume. She swallowed.

'I do hope you like that, Julia. You do recognise it, don't you? Oh, I can see you do! It was so kind of Emily to let me paint her, it took hours, and she sat so patiently. Though as you can see, she sometimes dropped off. We had such a lovely August, didn't we? I thought it was the heat that made her sleep so much, but I wondered afterwards if it was her heart condition. She only mentioned it once. She didn't like a fuss, did she?'

'No, she didn't.' Julia paused, puzzling again over her mother's failure to mention Linda. 'How often did you say you visited?'

'I couldn't say. Often enough that I miss her now.' Linda gazed at her with such intensity that Julia looked away, but not before seeing that the other woman's hazel eyes were glistening with tears. Linda rushed on, 'I didn't see her very often, but she did like to chat when I was there. She used to tell me about how busy you and James were, and talk about what she remembered of our family. She enjoyed reminiscing, but so do lots of older people, don't they?'

A flush rose above the shawl collar of Julia's pink and grey wool dress as she remembered the number of occasions she would steer her mother on to other subjects when she recounted anecdotes from her early years. She had tended to do so more frequently in her last months. Perhaps Linda's appearance had sparked Emily's memories.

Linda was speaking again, but Julia was still mulling over her previous comment, 'She used to tell me about how busy you and James were.' Was that why Emily hadn't told them about Linda? Since her mother's death, Julia had realised how preoccupied she had been with her own problems when her mother's health was failing. It was soon after Greg left in August that Emily's heart failure had been diagnosed, but she hadn't discussed it in any detail, dismissing it as 'one of those things.'

Gazing at the painting of the old woman in the rocking chair, Linda babbling on beside her, Julia remembered again the pang she had felt when she read on the Death Certificate, 'Stress cardiomyopathy.' The doctor had explained that her mother's heart failure had been more advanced than she had admitted. But when Julia researched stress cardiomyopathy she discovered that the condition was caused by the weakening of the heart muscle due to intense physical or emotional stress. She had wondered if the shock of her separation from Greg had accelerated her mother's death. Perhaps it was self-centred to think that her own difficulties could have caused such upset to her mother, but Emily had been fond of Greg and very concerned for Julia after their split.

Linda laid a hand on her arm, the multi-coloured nails freshly painted, recalling her to the present. She had stopped speaking and was evidently waiting for a response.

'I'm sorry.' Julia's cheeks burned again. 'I was miles away.'

'Of course, these paintings must bring back so many memories for you!' Linda tightened her grip on Julia's arm, drawing her towards her in an awkward embrace. Julia stiffened. The other woman released her immediately, turning to the paintings and not meeting her eye as she continued. 'I was just saying how I would love you to have these. You'll see they aren't priced. That's because I was keeping them for you. They would mean more to you than they could to anyone else. I so want to keep them in our family.'

'Oh, I couldn't. . .' began Julia. 'It's so kind, but you hardly know me.' She found she wanted to reinforce this point. Linda's talk about 'our family' set her teeth on edge. 'Besides, I don't know anything about art. I can see they are very good though.' She had overheard various people behind them murmuring their appreciation of the Open Door series during their conversation.

'Please, Julia, do say you'll have them. It's only right you should.' Linda turned back to her, hazel eyes wide and beseeching.

'Well. . .' Julia was casting around for a reply as the loud voice of the photographer from the local county magazine permeated the hum of conversation.

'There you are, Linda! Just come to take a few pics before I go to the hospice dinner dance!' For a moment the gallery fell quiet as people looked at him askance. He swept towards them, a tall, ungainly figure in an oversized navy waterproof, showering the wooden floor with raindrops. The buzz resumed.

'Hello, Chris.' Linda smiled at the young man warmly. 'It's good of you to come.'

'Can't miss an opportunity to publicise the most famous artist in town at the moment, can I? This damn rain, can't see a thing!' Chris removed his black framed specs, misted over in the warmth of the gallery, and groped around in numerous pockets before withdrawing a packet of tissues. He wiped his glasses vigorously, peering near-sightedly around. 'Now, where shall I take you – maybe over here, no glare from the light, lots of people milling in the background?' He indicated a spot to the right of the archway leading back into the outer area.

'Wherever you think.' Linda shrugged. 'Chris, let me introduce my cousin, Julia. I'd like her to be in the photos with me. We only met very recently. I knew her mother, though. These paintings are of her front door. And finally of her.' She waved a hand at the final painting. Julia noticed a shadow pass across her face. She shut out the uncharitable thought that Linda had no right to miss her mother so much.

'Cool,' said Chris. 'Long-lost family story, that'll add a bit of interest to the piece. If you stand right next to Linda, Julia. . .' He busied himself with the camera.

Julia opened her mouth to protest, but again Linda placed a hand on her arm, steering her towards the archway. 'This is so lovely, Julia. To have you in the photo, the first time I've had family with me at an exhibition!' She adjusted her lilac wrap and flung an arm round the other woman's shoulder. Julia resisted the impulse to draw away, forcing a smile.

'That's it, just relax,' said Chris. Julia tried not to blink as he snapped away. 'Great! I'm done. Hey, there is a family likeness you know, both the same heart-shaped faces, similar upturned noses too. How did you say you found one another, then?'

'It was Genes Reunited. . .' Linda began, as Julia moved away to look at some of the other paintings. She swayed slightly and wished she had had time to eat before coming to the gallery. The alcohol on an empty stomach had made her tipsy.

Curiosity about Linda and her relationship with her mother was beginning to outweigh her sense of unease about the older woman. Besides, she reasoned, her disquiet might have been exaggerated by Linda turning up so unexpectedly at the funeral. She hoped that they might have a further opportunity for conversation that evening, and decided not to rush home after all.

To her right the couple who had identified the farmhouse painting as consistent with the Gothic atmosphere of Linda's early work were contrasting it with the Open Door series.

'Such a sense of peace,' breathed the woman. 'So different from that sinister mood earlier on.'

'Quite a transformation,' agreed her husband.

'You wonder, don't you,' mused the woman, 'about how much one's own experiences are reflected in one's art? I wonder if she has moved on herself, from a more –' she circled her right hand, seeking the word, '– a more *disturbed* state to one of serenity? Remember those first paintings we saw of hers, in that little gallery on the Norfolk coast, all those years ago?'

'Ugh.' Her husband wrinkled his bulbous nose. 'Those the critics described as a feminist revolt against traditional Madonna and child images?'

'Exactly, full of blood and suffering, Jesus ripped from Mary's womb, or holding a knife above her heart, flames leaping around them. Very controversial. But maybe they were expressing the artist's inner torment. Maybe now, as she gets older, she's accepting who she is, like this old woman, so at peace. Whoever she is.' She nodded towards the final painting.

Julia took a deep breath. 'Excuse me,' she said, keeping her voice as level as she could. She placed her left hand over her right on the stem of the now empty wine glass, trying in vain to still the trembling.

'Yes?' The woman turned to her, plucked eyebrows raised.

'That "old woman" was my mother.'

'Oh.' The woman looked away, a faint flush on her cheeks.

'Yes,' continued Julia. 'She died six weeks ago.'

'Oh,' said the woman again, fingering her pearl necklace. 'I'm sorry,' she muttered lamely. Her husband placed his hand in the small of her back and steered her towards the archway.

Left alone in front of the Open Door paintings, Julia reached inside her coat pocket for a tissue, scrubbing at her cheeks and hoping her mascara hadn't run. She knew she was being irrational to resent the woman speaking so impersonally about her mother. She had successfully locked away her grief during her first day back at work. It had been a shaky start when Pete told her about the landlord terminating their lease, but she had managed to remain focused during her first appointment with Grace and throughout her other three sessions. Now, standing in the nearly deserted gallery, the sadness and loneliness which had affected her since Emily's death threatened to overwhelm her.

Suddenly Linda was at her side, hazel eyes wide with sympathy. 'Julia, what is it? Is it the paintings? I'm so sorry, I never thought how much they might upset you. So insensitive of me.'

'No, it was just something someone said.' Julia tried to smile, aware that she couldn't deal with Linda's sympathy. Nor did she want to witness any further sign of distress at Emily's death from her newly-discovered cousin. Linda couldn't begin to understand what her mother's loss meant to her.

'I am so sorry,' Linda repeated. She stepped closer to Julia. Fearful of another attempt at an embrace, the younger woman took a step backwards. Linda seemed not to notice. 'I was wondering, have you eaten yet?'

Julia shook her head.

'Well, let me treat you to dinner at the Italian around the corner. Everyone's left now and it's time we closed. I'd been planning to ask you to join me, a kind of celebration of the exhibition and seeing you again. Oh, I can't tell you how much it's meant to have you here!' Again Linda placed a hand on Julia's arm, smiling warmly, nudging her towards the door.

Julia didn't have the strength to resist. Besides, she had already refused the paintings, and hunger might be contributing to her low mood. Interest in her new artist relation edged out her sense of being overpowered by the older woman as Linda locked the gallery and they stepped out into the wet and windy January night.

– CHAPTER 4 –

Julia hadn't been to Giuseppe's before. It was tucked away along an alley towards the cathedral. The quarter hour chimed above them as they paused on the corner below an unlit street lamp. Both were breathless from the climb up the well-named Steep Hill. The cobbles were slippery with sleet, and they were walking into the wind. Linda led the way into the dark passage. Julia shook off a moment's misgiving as she followed.

A 'To Let' sign creaked above Julia's head as she stopped outside an empty shop with boarded windows. Her umbrella had turned inside out in the wind. She jumped when a bundle stirred on the doorstep. A man's voice rasped, 'Any spare change?' She moved on quickly, nearly bumping into Linda who halted, rummaging around in her bag. Julia didn't look back, focusing on the pool of light spilling out on to the cobbles a few doors further on. She hoped it was the restaurant, where they could take refuge from the hostile weather and dingy street. Behind her, she heard the man's, 'God bless, duck,' and Linda's warm reply, 'And you!'

Alongside her again, Linda lowered her voice, 'I always think, "There but for the grace of God," don't you? I know not everyone does, that people worry what the money might be spent on, or talk about the few who aren't genuine, but who knows where we might be if our circumstances were different. Do you ever think that, Julia?'

'Well, I. . .' Still battling with her umbrella, Julia was assailed by another memory of Greg, pulling her on past a rough sleeper when she had been reaching into her pocket for some coins. *'Come on, Julia, we'll be late for the film. Most of them are frauds anyway!'* Seeing her expression, he had smiled, tempering his words. *'But, of course, you being a do-gooder, not a cynic like me. . .'* He had left the sentence unfinished and patted her head, still smiling. She had smiled back, even though she had felt patronised by the gesture. That had been in the early days of their relationship, the golden time when she had ignored any misgivings about Greg, caught up in the whirlwind romance as he lavished flowers and chocolates upon her.

Thinking back, Julia realised that she had never given spontaneously since, preferring to organise her charitable giving through her bank account. She wondered how much Greg had influenced her during their years together. Had he changed her?

'Here we are!' Linda interrupted Julia's thoughts, pushing open a low black wooden door. 'I'm sure you'll love Giuseppe's, Julia. It's one of those magical places where you think everything will turn out well, whatever's wrong, you know?'

Julia bit back the tart reply that it *would* take magic for her life to turn out well at present. Inside the doorway, Linda was looking round at her expectantly. Julia was spared the need to answer when a man in black evening dress emerged from behind the bar. *'Signora* Linda!' he beamed, kissing her on both cheeks. 'How did the exhibition go? And you must be Linda's cousin!' He turned to Julia. She froze momentarily, her umbrella extended in front of her on the doorstep, water trickling on to the terracotta tiles. How did he know she would be here this evening? She turned to Linda, eyebrows raised.

'Oh, I was so excited that you were coming to the exhibition, Julia! I told Giuseppe all about finding you and Emily when I booked, how much it means to me to have found my family.'

Julia prickled again at the mention of 'family,' and at the presumption that she would accept Linda's invitation. 'I see,' she said, in a tone which matched the weather.

Advancing inside the low-ceilinged restaurant with its yellow walls, Julia felt she might be overpowered by the sudden heat from the log fire and flaming brazier where the stout red-faced chef stabbed at a pizza. The mingled odours of cheese and garlic nauseated her. *What was she doing here*? She closed her eyes, momentarily dizzy. For the third time that evening, Linda laid a hand on her arm. Struck by another memory of her mother along with a fresh waft of the older woman's jasmine perfume, she clutched the back of a chair.

'Are you all right, Julia? It must have been a long day, your first day back at work since Emily. . . and of course you've not eaten. Have you given me my usual table by the window, Giuseppe?' When the Italian nodded, she led Julia over to a square table laid for two and helped her remove her coat. Julia sat down, smiling her thanks when Linda returned from hanging their coats on a mahogany stand by the door. The small leaded window was misty with condensation, adding to her claustrophobia.

As she sipped the glass of water brought over by a

concerned Giuseppe, it occurred to her again how little she knew about Linda. The other woman seemed to know so much more about her. Despite the warmth, she shivered.

'Oh, I do hope you're not coming down with something, Julia! There are so many infections around at the moment. I wonder if you're running a temperature?' Linda leaned across the table, placing a cool palm on Julia's forehead, as her mother used to when she was a child. But this was not her mother. Julia shrank back into the bent-wood chair, blinking back the tears which were always near in these early weeks of grief.

To escape the older woman's scrutiny, she opened her black handbag and bent her head over it, making a show of checking for her purse and house keys. When she glanced up, Linda was still looking at her solicitously. Julia smiled weakly and reached for the menu. 'Just hungry, I expect. What would you recommend?'

'Everything I've ever tried here is so good!' enthused Linda. 'If you like seafood, I'd recommend the *linguine ai frutti di mare*, but the Bolognese is one of the best I've ever tasted, and the butternut squash risotto is delicious, creamy without being heavy. And the pizzas, well, what can I say? I'll order wine, I usually have the Chianti, would you like that?' Without giving Julia time to reply, she requested a bottle from Giuseppe.

When the proprietor brought the wine over, the women ordered their food. By the time their meals arrived on bright yellow plates edged with an intricate pattern of olives, they had consumed over half the bottle. Julia, usually a light drinker, knew that she was using the alcohol to relax. There was still something about Linda – her constant chatter, her concern to establish their family connection, her repeated references to Emily – which she found disquieting. But the other woman also challenged her with her optimism, her generosity, and maybe that was a good thing. The incident with the rough sleeper had reminded her how she used to be before she met Greg. She had been more open, less wary. Recognising these qualities in the older woman, she found herself growing wistful.

As they ate the food which was as excellent as she had promised, Linda spoke again about how much she had enjoyed visiting Emily in the summer and how delighted she had been when Emily agreed she could paint her. Julia wished they could talk about something else. It pained her to think that her mother had kept the visits to herself. Presumably she had thought Julia was too wrapped up with her own problems at the time to be interested in the news of the recently discovered cousin. But from what James had said at the funeral, their mother hadn't mentioned Linda's visits to him either, which seemed odd, unless Emily had simply been preoccupied with her own deteriorating health.

As if she could read her thoughts, Linda turned the subject to Julia's half-brother. 'I'd love to meet James properly some time, Julia, if you could arrange that? Did you mention me to him last week, after we met?'

'Yes.' Julia picked up the opportunity to find out more about her new relation. 'So, do you have any brothers or sisters, Linda, any more cousins we don't know about?'

For the first time since they met, Julia saw Linda's face close down, her usual animation drain away. She suddenly looked much older, the wrinkles around her eyes accentuated in the flickering light from the candle between them. 'No.' She paused. 'Well, not full blood siblings, anyway.'

'Oh?' Julia was struck by the choice of words, sensing at the same time that she should tread carefully. She hoped her questioning tone might prompt a response as it so often did in her counselling room. But they were interrupted by Giuseppe, who glided over to check that everything was satisfactory. Linda's face brightened again as she complimented him on the food.

After the proprietor had moved away, Linda took over the conversation, turning the focus back on Julia. 'I'm sure you must miss Emily dreadfully. How are you getting on, really? With Greg leaving so recently too, you've had such a difficult time, haven't you?'

Julia didn't refuse more wine as Linda reached over to top up her glass again, draining the bottle. She found that for the first time in months she was rather enjoying herself in the cosy restaurant. She could see what the older woman meant about the mood-enhancing quality of Giuseppe's. Taking a deep breath, she began to speak more openly to her new relative. She acknowledged what a shock it had been when Greg left. But when she admitted how much she missed her mother, she stopped mid-sentence as she saw Linda's eyes misting over.

Suddenly the older woman was sobbing, 'I miss her so much too. We'd grown so close.' She lay down her knife and reached her right hand across the table, seeking Julia's. Julia pretended she didn't notice, concentrating on loading the final grains of risotto on to her fork. Something twisted in her chest, reminding her of a feeling she'd had as a child when her infant half-brother had toddled into her bedroom and grabbed her favourite teddy bear. '*It's mine!*' she had shouted when her mother remonstrated with her for making a fuss. '*It's my teddy!*'

Now she raised the fork to her mouth, staring at Linda whose shoulders were shaking. She spoke very slowly before taking her last mouthful. 'But she was *my* mother, Linda. Surely you understand I must miss her more than you?'

As soon she had spoken, she bit her lower lip, ashamed of how childish her words sounded. But it was too late to unsay them. Tears continued to pour down Linda's cheeks, tracks of black mascara in their wake. After a long moment she gasped out, 'You don't understand. Now isn't the time to explain about our family. I don't want to upset you, to shock you, not with everything else you're dealing with.'

'What do you mean, "our family"?' Julia lowered her voice as the couple two tables away turned to look at them. Giuseppe cast an anxious glance in their direction. She inhaled, lining her cutlery up on her empty plate. She wanted to clear this up, to establish some distance, even as she knew that the alcohol was making her more confrontational than usual. 'I'm sorry, Linda, but we're only distant cousins. Isn't "our family" stretching it a bit?'

The older woman reached inside her colourful jacquard bag for a tissue. She massaged her temples. 'No,' she said quietly. 'No, I don't think it is. But I really can't explain tonight. One of my headaches is starting. I've been having them a lot recently. I'm sorry. Now, please let me settle the bill. This is my treat. It really was lovely to have you at the exhibition. Thank you so much for coming.'

Julia was shocked by the speed of her dismissal. She opened her mouth to insist on paying her share and to push Linda further to tell her what she knew about 'our family.' But taking in her companion's strained white face and swollen eyes, she held back. She had already refused the paintings and didn't want to be ungracious. 'Thank you,' she said. 'That's very kind of you. I'll head off now. I've got an early start tomorrow.'

Linda nodded. 'I'll be in touch, Julia.'

Julia shivered as she took her coat from the stand by the door. A young couple entering the restaurant had let in a blast of cold air, but Linda's promise of further contact had also chilled her. Giuseppe came across to help her into her coat, expressing his delight at meeting her and the hope that she would soon return with '*Signora* Linda.' But he was not smiling as widely as he had when they arrived, and she put this down to his having witnessed Linda's distress a few moments earlier.

She paused with her handle on the door, looking back to acknowledge Linda one last time. But the older woman was looking down into her empty wine glass, her right hand still pressed to her forehead. She really didn't look well. Julia briefly contemplated going back to see if she could help her find a taxi. Then, thinking how Linda had dismissed her, and how drained she was herself, she decided against the idea.

Out in the alley, the sleet had stopped and the wind had dropped, leaving behind an eerie stillness. Julia wondered if it might snow as she turned right along the alley, away from the hill up to the cathedral. She calculated she would come out on another street which she knew circled back round to the church. It would add an extra five minutes to the walk home, but she had no wish to pass the rough sleeper again. It wasn't that she was afraid that he would harm her; she simply didn't want to encounter the evidence of human misery again.

Treading carefully over the glistening cobbles, she chided herself for her weakness, but this long day had shown her how fragile she was following her mother's death. The news that her landlord was terminating the lease of her office had thrown her more than she would have expected, and she didn't feel she had coped well with Linda.

She emerged from the alley and turned up the well-lit street towards the cathedral, mulling over the second encounter with her cousin. In the back of her mind, something Linda had said was niggling her, something besides those irritating references to 'our family.' As a professional listener, Julia had an accurate recollection of conversations. Hunched inside her trench coat against the cold as the warming effects of the wine wore off, she replayed the last few minutes of their conversation.

Now the cathedral loomed above her, its precincts deserted on the cold night. She paused for a moment, gazing up at it. It never ceased to astonish her, this magnificent nine-hundred-year-old Norman church. She started as the first stroke of ten boomed out. It carried with it the memory of Linda's unsettling words. They ran over and over in her mind, magnified with each stroke of the cathedral bell: *'Now isn't the time to explain about our family. I don't want to upset you, to shock you, not with everything else you're dealing with.'*

Turning away from the cathedral, she picked up her pace. She was almost running, sliding on the icy paving stones, trying to escape that last dong of the bell which reverberated in her mind along with Linda's words. What had the woman meant? What could there possibly be in their family history which might upset or shock her? Wouldn't her mother have told her?

Groping in her bag for her key as she reached the cottage, Julia shivered as the first snowflakes fell. One settled on her ear like a whisper, echoing the murmur of the thought that here was the reason for Emily's silence about Linda. The artist carried with her a disturbing family secret. Julia shook her head, trying to dispel her anxiety with the snowflake. But the unsettling thought refused to be dislodged, a troublesome companion during another sleepless night.

– CHAPTER 5 –

The knocking grew louder, more urgent. Julia opened her mouth to shout, to scream, but no sound came. Surely everyone else could hear? Didn't they realise what was happening? Why was the vicar pulling the cord, closing the curtains? Standing next to the coffin, he *must* be able to hear. Despite the pounding, he continued his steady intonation, 'Earth to earth, ashes to ashes. . .'

She tried to move, to run forward before it was too late. Why wouldn't her legs respond? She could feel them twitching, but that was all. Then a voice broke through the banging. It was muffled, but she could make out her name: 'Julia! Julia!' Gradually she realised it wasn't her mother, shouting to her to come to her rescue before the coffin rolled into the furnace. It was Greg. Greg? That couldn't be right. He wasn't there, unless he'd slipped in late. She'd scanned the congregation as she processed in behind the coffin. She turned her head to check and met something soft beneath it. Her pillow. Gasping for breath, heart pounding, she surfaced into consciousness.

Disoriented by the nightmare, it took a moment for Julia to realise that the knocking was real. Someone was rapping on the front door. It *was* Greg calling her name. She didn't move immediately, trying to separate reality from her dream world. She must have overslept, because there was too much light percolating through the curtains for a January morning. What day was it? What was Greg doing here? Slowly she sat up, pushing a strand of hair out of her eyes, her pulse still racing. She reached for the alarm clock on the bedside table and was shocked to see it was 9.35 a.m. In a rush she remembered: it was Saturday, the day Greg had arranged to call to collect the rest of his belongings.

'Damn!' Julia padded over to the window, pulling on her dressing-gown. This wasn't how she had wanted Greg to see her, dishevelled, half-asleep. She drew back the curtain and raised the sash window further. She had woken in the night, her body bathed in sweat, opening the window. She didn't think she would ever get used to the hot flushes. Now an icy blast hit her. She shivered, tightening the belt of the dressing-gown. Alerted by the noise, Greg looked up. Behind him, the postman was making his way up the path.

'Julia! I thought we said 9.30? Why aren't you up yet?'

'I overslept,' she replied coolly. 'I'll be down in five minutes.' Noticing Greg reaching his hand towards the postman, she added: 'Please put my mail through the letterbox.'

The postman didn't look at Greg as he followed her instructions before retreating to the street.

'Can't you at least let me in? It's freezing out here!'

'Then why don't you wait in the car?' Julia slammed the window down before he could reply, registering his indignant expression with satisfaction. She knew she was being awkward, but she wanted this meeting to run on her terms as far as possible.

She used the bathroom quickly, frowning at the dark rings below her brown eyes as she splashed water on her face. She pulled on jeans and a black polo neck jumper before running a hairbrush across her brunette bob. Downstairs she picked up two letters from the doormat before unlocking the door. Glancing at them quickly, she saw one of them was addressed to her and Greg. It bore the blue stamp of the mortgage company.

On the doorstep Greg stood with his arms folded across his chest. His lower lip jutted out in the way Julia remembered well, especially from their last months together. The grey sky was heavy with unshed snow.

Silence hung between them like a curtain. Greg finally spoke. 'So I can come in now, can I?'

Julia stepped back into the hall. Confronted by her ex-partner for the first time in five months, she found her legs were shaking. Her stomach flipped as he brushed past her. It seemed that her every nerve was fizzing, her blood burning inside her. She was grateful that she had chosen the polo neck as she felt a flush rising from her chest. It came to her that his betrayal didn't matter to her physically. He would only have to touch her and she would fall into his arms again.

She was shocked at her body's treachery. *We are all animals*, she thought. She closed the front door. 'You're right, it's freezing,' she said, shivering.

Greg glanced at her, then away again. She hoped he hadn't read any of her feelings in her face. She heard him swallow, and realised he was nervous. She'd assumed he would be in complete control of this meeting, having reflected, with bitterness, that he had experience of collecting belongings from an ex's house. He had, after all, left his wife for her.

'So, how are you?' he asked.

'Fine. And you?'

'Well, thanks.' Greg indicated the letters which Julia was clutching tightly, as if they would give her strength. 'Anything for me?'

'I thought you'd had your post redirected?'

'I have. But if there's anything addressed to both of us, anything that I need to know about. . .'

'Like what? All the bills were in my name anyway. The bank has sent something about the mortgage, but it's probably just the annual statement. And you know I've taken over the payments since you left.' Julia tapped the envelope carrying the bank's stamp. 'I'll deal with it later.'

'Right.' Greg exhaled, seeming to relax. 'So where's my stuff?'

'There are five boxes in the dining-room, and some clothes left in the wardrobe in the back bedroom.' Julia had no intention of telling Greg that she had opened the wardrobe to pack his clothes but had been unable to. For as long as they hung there, she had been able to cling to the hope that he might return.

'OK.'

'I'll be in the kitchen. Coffee?'

'Yes. Actually, there's something I want to tell you. I'll just get everything packed.'

'I'll put the kettle on.' Julia went into the kitchen, her heart pounding. What could Greg have to tell her? For a mad moment she fantasised he was going to tell her he had made a terrible mistake and wanted to come back to her.

47

But obviously he would delay packing if that was the case. She filled the kettle with shaking hands and spooned coffee into the cafetière. She could hear his footsteps above her, the rattle of coat hangers. This would probably be the last time he would be in this house they had shared together. Would they even meet again? Her eyes blurred with tears as she poured the boiled water on the coffee grounds. She swallowed. She had promised herself that she would not, absolutely would *not*, give him any hint of her desolation. She blinked away her tears as Greg came downstairs into the hall. Three plastic bags rustled as he set them down by the kitchen door.

'Think that's everything.' He attempted a breezy smile, as if he were vacating a hotel room and Julia were the receptionist. 'Coffee ready?'

'Just about.' Julia plunged the coffee and poured it into two turquoise Denby mugs usually reserved for guests. She saw Greg glance at the mug tree where his Arsenal Football Club beaker used to hang.

'Is my mug in the boxes?'

'It broke,' said Julia. In fact she had flung it on to the kitchen tiles the night he left the house. She handed him a steaming mug and retreated to the sink.

'Oh.'

There was a pause. Greg, still standing in the doorway, was taking quick sips of his coffee. Julia waited in silence. She wasn't going to make this easy for him.

He cleared his throat. 'The thing is, what I've got to tell you, well –'

'Yes? What is it? It can't be any worse than telling me you were leaving on our way back from holiday, can it?' Julia was pleased to get that in. They had spent what she

48

thought was a happy few days with friends in Norfolk. It was on the drive home that Greg had told her, eyes glued on the slow-moving traffic ahead, that he thought they should 'take a break'. He had omitted to mention his new girlfriend to her. In fact he had denied there was anyone else when she asked him, only admitting later that he had already met Lisa.

He looked down at the tiled floor, refusing to meet her gaze. 'Lisa's pregnant,' he said flatly.

'Pregnant? How pregnant?'

'Seven months.'

'*Seven months*?' A thought occurred to Julia, though even as she voiced it she guessed she was clutching at straws. 'You're sure the baby's yours?'

'Yes. Of course it is.'

'Of course? You told me that you hadn't slept with her when we separated!' Her hands were trembling again. She set her mug down on the counter.

'No. I know. I shouldn't have done. Sorry.'

'Sorry? You think that makes it all right, do you?'

'No, but. . .'

'But nothing! And you told me you didn't want children!'

'Well, you didn't, did you? We talked about it when we got together.'

'Five years ago! And you made it absolutely clear that you never wanted any.' Julia covered her eyes with her hands.

'You seemed fine with it,' muttered Greg.

There was a long pause. Finally Julia broke it. 'You never asked again, did you?'

'No. Nor did you.'

'But you were so certain!' Julia shouted. 'You were always saying how much you valued our freedom because we weren't tied down with kids. You even said you didn't understand why Clare was so bothered about it all! And remember, I was nearly forty-four when we met. It wasn't like I had a lot of time to play with, was it?'

Greg didn't respond, taking a large gulp of his coffee. Julia tried to speak more calmly. 'So when did you change your mind?'

'I couldn't say,' he muttered. 'It had crossed my mind the last couple of years, but by then. . .'

'By then it was probably too late for me?'

Greg glanced at her quickly, then away again.

'So. . .' Julia paused, unsure if she wanted to hear the answer to her next question, but a masochistic impulse drove her on. 'So did Lisa get pregnant to make sure you left me for her, that you did the honourable thing?' •

Another moment of silence passed before he replied. 'I'm doing "the honourable thing" as you say, because I love her.'

'But I thought. . .' Her voice trailed off in a strangled sob. 'I thought you loved me.'

'I thought I did.' Greg spoke slowly, as though he were trying to work out his feelings as he went along. 'But with Lisa it's different.'

'It always is, isn't it? Just as I was "different" to Carol. Who's going to be "different" to Lisa, Greg? I should have listened to my mother, shouldn't I, at the beginning, when she warned me that you might leave me just like you left your wife?'

'Oh, your sainted mother! Don't tell me all over again

what a perfect relationship she and your father had until his tragic early death!'

Julia stared at him. Out of the corner of her eye she could see the block of knives by the electric hob. For a moment she understood why Agatha Christie had believed that everyone was capable of murder. She took a deep breath.

'My father's early death *was* tragic,' she said. 'And how dare you speak of my mother like that? That's the only reservation she ever voiced about you. She was very upset when you left, she'd grown fond of you.'

'You make me sound like a favourite pet!'

'That's not what I meant. It's just. . .' She gulped, before voicing for the first time the thoughts that had troubled her since she researched her mother's medical condition. 'I've worried that the upset might have been such a shock that it contributed to her heart failure in the end.'

Greg gave an incredulous laugh. 'Don't tell me that you're trying to lay your mother's death at my door as well! She was sick, Julia, sick and old.'

'No, I'm not blaming you. It's just. . . I miss her so much.' She pushed a strand of hair behind her right ear. 'I miss you too,' she whispered, unable to stop herself.

'For God's sake. . .' He turned his back on her and went out to the hall. She heard the carrier bags crackle as he gathered them up, the squeak of the front door opening.

Julia gripped the kitchen sink, resisting the impulse to follow him. What more was there to say? His dispassionate words about her mother's death had shocked her to the core. Even as she wondered how it could be that the man she had loved so much could have become this stranger, she recognised the cliché.

Staring across the kitchen towards the empty doorway, her eyes fell on the envelope which had arrived from the bank. She noticed, with a strange detachment, that her hands were still shaking as she picked it up from the counter and opened it.

She had to read the letter twice before it made any sense. Then she walked slowly out to the hall.

Greg emerged from the dining-room carrying the last two boxes. His eyes travelled from Julia's face to the letter in her hand. His face drained of colour.

Julia's voice seemed to come from far away. 'So when exactly were you planning to tell me about this?' She tapped the letter.

He shrugged his broad shoulders, but she had registered the twitch of his left eye which always signified tension. 'I don't know what you mean.'

'Don't give me that!' Julia yelled. 'No wonder you wanted to intercept the mail! Six months arrears from when you were living here and supposed to be paying the mortgage! They're threatening to repossess!'

Again he shrugged. 'I'm sorry,' he muttered.

'Sorry!' stormed Julia. 'Sorry!' She advanced across the hall, waving the letter in front of his face. 'It wasn't enough for you to cheat on me with that woman, was it? You had to cheat me financially as well!'

'It wasn't like that.' He set the boxes down between them. 'You know things got a bit tight for me when the school didn't renew my contract for the summer term. I only had a few hours' tutoring a week. I wasn't making enough, missed a couple of mortgage payments.'

'A couple! It says six months here! And I don't understand why the bank hasn't written before now.'

He looked down at the boxes. 'I've been trying to hold them off,' he said quietly. 'I told them I planned to pay off the arrears and asked them not to take proceedings. My time ran out last week. I've not managed to get the money together. I could give you a couple of hundred. That's all. They might delay, if you explain you'll have some money coming from your mother.'

'Not within twenty-eight days!' shouted Julia. 'And a couple of hundred doesn't exactly make a big impression on three thousand, does it?'

Greg bit his lip. 'Like I say, I'm sorry. But I can't offer anything else, not with the baby coming.'

'So let me get this right.' She spat the words. 'You get a new girlfriend, a new home, a baby, and leave me not only alone but also homeless?'

'Oh, don't be so bloody melodramatic! This place will sell tomorrow, no problem. You know houses near the cathedral are always snapped up. You'll soon find somewhere else. Look on it as a fresh start.' He bent to pick up the boxes. 'I've got to go.'

'And that's it? We spend five years together and you tell me to make a fresh start whilst you waltz off to play happy families with another woman?'

Greg sighed. 'I don't have time for this. It's over, Julia. People break up all the time. You'll get over it.' He turned his back and stepped towards the front door, the boxes balanced precariously in his arms.

For a moment Julia stood rooted to the spot. Then, overtaken by an anger she had never known, she lunged at him, pushing him over the threshold. He stumbled but didn't fall, dropping the top box which collapsed where it landed. CDs and books cascaded along the icy path. The glass cover of a photograph shattered, scattering shards of glass in all directions.

She felt a moment's compunction. She knew Greg had treasured the picture of himself as a young boy with his parents who had died in a car crash ten years ago. But when he spun furiously round on her, she said sweetly, 'And glass breaks all the time. You'll fix it soon enough.' She stepped back into the hall, slamming the door and turning the key in the lock.

Back in the kitchen she set about washing the cafetière. It was only when her trembling hands failed to reassemble the filter that the tears came and she sank to the floor in a shuddering heap.

– CHAPTER 6 –

Julia didn't know how long she lay on the kitchen tiles. The worst of the storm of weeping over, she pulled herself to a sitting position, leaning back against the washing machine. Her body shook with a few final sobs. She tried to keep her mind blank, shutting out the thoughts which crowded in. She didn't want to replay the scene with Greg, to confront the fact that their relationship lay irrevocably in the past. She had tried to reason away her hope of a reconciliation before his visit. But it had been there all the same, helping her through the lonely months without him and the recent grief-stricken weeks since her mother's death. Nothing but a foolish fantasy. When she faced reality, she knew she would see she had been in denial about the end of the relationship. How many times had she discussed how denial was a classic symptom of grief with her clients? She had never known its delusive power for herself as forcibly as now.

So she knelt there, numb, staring unseeingly towards the doorway to the hall. She felt raw and empty, as if the tears had scraped away her insides. The cold tap was dripping, but she made no effort to stand and turn it off. There was an odd sense of comfort in the rhythmic drip, drip, drip. It was like a heartbeat, reminding her of life continuing even in the midst of her devastation. Only when the old-fashioned corded phone in the hall began to ring did she drag herself up, placing her weight on her right leg because her left leg had frozen beneath her.

By the time she had limped out to the hall, the answerphone was clicking in. She picked up the receiver and waited for her recorded greeting to end before speaking. 'Hello?'

'Hi Julia! I'm so pleased I caught you. I thought you might be out on a Saturday morning. But I decided I'd try anyway, just in case. It's Linda, by the way.'

'Yes. Hello.' Julia closed her eyes, wishing she hadn't answered the phone. Linda didn't need to identify herself. She would recognise that breathless nasal tone anywhere.

'How are you? Are you getting on all right?' Characteristically, the other woman rushed on without waiting for a reply. 'Listen, I'm so sorry that we parted awkwardly at Giuseppe's the other night. These headaches seem to come from nowhere. I think that one might have been triggered with the excitement of the exhibition and seeing you again. Such a nuisance! I hope it didn't spoil your evening. We were having such a lovely time, weren't we, getting to know one another better?'

Julia twisted the cream phone cord in her hand without replying.

After a moment Linda resumed, 'Anyway, I wondered if we could arrange to meet again, maybe next Saturday? What about lunch, or coffee?'

'I'll check the calendar,' Julia said. 'I won't be a moment.' She retraced her steps to the kitchen. She had no intention of seeing Linda again any time soon, if at all. But nor did she want to hurt the older woman's feelings by an outright rejection. She was relieved to see that Aunt Ada's eightieth meal was pencilled in for the following Saturday. She wasn't looking forward to it, but at least it gave her a valid reason to refuse the invitation.

Back on the phone, she apologised with as much false sincerity as she could muster. 'I'm sorry, Linda. I've got something on next Saturday.'

'Oh.' Linda's disappointment was palpable as she drew out the single syllable. 'What a pity. But it's good you're getting out, isn't it? Better than staying at home after everything you've been through. I hope you're going somewhere nice?'

Julia cringed. Linda's concern for her wellbeing and the frequent references to her recent difficulties struck her as over-familiar. And she didn't appreciate the curiosity about her social life. But as Linda waited for a reply, Julia reminded herself that at least she had managed to postpone this meeting. Relief made her more voluble than usual.

'Actually, it's my aunt Ada's eightieth. Back at The Wingate where we had Mum's reception. I could do without it, to be honest, but family duty, you know.'

She regretted the final sentence as soon as the words were out of her mouth. There was a pause before Linda spoke again, a strange edge to her tone. 'Family duty. Emily mentioned how your aunt Ada set a great deal of store by family duty. Like her mother, she said.'

'Oh?' Again Julia found herself taken aback by the extent of the conversations between Linda and her mother. That niggling question, '*Why did you never tell me about Linda?*' passed through her mind again as she looked up at the wedding photograph of her parents hanging above the walnut bookcase. Leonard stood handsome and upright in his naval uniform, his arm around Emily who stared back at the camera, stiff in her satin wedding gown and lace veil. Leonard was grinning broadly and Emily's lips were parted in a shy smile. She had never enjoyed being the centre of attention.

'Yes,' Linda went on. 'Emily said her mother and sister were very concerned with respectability and keeping up appearances.'

'Well, yes, I suppose they were. Not that I remember Grandma very well.' Julia was interested that her mother had differentiated herself from her own mother and sister in this way. 'Mother was certainly more relaxed than Aunt Ada. My father had very high standards. He was always concerned about duty, commitment, doing the right thing. He was a captain in the Navy, you know.'

'Yes. I did know. Emily told me.'

There was an interval, oppressive to Julia as it lengthened. After the scene with Greg, this conversation was something she could do without. She found herself babbling in her turn, drawing the call to an end. 'Anyway, Linda, I'm sorry about next Saturday. Maybe some other time, when things have settled down. I'd better go. I'm going over to Mother's with James this afternoon to start clearing the house.'

'Of course. I'll be in touch again soon. Bye!' Linda rang off with unexpected alacrity, and Julia heaved a sigh of relief. A lucky escape, she told herself as she headed back towards the kitchen. If Linda had been put off by her unwillingness to make alternative arrangements, that could only be a good thing. Life was complicated enough without the woman's rather needy presence and her allusions to a family secret.

The confrontation with Greg had dulled her appetite but she knew she should eat something before going over to Emily's cottage. It was already midday and she had missed breakfast. She would be glad to see James. Even though their task was a dismal one, her half-brother's company always cheered her. She wanted to talk over the situation about her house with him, gain an outside perspective.

She was taking the final mouthful of poached eggs on wholegrain toast when the phone rang again. This time she waited for the caller to speak into the answerphone, not wanting to risk another conversation with Linda. But when she heard her sister-in-law Clare's greeting, she picked up.

'Hi, Clare. Sorry, just finishing eating.'

'Hi. James asked me to call. He's had to go into the department. Some student having a crisis. He asked me to let you know he won't be able to make it this afternoon.'

'Oh,' Julia felt a stab of disappointment. She told herself not to be selfish. 'I hope it's nothing too serious?'

Clare didn't reply immediately. 'I'm not sure,' she said. 'He went out quickly after getting a call without going into any details.' She paused. 'Anyway, we'll see you at Aunt Ada's lunch next week, won't we?'

'Yes.'

'Bye then,' Clare hung up, leaving Julia listening to the dialling tone.

She replaced the receiver, frowning. Clare would usually have had a chat, but she seemed in a rush to end the call. Perhaps she'd felt awkward about leaving Julia to begin the task of sorting through Emily's personal effects on her own. Not that she had offered to help in place of James, Julia noted. She could put off the unpleasant duty, wait until James was free, but they had agreed they needed to make a start before getting a valuation and putting the house on the market. And it would be good for her to have something to occupy her on a cold January afternoon. If she stayed at home, she would only end up brooding.

Forty minutes later she pulled up in the lane outside her mother's cottage. She shivered as she stepped out of the car. The temperature had dropped even further during the twelve mile drive. The sky was the same pewter of the morning. She would need to keep an eye out for snow: the minor road which wound along the limestone ridge back to the city would soon become treacherous.

She paused for a moment with her gloved hand on the gate, looking at the modest house where her mother had spent the final seven years of her life. She had moved here following the death of her second husband, Nicholas, James's father. Julia still half-expected Emily to be looking for her from the window, moving to open the door as soon as she arrived. Even in her last months she had insisted on greeting her visitors at the door. By then she had needed the aid of a frame and Julia had assured her she could let herself in, but Emily had refused. Julia still found it difficult to believe that she would never again see that gentle smile light up the faded blue eyes. Her mother's warm welcome was one of the things she missed most. She shivered and stepped carefully down the path, still icy from the overnight frost.

She had just taken the key from her pocket when she

heard knocking. She jumped, dropping the key to the stone doorstep, transported back to the waking nightmare of her mother banging for release from her coffin. Then the porch door of the neighbouring terraced cottage opened.

Julia's heart was still hammering as she greeted her mother's neighbour before stooping to pick up the key.

'Are you all right?' Edith stood in the porch doorway, craning to see over the six-foot-high panelled fence which separated the two properties.

'Yes. I just dropped the key. How are you, Edith?'

'Not bad, apart from my arthritis. Always worse in the cold.' The old woman shivered dramatically. 'Come over to check things, have you? You need to be careful with empty houses in this weather, always a risk of frozen pipes, isn't there? I expect you'll be wanting to make a start on clearing your mother's things soon, won't you?'

Julia answered the last question. 'Yes. That's why I'm here this afternoon.'

'Oh. Is your brother coming too?'

'No. He couldn't make it. Anyway, it's nice to see you, but I mustn't keep you out in this cold, Edith.'

'Just wanted to see how you were, duck. I know it can't be easy, with your boyfriend gone and now your mum. If ever you want a chat. . .'

'Thank you, Edith.' Julia turned away, inserting the key back in the lock.

'By the way, I meant to ask. . . I know it's none of my business, but. . .'

Julia sighed as she pushed the heavy wooden door. The timber had swollen in the winter weather and she had to press against it with her shoulder.

'It was just that woman who was round the other day,

61

the one who started visiting your mum in summer, you did know she was here, didn't you? I thought it must be all right seeing as she had a key. Still, I thought I should mention it when I saw you.'

Julia stiffened. 'Which woman, Edith?'

'She came to talk to you at the funeral. A distant relation, isn't she? I always find myself looking at her nails, really bright she has them, different colours.' Edith wrinkled her nose.

Linda. Julia had known as soon as Edith asked. She looked properly at the old woman for the first time in their exchange. 'You said she was round the other day?'

'Yes. She wasn't long inside. Didn't you know she was coming?' Edith's beady brown eyes scanned Julia's face.

She sidestepped the question with one of her own. 'I don't suppose you noticed if she brought anything out of the house, did you?'

'No, not unless she put it in that bag she had with her. Ever so garish it was. She wouldn't take anything she shouldn't, would she? Shouldn't she have been here?'

Again Julia didn't answer the barrage of questions. 'And you saw her when she visited Mum in the summer?'

'Yes. She first turned up one Tuesday afternoon in August. I remember because the bin men had been. I was wheeling my bin back in when I saw her standing at your mum's gate. Just looking at the cottage, she was, not going up the path, so I asked if she needed help. I thought maybe she'd got the wrong house, seeing as I'd never seen her before. She asked if your mum lived there, so I told her she did. Then she went and knocked on the door and I came back in. She was often here after that, but we never had a proper chat. Your mum didn't say much about her either, just that she was a relation. She didn't seem to want to talk about her, and I didn't press her. It was around then that she got diagnosed with her heart condition, wasn't it? So I didn't want to upset her by talking about the woman if she didn't want to. But I was surprised when she turned up on her own on Wednesday. I did think of phoning you, but didn't want to interfere. I hope I did right. Like I say, I thought if she had a key it must be all right for her to be here.'

The old woman looked expectantly at Julia, who pushed a strand of hair behind her ear, thinking. 'I see,' she said slowly. 'You got the impression Mum didn't want to talk about Linda?'

'I don't know for sure. It was just a feeling I had. She seemed to clam up when I asked about her the first time and after that, well, as I say, with her getting the bad news from the doctors, I thought it was best left.'

'Yes, it was probably for the best.' Julia looked up at the leaden sky. Her concern about Linda had mounted during the exchange. She'd thought it strange since first meeting the woman at the funeral that her mother had never mentioned her. Now here was Edith saying she had a key, which Emily must have given her. But surely Linda realised that she had no business at the cottage now Emily had died? And why would Emily have given her a key without mentioning it to her or James?

'I did do right, didn't I?' Edith's lined face creased further with anxiety.

'I'm sure you did,' Julia reassured her. 'I'll try and get in contact with her when I get home.' She paused, realising she had no contact details for Linda. 'If you see her here again, would you mind phoning me?'

'Of course,' said Edith. 'I did think of it on Wednesday, as I said, but I didn't want to interfere.'

'No, I understand. Thanks, Edith. I'd better get on, and you really should get in, out of this cold.'

'Yes, I'm surprised it's not snowed yet.' The old woman glanced up at the snow laden sky. 'Strange, isn't it?' she mused.

'That it's not snowed?' asked Julia, one foot now over her mother's threshold.

'No, not that,' said Edith. 'Probably just coincidence, but when your mum started with her funny turns in summer, it struck me that it was around the time that this woman turned up. I always had the sense she upset your mum somehow.' She shrugged, stepping back into her porch. 'Just a feeling, probably nothing. Anyway, if I see her again, I'll phone.'

'Thanks, Edith. You take care now, won't you?'

Julia stepped inside the empty cottage, her mind churning with further questions about Linda. Had her appearance somehow precipitated Emily's ill-health, even her death, as Edith implied? Why had she come back to the cottage after Emily's death? If she had left something behind on a visit, surely she could have asked Julia about it at the gallery and handed back the key? Linda had never struck Julia as dishonest, but the fact was she scarcely knew the woman. She and James had removed a small amount of cash, their mother's cheque book and financial statements from the cottage when Emily was taken into hospital on New Year's Eve. There were no other valuables.

But it wasn't just the possibility that Linda might be a thief that was the problem, thought Julia switching on the electric fire in the cold sitting room. There was the fact that the older woman knew so much about her. Let alone that hint about a family secret on Wednesday evening. . .

Crouching over the two orange bars of the fire, Julia shivered. What was it that Linda knew? And just why had her mother kept her visits a secret?

– CHAPTER 7 –

No matter how much she told herself that the old woman was being melodramatic, Julia was troubled by Edith's suspicion that Linda's appearance had hastened Emily's death. Climbing the narrow staircase to her mother's bedroom, she regretted putting off meeting Linda earlier. Maybe she had planned to share whatever it was she knew about the family.

Julia opened the teak wardrobe in her mother's bedroom. One glance inside convinced her to wait for James's help to empty it. Tears pricked the back of her eyes as she contemplated the pastel coloured blouses, skirts, dresses and cardigans. The faint fragrance of jasmine lingered. She ran back downstairs to begin the less emotional task of clearing the desk in the sitting room.

The Edwardian walnut desk had belonged to Emily's father, and matched the bookcase in Julia's hall. It had been battered and scratched for as long as Julia could remember. She had never known her maternal grandfather who had died before her parent's marriage. Emily had rarely spoken of him, although she had faithfully taken flowers to his grave on the anniversary of his death each year. He was buried in the churchyard of a nearby village. Even as a child Julia had been sensitive to the shadow which passed over her mother's face when she asked, 'Why do I only have one grandpa, Mummy? Susan and Jennifer have two.'

'Your other grandpa died a long time ago.'

'Oh.' Aged six, the closest Julia had come to death was when the cat was run over by an elderly neighbour. Watching her mother chop the onion for the cottage pie, she digested this new idea that people also died. 'So is he in a box in the garden too, Mummy?'

'No.' Her mother paused. Emily had a gift for using a child's frame of reference. 'He's in a box in a church garden not very far away.'

'Oh.' Julia chewed her thumb nail, thinking. 'I wish he was still here, Mummy.'

Emily sighed. 'So do I, sweetheart, so do I.' She brushed the back of her hand across her eyes. 'These onions!' she said.

'Naughty onions, making Mummy cry!' said Julia. But her mother didn't smile as she usually would. Instead she turned her head away as she passed Julia on her way out of the kitchen. When she came back a few minutes later, her eyes were red-rimmed. She was holding a sepia photograph with curled edges. 'This was your other grandpa.'

Julia studied the photograph of the head and shoulders of a young man in army uniform. His hair was combed back from his forehead and parted in the middle. Julia could see he shared her mother's fine features. His head was turned slightly to the left, and he seemed to be looking beyond the camera. 'He looks all dreamy like you do sometimes, Mummy.'

Emily smiled. 'Do you think so, sweetheart?'

'Yes. Was he always a soldier?'

'No, just during a terrible war a long time ago. He was a vicar when he came back.'

'A vicar?' Julia thought of Reverend Lacey, the plump middle-aged vicar in the village. The young man who had been her grandfather looked very different. 'Did he have a loud voice like Reverend Lacey?'

Emily laughed. Julia beamed her gap-toothed smile, delighted to have cheered her mother up.

'Reverend Lacey does boom a bit, doesn't he? No, my father spoke softly most of the time. He was a quiet man, very kind.' She raised her hand to her eyes again, before sending Julia out to the shed to fetch some potatoes. When the little girl returned, Emily didn't say anything more about her grandfather. But the following November she took Julia to his grave for the first time.

Running her hand over the desk's scarred surface over forty years later, Julia shivered. It wasn't only the empty house that was making her feel cold this January afternoon. Since Greg's visit, she had been pushing aside the thought of the child she would never have. It had been niggling at the back of her mind since her mother's death. Now the regret roared into her consciousness, like a nagging toothache suddenly overtaking her with the full force of pain. Even as she chided herself for self-pity, she regretted that there would be no one to remember her as she remembered her mother, or as her mother had remembered her grandfather. There would be no one to inherit this shabby old desk. Unless James and Clare had a child after all, if they were lucky with another IVF cycle.

Julia swallowed hard as she pulled open the top middle drawer of the desk. It contained a stack of household bills bound by a bulldog clip. She drew them out, extracting the most recent. She hoped James had remembered to notify the utility companies of their mother's death as he had promised. Placing the rest of the bills in a bag for recycling, she took her mother's turquoise leather address book from the drawer. The younger Emily's beautifully rounded handwriting brought a lump to her throat. It had become so shaky in recent years.

Some of the names in the address book meant nothing to her. Others conjured up images of people she vaguely remembered from childhood: Arthur and Moira Anderson, Sybil and Nicholas Browning, Peter and Olive Duffy, Hazel and Timothy Fielding, Rodney and Vera Galbraith. . . She recalled that Reverend Lacey's daughter Eileen had been a regular babysitter when her parents went out to evening functions with their friends. Emily had often been late, frequently changing her mind about her dress, shoes or jewellery. Julia remembered her father saying on numerous occasions, 'You know I always think you look lovely, Em,' as he steered her firmly towards the door. He had never been impatient with Emily's dithering, for all his habitual concern for punctuality. To Julia that had been a sign of his love for her mother.

She flicked through the alphabetical lists, thinking how some of her parents' friends must have withdrawn after her father's death. The discovery that couples with whom she and Greg had socialised were less forthcoming with invitations after their separation had been painful, and she wouldn't allow herself to speculate whether some of their so-called friends had welcomed Lisa as Greg's new partner as readily as they had welcomed her when Greg had left his wife.

As a widow with a young daughter forty-one years ago,

Julia suspected her mother would have been even more isolated. Not that she would have minded necessarily, she thought, her eyes running over entries under 'M' and 'N.' Emily had always been self-contained, which was another reason why the apparent frequency of Linda's visits surprised Julia. Leonard had been the more sociable. With a distinguished naval career behind him, he had resumed work as a solicitor in the small legal practice on the northern edge of Lincoln after the war. His father had been a partner there before him. Leonard had been active in the village too, serving as churchwarden and on the Parish Council. Julia remembered how crowded the church had been for his funeral. She had clung tightly to her mother's hand as they sat together on the front pew, staring straight ahead as Reverend Lacey rumbled on. She refused to look at the wooden box which four ex-naval officers had carried in from the horse-drawn hearse. A cross of lilies lay on top. She would hate their overpowering scent for ever after.

One of the bearers was the same William Prescott whose name Julia came across now in her mother's address book. The details were crossed through, so either he and Emily had long since lost touch or he had predeceased her. Tapping her thumb against the name, she carried the address book over to the small window. Outside the first snowflakes were beginning to fall. The last time she had seen William Prescott was on another snowy Saturday many years ago, the winter after her father died. Her mother had persuaded her to join the other children building a snowman on the village green.

'But Mummy, I need to do my homework,' Julia protested.

'There's plenty of time for that later,' Emily replied. 'Besides, I haven't seen your school books since you came home yesterday. Leave the drying up, I can do that while you're out.'

'You know I like helping you.'

'I know, sweetheart, and you're a big help. But it's important that you get some fresh air and spend some time with the other children.'

'But I want to be with you, Mummy.' Julia's voice wobbled.

Emily paused in scrubbing the casserole dish. She turned from the greasy enamel sink to look at her eight-year-old daughter. 'I know, sweetheart,' she said again. 'And I'll be right here when you get back, won't I, just like I'm here when you come home from school?'

Julia gazed back at her mistily without answering. Her heart beat faster with the knowledge that her mother did understand, after all.

'I'll be here when you get back, won't I?' Emily repeated, laying her left hand, reddened from the hot water, on Julia's shoulder. Julia leaned her head against it, not minding the damp prickle of her red woollen jumper against her skin. Very softly, her mother said, 'Your father wasn't strong because of the war. We always knew that he might not have long.' She let go of Julia's shoulder, plunging her hand back into the water. 'Now you wrap up well, and go and enjoy yourself with your friends.'

An hour later, Julia slid home rosy-cheeked and breathless, dodging snowballs from Eddie Gibson and Frank Norris as she rounded the corner of the drive. She barely noticed an unfamiliar blue Ford Anglia parked outside and flung open the front door. 'Mummy. . .' she began, then stopped. Her mother was standing at the foot of the staircase which led from the hall. Her face was drained of colour. She was holding on to the lowest banister so tightly that her knuckles were white.

Emily's blue eyes flickered towards Julia, then back to her left. For the first time Julia remembered, her mother's face didn't light up at the sight of her. It was as if she hadn't seen her. The little girl followed the direction of her mother's gaze. A slight ginger-haired man wearing a brown wool tweed overcoat was leaning against the wall, arms folded across his chest. Julia recognised him as William Prescott, her father's friend. She hadn't seen him since the funeral.

Then her mother spoke in a tone Julia had never heard before, a low moan which made Julia shudder. 'You had no right,' she said. And then, more loudly, 'You had no right!' Emily drew herself up, raising her heart-shaped chin. She advanced towards William Prescott, shouting the words now. 'You had no right!'

For one breathless moment Julia was certain her mother was going to strike the man. He must have had the same thought as he took a sideways step into the umbrella stand. It clattered to the floor, banging against his leg. But he ignored it. He didn't take his eyes from Emily's face as he said, a strange smile playing about his small mouth, 'He was my friend. I judged it right to tell him. It was my duty.'

'Duty!' Emily spat the word. 'And your sense of duty ki–' She raised her right hand as Julia suddenly found her voice. 'Mummy!' she screamed.

Emily's hand fell to her side. She looked round to where Julia stood by the half-open front door, snow puddling on the tiles from her grey duffle coat. 'Julia. . .' Her voice trailed away and she took a breath. 'Mr Prescott was just leaving.'

Emily turned and began to move slowly towards the kitchen, her shoulders slumped beneath her blue-and-grey-checked handknitted cardigan. From the rear she looked like a much older woman. 'Take off your wet things, sweetheart. I don't want you catching cold,' she added, without turning.

'Yes, Mummy.'

Julia glanced uncertainly at William Prescott. He managed a half-smile as he edged past her through the doorway, placing a hand briefly on her shoulder. She stiffened and the smile vanished.

'Sorry I can't stay, Julia,' he said coldly. 'I'll call again some time.'

But he never did. That was the last time Julia saw him. In fact she hadn't spared him a thought until finding his details in her mother's address book on another snowy afternoon over forty years later.

She traced a diamond in the window with her forefinger. Outside the snow was falling thicker and faster. It was beginning to settle. What little daylight there had been was already fading. It was only three o'clock, but she would need to go soon to avoid difficulties on the cliff road. She should at least empty the desk before setting out.

She crossed back to the desk, chewing on her thumbnail. What was it William Prescott had done which had made Emily so furious? And what would her mother have said if Julia hadn't interrupted? Reaching under the desk to switch on the antique brass lamp, she jumped as the bulb popped, and banged her head against the wood. 'Damn!'

She went through to the kitchen. The fuse box was in the cupboard below the kettle. She groped cautiously behind an assortment of packets, tins and jars, hoping she could reach the trip switch without emptying the cupboard. Or, much worse, encountering anything furry. A mouse had taken up residence in the cottage two years ago. She shuddered at the thought.

Then she gave another start, banging her hand against a can. The phone, which hadn't yet been disconnected, was ringing through the silent house.

She went back into the sitting room and picked up the receiver. 'Hello?' There was no response. 'Hello?' Silence. A click. The caller had rung off. She tutted to herself. Probably a wrong number, but she wished the person had at least spoken.

Julia shivered. The fire had done little to warm the room and now that it had failed with the circuit tripping, the temperature was dropping rapidly. She was on her way back into the kitchen when a knock at the front door made her jump again. 'For goodness' sake!'

Edith was standing on the doorstep, shrunken against the snow inside a grey coat.

'I was thinking,' she said, 'about that woman. Your mum kept a diary, didn't she?'

'Did she?' Julia had forgotten or not known this. The now familiar self-reproach, that perhaps she hadn't paid as much attention to her mother as she might have, assailed her again.

'Yes. She used to tell me she wrote in it every day, nothing in particular, she said. I wondered if maybe there'll be something about her, this Linda woman, in there.'

'Thank you. That's a good idea, Edith. I don't suppose you know where Mother kept her diary, do you?'

'In her desk. That's where she kept everything important, isn't it?' Edith raised a pencilled eyebrow, surprised that Julia didn't know this, adding to the younger woman's sense of guilt. 'You're on your way, are you? Turned the lights off?'

Julia sighed. 'They've fused. The desk lamp's blown. I was just trying to fix it. But I'll leave after I've done that, I don't want to get caught on the cliff road in the snow.'

'No, you should be going, duck,' said the old woman solicitously. 'And next time, if you want a cup of tea. . .'

'Thanks. I'll do that.' Edith had been kind to her mother in her last months, fetching essential groceries between Julia's and James's visits. 'Now you take care on the path, it's getting slippery.'

'Will do. Bye, duck.' Edith turned and shuffled slowly back to her house.

Julia waited until she saw her white head disappear into the porch before going back to the narrow kitchen, shadowy now in the gathering dusk. Reaching inside the cupboard, she felt along the switches until she found the one which had tripped. As she flicked it up, causing light from the sitting room to spill into the kitchen, her mother's long ago words to William Prescott came back to her. With a sudden burst of clarity, she knew how Emily would have completed her sentence if she hadn't interrupted her, '*And your sense of duty killed him.*'

– CHAPTER 8 –

'*And your sense of duty killed him.*' The words echoed in Julia's mind as she returned to the sitting room. She had never seen her mother so shocked or angry as she was that afternoon. The scene had long been buried in her subconscious, reawakened on this snowy January afternoon four decades later by a forgotten name in her mother's address book. William Prescott. Was he still alive? Was there a connection between what Linda knew and her mother's accusation towards the man?

The questions tumbled around her mind as she pulled open the drawers in her grandfather's desk, searching for her mother's diary. Maybe the diary would shed some light on Linda's sudden appearance as Edith had suggested. But even as she rifled through the mixture of stationery, correspondence and packets of photographs, another question drowned out the others: *Do I really want to know?*

Finally, in the third drawer down on the left side of the desk, she discovered an assortment of notebooks. Some were leather, some hardback, others spiralbound with patterned fabric covers. Opening one at random, her fingers trembling, Julia saw pages covered with her mother's rounded script, interspersed with dates from five years ago. Dipping into them, Julia smiled despite her agitation.

Invariably Emily mentioned the weather, a topic never omitted in her conversations. Emily also wrote about places she had been to, people she had seen, visitors who had called. The simple details of an older person's increasingly circumscribed world, Julia thought with a pang. The entries included visits to the single remaining village shop, encounters with Edith and other neighbours.

She flicked through the diaries, checking the dates. The oldest went back to 1987, fifteen years ago. She piled them up in chronological order. The last one she opened began in December 2000. Turning the pages through the early months of the previous year, 2001, her heart began to beat faster. April, May, June, July, August. . . It was August when Edith said Linda had made her first visit. Her mother's handwriting became increasingly shaky as the months passed. Julia caught her breath when she skimmed the entry for the 8th of August: 'Julia called. She told me Greg has left. I haven't seen her so lost and uncertain since Leonard died.'

Julia's eyes swam with tears as she turned the page. She had reached the end of the cream notebook. The last entry was dated 14th of August. Was this the final entry her mother had ever made? Or was there a later diary which she had kept somewhere else?

Glancing towards the window, Julia saw that a good inch of snow had settled on the sill. She should leave. But it was frustrating to think that there might be another diary offering a clue about the family secret Linda had alluded to. Or was it better left hidden? Again she heard her mother's low, furious voice to William Prescott nearly half a century earlier: 'And your sense of duty killed him.'

She shuddered, shoving the diaries into the carrier

bag. She had had enough for one afternoon. Switching off the fire and light, she tried to convince herself that it was the combination of the empty cottage, the hostile January afternoon, and the scene with Greg that morning, which had filled her with foreboding.

But as she locked the door and made her way up the white path, she found she couldn't dispel the image of her mother, hand raised to strike William Prescott, shouting her accusation at him. It seemed impossible that her gentle, rather passive mother, could ever have acted in such a way. There again, Julia reminded herself grimly, she had never believed herself capable of the slightest violence until she had launched herself at Greg that morning.

There was never much traffic around the village green as the road petered out into fields beyond it. In the gathering gloom of the snowy evening no one was around. She followed the tracks of another vehicle up the steep lane to the cliff road. A surprising amount of snow had already accumulated. Even the usually busy road towards Lincoln was almost deserted, and she regretted not setting out sooner. She turned on the radio, tuned in as usual to Classic FM. Allegri's *Miserere* was playing. It was one of Julia's favourite pieces. But the haunting tones did nothing to allay the sense of unease which had settled on her as deeply as the snow which lay in the surrounding fields. She switched to Lincs FM. The chirpy-voiced presenter was providing a traffic update, urging people not to travel unless absolutely necessary. Heavy snow was forecast well into the evening.

She relaxed after she had made her way up the sharp incline from the village of Scampton where her grandfather had been vicar. But as she approached the traffic lights at the final village before the city and Celine Dion launched into 'My Heart Will Go On', Julia's eyes flooded with tears again. She and Greg had been to see *Titanic* together. He had sung the song to her, badly, after they had made love that night.

At the time she had believed the sentiment of the song, that she and Greg were soulmates, whose love would last for ever. Now she never wanted to hear the maudlin ballad again. She took her left hand off the steering wheel and reached over to switch off the radio.

Too late, she registered the lights turning from amber to red. She hit the brake hard. Too hard. The Mondeo skidded onwards in the snow. She drove into the skid to correct her trajectory. A vehicle was mounting the hill to make the right turn in front of her and her car was sliding directly towards it. The driver honked. Panicking, she over-corrected. Her front wheels slewed to the left. She closed her eyes, preparing for the crash into the stone wall which ran alongside the road.

The crash didn't come. When she opened her eyes again, she saw that she had stopped inches short of the wall. She took some steadying breaths, resting her head on the steering wheel.

For the third time that day, she was startled by knocking, this time on the driver's window. Jerking upright, she turned her head. Someone was opening the door. Her heart pounded.

'Hey, are you OK? What the hell. . . Julia?'

Julia recognised Pete, the reflexologist, staring at her wide-eyed beneath a black beanie.

'It was Celine Dion. . . I didn't see. . . I skidded. . .' Incoherent, in shock, relieved to see a familiar face, she began to cry again.

Pete hesitated, then moved round to the passenger door. He climbed in beside her and placed his gloved hand gently on her left arm. Julia leaned towards him, resting her head against his shoulder as she continued to weep. She was grateful that he didn't speak. The windscreen was covered in snow by the time her sobs subsided. She moved away from him, suddenly self-conscious.

'It's OK,' he said.

'No. I'm sorry,' said Julia.

'Why?'

'Well. . . getting into this state. Where did you come from?'

'I was the driver turning when you spun across the road. I parked up to see if you needed help.'

'How embarrassing!'

'Don't worry about it. But you must have come through a red light, you know. And I'd have had you down as a cautious driver.'

'I am. I didn't see it till too late. I. . .' She swallowed hard and turned her face away.

There was a pause before Pete, with a sensitivity which surprised her, turned into practical mode. 'Not a problem,' he said. 'No harm done. Are you OK to drive home? You should be able to reverse off the verge. But we'd better make a move soon.' Thick snowflakes, driven by the wind which had risen during her short journey, were beginning to cover the windows.

'I'll be fine now. Thanks.' Julia wished her voice

wouldn't wobble. She scrabbled in her pocket for another tissue.

Pete detected her uncertainty. 'Tell you what,' he said, 'shall I follow you home, make sure you get back safely?'

'You don't need to do that.' She blew her nose.

'I don't need to. I'd like to.'

'I don't want to intrude on your Saturday evening. Won't Xanthe be expecting you?'

Another silence. 'Xanthe left last summer,' said Pete.

'I'm sorry. I didn't know.'

He shrugged. 'Don't worry about it,' he said again. 'You had your trauma with Greg at the time.'

'Yes, but you listened to me about Greg.' Julia remembered how kind Pete had been when he dropped into her office begging milk the day after Greg left and found her crying. She had spilled out the story to him and he had listened patiently, without interrupting.

'You didn't need my troubles as well.' He hesitated. 'It was my fault anyway.'

'That Xanthe left?'

'Yep.' Pete took a deep breath, staring in front of him. He ran his hand over the door to the glove compartment, leaving a watery trail. 'The thing is, there's someone else.'

'There always is, isn't there?' She bit her lip as soon as the words were out.

'Excuse me?' He turned towards her.

'Someone else,' she said. 'Sorry. It's none of my business. Anyway, aren't you planning to see her tonight?'

'Who?'

'The "someone else."'

Pete faced forward again. He spoke slowly, seeming to

choose his words carefully. 'Actually, I don't have plans to see her. And for the record, I wasn't unfaithful to Xanthe.'

Julia was grateful for the twilight which hid her blush. 'No, I. . . It's just. . . Greg called earlier for his stuff and. . .' She gulped and then blurted out, 'His girlfriend's seven months' pregnant.'

He jerked round in his seat, knocking his right knee against the gear lever.

'Seven months? But that means. . . ?'

'Yes. She was pregnant when he left me.'

'Shit, Jules, I'm sorry.'

'Thanks.'

They sat in silence for a moment. Then Pete said, 'The offer still stands. I'd be more than happy to follow you home.'

'OK.' She hesitated. The prospect of her empty cottage on the hostile winter's night wasn't appealing. Besides, Pete had been very kind. 'Would you like to stay for dinner?'

'That'd be great!'

Julia smiled at his enthusiasm. They'd both occupied offices in the old school for five years without ever socialising. In fact apart from that time last summer when she had poured out her heart about Greg, they'd had few meaningful conversations.

Pete opened the passenger door, brushing snow from the window. A flurry of snowflakes blew onto the dashboard. 'Have you got a scraper? You might damage the wipers if you try and shift the snow with them.'

'I think it's in the boot.' Shivering in the icy blast, she unclipped her seat belt.

'I'll get it.' He vanished before she could protest. She

heard a soft thud as snow fell from the boot. He rustled among the carrier bags from her mother's house. 'You've got a lot of stuff in here,' he called.

'From Mum's.' Thinking of the diaries, her recovered memory of her mother's confrontation with William Prescott, Julia was overcome with a sudden weariness. She closed her eyes.

'I'm sorry.' Pete continued to rummage around. 'Found it!' He slammed down the boot lid. A moment later his face loomed at her through the cleared windscreen. He scraped the snow from her side window before reoccupying the passenger seat. 'You won't have a problem getting off the verge. Just make sure you stop for the red light this time, will you?'

'Ha, ha.' She switched on the engine and edged cautiously back into the road. A hundred yards on she pulled in so Pete could pick up his Fiesta. He followed her as she drove slowly back towards the city, taking extra care on the mini-roundabouts as she approached her house tucked behind the cathedral. As she climbed out of the Mondeo on to the slippery pavement the bell chimed seven.

'Great place, Jules. Bags of character.' Pete glanced round her hall, taking in the beams and oak flooring, the walnut bookcase and grandmother clock, matching pieces to the desk in Emily's sitting room. He took his beanie off and ran his hand over his newly-shaved head. Stepping out of his brown suede boots, he placed them beside her discarded ankle boots on the doormat.

'Thanks. Sorry it's so cold. I'll put the heating on.' Julia went through to the kitchen and flicked the switch on the boiler. She didn't hear Pete padding in behind her in his socks as it fired up. She started when he spoke again.

'How long have you been here? Hey – you're a bit jumpy, aren't you?' He moved back to stand in the doorway as Greg had done that morning. She turned away, not wanting to recall the earlier scene, and reached for two crystal wine glasses from the cupboard.

'Still a bit shocked from the skid, I expect.' She contemplated telling him about Linda and her memory of the scene between her mother and William Prescott, how she had felt spooked in Emily's cottage earlier. But in the reassuring surroundings of her kitchen it sounded melodramatic in her own mind.

'I've been here six years,' she said. 'Not for much longer though.'

Her stomach fluttered as she remembered the letter from the bank. She had forgotten about it during the afternoon. It still lay on the counter beside the fridge freezer.

'Oh?' Pete looked at her questioningly. 'Making a new start, now that Greg's gone?'

'No. Not that. He's the one making the new start.' She couldn't keep the bitterness out of her voice. 'We arranged it so that he paid the mortgage, I paid everything else. Only he didn't pay the mortgage the last few months he was here. Something else he didn't bother to tell me. So this morning I got this.' She handed him the letter and went across to the well-stocked wine rack. 'White or red?'

'Red please.' Pete reached inside the pocket of his insulated jacket. Julia was surprised to see that he needed reading glasses. She hadn't thought he was old enough. She'd always assumed the creases in his forehead, the lines etched around his eyes and mouth, were the usual symptoms of skin ageing prematurely associated with smoking. Maybe he was closer to her age than she'd thought.

84

The gold stud in his left ear lobe gleamed under the spotlight as he raised his head from the letter. 'Shit, Jules, I'm sorry,' he said, for the second time that evening.

Again the abbreviation of her name. 'Please don't say that,' she said.

'What? Sorry. You never swear, do you?'

'Not that. I'm not keen on "Jules,"' she said. 'Sorry, I don't mean to sound precious about it. It's only family or really close friends. . .' She bit back the rest of her sentence as he raised a blonde eyebrow. She hadn't noticed how bright his blue eyes were before.

'I see,' he said. 'And working alongside one another five years doesn't qualify for "close friends"?' He was looking at her with a strange intensity.

Julia tucked a section of her brunette bob behind her right ear and dropped her gaze. 'Sorry. Just me.' She turned away and opened the drawer where she kept the corkscrew.

'Don't worry about it, *Julia*.' She winced at his ironic emphasis. But when she glanced round at him, the metal corkscrew cold against her palm, he was smiling again. Then he spoke more seriously. 'Sounds like Greg turned out to be more than a bit of a bastard.'

'He's not, not really,' she said quickly.

'Isn't he? He lied to you about this other woman, he's left you with mortgage arrears. Can you pay them back?'

'No.' Julia bent her head over the bottle of wine, tears welling up again. She began to press the corkscrew into the cork and then withdrew it when she saw she hadn't centred it. 'Damn,' she muttered.

Pete crossed the kitchen. He was close enough for her to feel the warmth of his breath on her neck. She stiffened.

Then he reached round her to take the corkscrew. His hand brushed against the small dome of her breast. She stepped back quickly.

'Let me do that,' he said. 'Why don't you sit down? You've had a hell of a day. And instead of cooking, why don't we order takeaway? You're close enough to the Man Yuen for them to deliver, even in this weather.' He withdrew the cork with a gentle pop.

'Yes, but I. . . OK. My treat, though.' She sank wearily into one of the two dining chairs at the table by the window, leafing through the pile of newspapers, magazines, charity bags and takeaway menus which had accumulated over recent weeks. She saw Pete glance at them as he set a glass of red wine down in front of her.

'It's not what I expected, your house,' he said, settling into the opposite seat.

'Oh?' She savoured the spicy aroma of the wine before taking a sip.

'No. I imagined you in some minimalist apartment, or at least a modern town house.'

'Did you? Why?'

His smile emphasised the lines at the corner of his mouth. 'You've always struck me as ultra-efficient,' he said. 'Very organised. And this. . .' he waved his hand at the jumble which lay between them.

'I am usually more organised,' she said quietly. 'It's just since Mother. . .'

His smile vanished. He looked stricken. 'I'm sorry,' he said immediately. 'That was tactless.'

There was an awkward pause. Then he reached across and touched her arm. She looked at his hand resting on her black sweater, noticing how long and slender his fingers were with their short square clean nails, how sensitive. He would need a sensitive touch, she supposed, as a reflexologist. Not that she knew very much about reflexology.

'You know, I've never had a massage,' she said, glancing across at him.

'Haven't you?' His voice sounded softer to her, as soft as the falling snow. He moved his hand down her arm and gently began to massage the inside of her wrist. She closed her eyes, relaxing for the first time in what felt like months. When she opened them and looked at him, he was watching her intently. She withdrew her arm abruptly.

'I'm sorry.' She forced a smile. 'We seem to keep apologising, don't we? But it's been a long day. I'm not sure this is a good idea. And even if you hadn't made plans with your. . . friend tonight, I don't think she'd be too happy to know you're here offering your services free of charge.'

'"Offering my services free of charge?"' Pete repeated, both eyebrows rising this time. 'Now there's a thought.'

The colour rushed to Julia's cheeks. 'Not *that*. You know what I mean.'

'Do I?' A smile played about his lips, making her wonder if she had imagined the intensity of his gaze before. She pushed away the thought of how much she had enjoyed the touch of his hand on her wrist.

'Pete! Look, I am sorry, but I think I'm better on my own now. And as I say, your friend. . .'

'I can take a hint.' He rose. 'And just so you know, you've got the wrong idea about my friend.'

'Oh?' She followed him into the hall, surprised how disappointed she was that he was going. 'It's none of my business, of course,' she added as he laced up his boots, 'but if ever you wanted to tell me about her. . .'

He looked at her for a long moment, then retrieved his beanie from the table. She opened the door. The snow had finally stopped and lay in drifts around the small garden. The patio planters and shrubs were shrouded in white. A taxi swished slowly along the road.

Pete stepped over the threshold and turned, gently planting a kiss on her cheek. 'Maybe one day I will,' he said.

– CHAPTER 9 –

Julia slept fitfully again that night, troubled by dreams which faded away when she emerged into semi-consciousness. Half-awake, she pushed the fragmented images back into the recesses of her mind. When she woke fully, her body bathed in the familiar perspiration, her bedside clock showed 4.10 a.m. She sighed and pushed back the duvet, padding barefoot to the sash window. Raising it above her head, she leaned out and gulped in the icy air.

White shapes loomed below her. She knew they were only bushes and plant pots covered in snow, but still she shivered, unable to shake off the sinister atmosphere from her dreams. She jumped when the cathedral clock struck the quarter. She usually found the chime comforting, but tonight the bell sounded a warning to her troubled mind.

Teeth chattering, Julia closed the window. She knew from the broken nights which had plagued her since her mother's death that sleep would be elusive. She decided to make some green tea and take a look at Emily's diaries. She'd left them when Pete went, too drained by the unsettling visit to the cottage and the accident on the way home.

Pete. Her hand on the landing light switch, Julia recalled the pleasurable sensation of his hand circling her wrist. With the clarity of the insomniac she acknowledged her attraction to him. Warmth flooded her. How ridiculous! They'd worked alongside one another all these years without her being remotely interested. He was just Pete, for goodness' sake! Plus he'd told her he was involved, although the relationship sounded complicated. And there was no reason to suspect he was interested in her. Telling herself that her reaction had been due to her shaken state after the skid and the disturbing afternoon at her mother's, Julia went down to the kitchen.

She ran water into the kettle. Outside a car churned up ice as it came down the street, the engine dying as she flicked the kettle on. She heard the car door slam, the faint beep of the central locking. The squeak of someone opening her wrought iron gate. For a wild moment, her hand poised above the canister where she kept the green tea, she imagined it was Greg. Greg suddenly overcome with regret about their separation, impulsively coming round in the middle of the night to seek a reconciliation. . . Whoever it was wasn't making any effort to approach the house quietly along the frozen path. Footsteps crunched towards the front door, reassuring her that this was no stealthy would-be intruder. Heart pounding, she peeked under the side of the olive roller blind, hoping against hope to see Greg's bulky figure.

Her pulse slowed when she recognised the slight physique of her half-brother as he reached the doorstep. Then it began to race again. What had brought James here at this time of night? She crossed the kitchen, bumping her thigh against the walnut bookcase in the hall in her haste.

'James! What's wrong? Is Clare OK? What's happened? You look terrible. Come in – you'll catch your death.

Where's your coat? But you shouldn't have been driving, aren't you over the limit?' The questions tumbled out as she took in James's dishevelled appearance and bloodshot eyes, smelled the stale beer on his breath. He stumbled into the hallway and she put out a steadying hand.

'Jules. Sorry about the time. Nowhere else to go. She's thrown me out.' James rubbed a hand over his right cheek, scratchy with stubble.

'Thrown you out! Wouldn't she even let you stay till morning? That doesn't sound like Clare.' But even as she thought it was out of character for her placid sister-in-law to send James packing on the coldest night of the winter, she recalled how she had surprised herself pushing Greg out into the garden the previous morning. She caught her breath, wondering what could have sparked Clare's fury.

'Long story.' James wound his way into the kitchen. He slumped into the wicker chair which Pete had occupied earlier. 'Any chance of a coffee? The stronger the better.'

'Of course.' The kettle had come up to boil. Julia spooned coffee into the cafetière for the two of them, deciding against her green tea. She set the cafetière and mugs on the table, taking a seat across from her half-brother. He held his head in his hands, his fingers interlocked, massaging his forehead.

The silence stretched between them, broken only by the ticking of the walnut grandmother clock in the hall. Like the desk at Emily's cottage, it had belonged to Julia's grandfather. Her mind turned to the diaries again. She could have looked at them whilst she drank her tea. She experienced a moment's resentment at James's intrusion, then chided herself for selfishness as she contemplated his hunched figure.

Finally, as Julia plunged the coffee, James raised his head. He gave a crooked half-smile. 'Long time since I came round to see you because of trouble with one of my women, isn't it?'

Julia didn't return the smile. 'I didn't think Clare was just "one of your women,"' she said. 'Not when you married her.' She poured coffee into a mug and placed it on a rattan coaster in front of him.

James shrugged. 'Always the older sister, aren't you?'

She stared at him. 'What do you mean?'

'You know.' James took more quick sips of the coffee, his eyes darting around the untidy kitchen. 'Making judgements.'

Julia drew in her breath. 'Making judgements? All I was saying was that I thought Clare was different from your other girlfriends.'

'Whatever.' He shrugged again. 'So you brought that stuff from Mum's, did you?' He waved his hand at the carrier bags of correspondence and diaries which cluttered the table between them.

'Yes.' Julia pushed back the disturbing memories of William Prescott and the snowy afternoon forty years earlier, determined her half-brother shouldn't change the subject. She remembered the phone call with Clare, forgotten in the emotional turmoil of the day. 'I spoke to Clare before I went over,' she said. 'She told me you weren't able to come to the cottage. Some crisis with a student.' She paused, recalling her sister-in-law's unusual reticence. 'Actually she was pretty brusque.'

James took a gulp from his mug, then set it down on the table. 'Ah.'

'Ah?'

'So Clare wasn't fooled then.'

'Not fooled about what?'

James ran his hand through his floppy blonde fringe, a habit he had developed as a small boy when caught out in mischief. 'Not fooled by me saying a student had a crisis. Of course, if the stupid woman hadn't rung home, then. . . Not that I planned on it going on any longer anyway.'

'On what going on any longer? And what do you mean, if the stupid woman hadn't rung home?'

He didn't reply, swirling the coffee around his mug. Julia's eyes widened. 'James, you're not. . . ?'

He looked back at her, his jaw set, holding her gaze. ''Fraid so. Fling with a student. Nothing serious.' He laughed mirthlessly. 'The irony is I finished it this afternoon. Too late though. Clare suspected and challenged me as soon as I got in. At least I admitted it. Thought that would go in my favour.'

'Go in your favour?'

'Yeah. I mean, that was part of the problem with you and Greg, wasn't it? He lied about the other woman, didn't he?'

Julia didn't trust herself to speak. James pushed at his fringe again, glanced away. 'Of course I know it doesn't make it right,' he muttered. His thick lips formed the sulky pout Julia remembered from childhood. 'I thought it might help though. Since it was over.'

'But James, what were you thinking? Why chance your marriage for some fling with a student? What about the IVF and everything?'

'Oh, the IVF.' James raised his bleary eyes towards the ceiling. 'Have you ever thought what it's like living with someone as desperate for a child as Clare? How our whole life has been taken over by visits to the clinic, by tests and dates of the next appointment, the next procedure?'

'I know it must be difficult, a terrible strain, but. . .'

'"Difficult? A terrible strain"? Believe me, Julia, you have no idea. Before it started we hadn't had sex for two years without Clare telling me the exact point of her cycle. Can you imagine how off-putting that is?'

'Well, no, but since you both wanted a baby so much, surely. . . ?'

James looked at her, his mouth set in a hard line. 'That's just it. I didn't, not so much. It's Clare who wants a child so badly. I thought she was happy with how things were. Decent income, good social life, nice holidays, no ties. Then all of a sudden, she hit 35, and having a baby became her one goal, the be-all and end-all. How stereo-typical is that? The old biological clock kicking in.'

There was a long pause as Julia took this in. 'I had no idea,' she said eventually. 'I assumed you were both really keen.'

James turned his face away. 'I went along with it, tried to be as supportive as I could. But I'd have been happy enough carrying on as things were. If a child came along, fine. If not, OK.' He paused. 'Like you.'

'Like me?'

'Yeah. I mean, you've never bothered, have you? About children?'

She didn't reply, twisting her mug between her hands on the table.

'Jules?' He glanced at her sharply.

She took a deep breath. 'Don't even go there,' she said. 'How can you sit there, making assumptions like that?'

'Like you don't make assumptions?' James spoke quietly, but there was an edge to his voice. '*You* thought I wanted a baby as much as Clare.'

'Well, yes, but that's what everyone thought, what you let us think.'

There was another silence. In the distance the cathedral clock struck five, followed a few seconds later by the grandmother clock's brighter chime from the hall. 'Not everyone,' said James as the final note died away. 'Greg guessed.'

'Greg! When?'

'Last summer. Just before he left.'

'Why didn't he tell me? Why didn't you say something when I came round offering support, encouraging you both to try again?'

'Oh, I don't know.' James shrugged and yawned. 'You seemed too involved somehow.'

'Of course I was involved! I'm your sister, for heaven's sake! And I like to think I've been a good friend to Clare since you got together.'

'Oh, yes, no doubt about that. A good friend to Clare, the caring sister, what more could anyone ask from St Julia! Only –' he eyeballed her, before continuing with slow deliberation, 'only, has it ever occurred to you that as you go around dispensing support and care to your family and clients, your own life is a bit of a bloody mess?'

Julia paused in the action of raising her mug to her mouth. 'And just what is that supposed to mean?'

'Oh, come on!' James ran his hand wearily over his bloodshot eyes. 'I don't need to spell it out! You've been so busy trying to sort everyone else out – shoring up Greg who never intended to get a proper job, organising Mum, being a shoulder for Clare to cry on, taking responsibility for everyone – that you never noticed what was really going on, never thought things might not work out as you planned.'

She stared back at him, blood pounding in her ears. 'I never had a plan,' she said tightly.

'Didn't you?' James held her gaze unblinkingly. 'Didn't you want everyone to live happily ever after? You wouldn't even admit Mum was dying, forever ferrying her back and forth to the doctor for new tablets, when all she wanted was to be left in peace for her last few months!' Noticing her open her mouth to protest, he continued relentlessly, 'She did, Julia. She told me.'

'But why didn't she tell me?' The childish whine came out before she could stop herself.

'She could see how cut up you were about Greg. That was part of it.'

'Part of it?'

James slumped back in his chair and looked away, speaking more quietly as he continued. 'You must know you're always so definite about everything, so sure that your way is the right way, that people just fall in with you. It's the line of least resistance.'

'But Mum. . . We all thought Dr Smythe should have diagnosed her heart condition sooner, begun some treatment, referred her on, researched new medication. . .'

'No, Julia. *You* thought that. Granted the heart failure seemed to come on suddenly. What was it, just a month or so after her annual check-up when she seemed as fit as ever? But she was seventy-five years old, anything can happen at that age. And she wasn't exempt because she was our mother!' He massaged his temples with his hands. 'Our family isn't immune from human weakness.'

'Don't patronise me! And whatever you do, don't you dare try to connect Mother's illness with your – your despicable behaviour by talking about "human weakness"!' She slammed her coffee mug down.

'Oh, "despicable behaviour", is it? What condemnatory language from counsellor Julia! And here was I thinking you were supposed to listen to the full story before passing judgement. I've always suspected you were more your father's daughter than our mother's.'

'What do you mean? You didn't even know my father!'

She could see from the gleam in his eye that he relished scoring a point. 'Just something Mum said once.'

'And what did Mum say?' Julia was resting her hand on the carrier bag containing their mother's diaries. It rustled as she withdrew it. She shivered suddenly. James's reference to her father had rekindled the memory of William Prescott.

'I don't remember her exact words. She was commenting on your integrity, your sense of responsibility, of what was right.' His thick lips curled. 'It was last summer, soon after Greg left. She could see how it had thrown you. What was it she said? Something like, "Julia struggles to understand us mere mortals. It can be difficult living with someone with such high standards. I found that with her father."'

'Mother said *that*? It sounds as though she was excusing Greg!'

'No, not at all.' James's tone was more gentle as he took in his sister's stricken face. 'It was more that she was trying to understand how poleaxed you were. That's when she compared you to your father. She said that he was a very honourable man. It wasn't intended as a criticism.'

Julia's chest tightened as she contemplated the conversation between Emily and James. She'd always assumed she had been her mother's main confidant, not James. Even though she had sometimes resented her mother's indulgence of her youngest child, she had thought her bond with her mother had been closer. There had been those years alone together before Emily met James's father. And it pained her to hear that her attempts to find better treatment for their mother had been tolerated rather than welcomed by Emily. Her head felt as if it would burst with the revelations. She closed her eyes.

'Jules? Are you OK?'

Julia's eyes snapped open. 'Of course I'm not OK! You come round here in the middle of the night, tell me you're having an affair, that Clare's thrown you out, and somehow manage to steer the conversation to my inadequacies as a sister, a daughter and a partner. You even criticise my father.'

James shook his head. 'Now come on, Julia. That's not what happened here. If you hadn't been so judgemental, I wouldn't have said some of these things. You know that.'

'Can't you hear how you're trying to excuse yourself? Why is it you can never accept responsibility, never admit your guilt? Is it because,' she paused, but couldn't stop herself, 'you were always Mother's blue-eyed boy who could do no wrong?'

Brother and sister stared at one another. Then James pursed his lips, spat out his retort. 'Let me ask you a question too. How come you're so bloody smug that you can never understand why the rest of us find it impossible to meet your standards?' He paused, before going on with a slow deliberation which Julia knew was calculated to wound, 'You are smug, and exacting, and that's why you find yourself on your own at nearly fifty. Maybe it's your father's glorious upright naval genes coming out, who knows?'

There was a long silence. Julia's head was throbbing even more. She took a deep breath. 'Get out,' she said. 'Get out of my house. And don't you ever dare to speak about my father in that way again.'

James got unsteadily to his feet, bumping his thigh against the table. He cursed before weaving across the kitchen. He didn't look back.

His half-sister remained rooted in her chair, hugging herself in the chilly kitchen. It was only when she heard the front door thud that she realised that she had been holding her breath.

Suddenly dizzy, she placed a hand on the table and hauled herself up. She took the mugs and cafetière across to the sink, flicked the advance switch on the boiler. Every word, every gesture of the exchange was etched in technicolour in her mind, replayed as she washed up. Her mother's words, according to James, gnawed at her like a toothache: *It can be difficult living with someone with such high standards. I found that with her father.* The revelation of the gulf between herself and her mother, possibly between her parents, sat like a leaden weight in her chest. Finally overcome by exhaustion, she dragged herself back up to bed.

– CHAPTER 10 –

It was midday when Julia woke with a sore throat and high temperature later that Sunday. The combination of physical and emotional fatigue had taken their toll. Sneezing, feverish and with no appetite on Monday morning, she phoned clients booked in for the next two days and cancelled their appointments. Back in bed she dozed fitfully, disturbed by dreams of Greg, her mother and, once, a baby screaming in a burning house. Surfacing into consciousness, she remembered the nightmare from the evening of her mother's funeral.

She shook her head to dispel the disturbing image. How strange that her nightmare had preceded Grace's account of being rescued as a baby from a house fire, a fire started by her sick mother! Dismissing it as no more than coincidence – for what other explanation could there be? – Julia turned on her bedside light. It was nearly 7 p.m. She'd slept most of the day away. Still sneezing, but a little hungry, she hauled herself out of bed and reached for her fluffy white dressing-gown. It was the last birthday present her mother had given her.

'Definitely not sexy,' Greg had said when she unwrapped it.

'Mother probably thinks we're past all that after five

years!' Julia's laugh died on her lips as Greg looked away, thick lips curled in a sneer.

In the kitchen she switched on the TV. She hadn't heard any news for forty-eight hours. The headlines were grim reminders of conflict and suffering. Photographs of prisoners captured in Afghanistan at Camp X-ray in Guantanamo Bay. Suspicions that the recent foot-and-mouth epidemic had been caused by meat smuggled into the U.K. Footage of pyres of animal carcasses the previous summer flashed through Julia's mind, sparking the nightmare of the burning house yet again. Her hand was shaking as she put the last of a wholemeal loaf under the grill and sliced some Cheddar.

She flicked off the TV and turned on the radio. The tinny theme tune for *The Archers* struck up. Lifting a corner of the blind, Julia saw the garden gleaming white in the light of the crescent moon. The temperature must have barely risen above zero since she came home on Saturday. She pulled her dressing-gown tightly around her and turned the toast, arranging the cheese on top.

A phone rang faintly above the clatter of glasses and buzz of conversation in the Ambridge pub. It was only when she heard the muffled sound of her voice inviting callers to leave a message that she realised it was her own.

Out in the hall she frowned to hear Pete's voice. He'd never rung her at home before. 'Hi, Julia. It's me, Pete. Just wondering if you're OK. Missed you at the office today. Thought I'd check you've not skidded into a wall anywhere.' A pause. 'Sorry. Not funny.'

Julia grimaced as Pete continued, 'And I've come across some premises that might be good, if you've thought any more about us being partners.' An embarrassed laugh.

'In business, of course. Anyway, ring me back if you like. You've got my number.'

Julia picked up the phone, about to call back, if only to speak to someone after two days alone. But there had been something awkward between her and Pete on Saturday – she found herself steering away from acknowledging that momentary attraction to him – and she hadn't decided whether she wanted to take him up on his offer of sharing business premises yet. Another major decision, another change which seemed too much to cope with alongside a house move caused by Greg defaulting on the mortgage. She replaced the receiver, cursing as the acrid smell of burning toast drew her back to the kitchen.

The toast was too charred to eat. She sat nibbling at the remains of the packet of Cheddar, only half-listening to the reviews on *Front Row*. Thinking about what she was going to do regarding the house and relocating her counselling business made her head ache. The business itself wasn't going well at present – she had turned down several potential clients in the late autumn to give herself more time to spend with Emily. Grace, due again on Wednesday, was the first new client she had taken in two months.

It still shocked her to think of the speed of her mother's decline. James had a point when he said she'd been in denial about Emily's illness. Her mind veered away from the ugly row with her half-brother. He had been the one person she thought she could count on. He'd been very supportive after her split from Greg, and she'd thought their shared grief over their mother had drawn them closer. What he had said, his accusation about her smugness, about her always trying to fix people, had hurt her deeply. And she'd been so shocked by his casual dismissal of his affair with a student, his treatment of Clare – 'one of my women'! Julia ran her hands through her hair, her usually sleek bob mussed by two days in bed. . . James had certainly been right about one thing, her life was a mess. She'd certainly not expected to be sitting alone in a house about to be repossessed at forty-nine. Her milestone birthday in April was something else she pushed from her mind.

Trying to distract herself from her problems, she went across to the sink. The wine glasses she and Pete had used on Saturday night lay unwashed in the bowl. The mugs and cafetière from James's visit stood on the counter alongside the sink. No more rubbish would fit in the bin. Newspapers, magazines and junk mail for recycling were piled up behind the back door. By her standards, the kitchen was a tip.

Among the clutter on the table lay the carrier bags containing her mother's diaries. Setting about the washing up, Julia decided they would wait. She wasn't sure what she was looking for in them anyway. The unease evoked by the memory of William Prescott's long ago visit that snowy afternoon had receded. Running hot water into the bowl, registering from her ability to smell the pomegranate washing-up liquid that her cold was improving, she reasoned that her distress over the scene with Greg had caused her to be over-imaginative at her mother's house.

She remembered that she needed to contact Linda somehow to find out why she had returned to the cottage after Emily's death. Maybe someone at the gallery where her exhibition had been held would have contact details? It was possible there was a simple explanation for her visit – perhaps she'd left something there? She was still surprised her mother had given the woman a key, and never mentioned her visits, but that didn't mean there was anything mysterious about her. The most likely explanation was that Emily hadn't thought it significant enough to trouble Julia about it when she was struggling to come to terms both with her separation from Greg and the news of her mother's illness.

Front Row had come to an end. The female radio announcer was introducing the book of the week in her neutral accent: 'A deeply personal account of one woman's reconciliation to childlessness after fertility treatment failed.' Julia lunged across the sink to switch to Classic FM, soapy water dripping on to the chrome radio from her yellow rubber gloves. 'I hope Clare isn't listening,' she said aloud as the pure flute music of Vaughan Williams's 'Lark Ascending' filtered through the kitchen.

That night she dreamed of Greg cradling a baby in a pink sleepsuit. She had never seen such tenderness and pride on his face. A surge of love rose in her for Greg and the little girl, their daughter. . . But no, not their daughter, because as the baby turned her head, her mouth open in a toothless smile, saying, 'Mama, Mama,' she was gazing at a young woman with long chestnut hair. The woman bent to take the baby from Greg, and Greg placed his hand round her waist, pulling her towards him. . .

Jerking awake, Julia buried her head in her pillow and wept for a long time before sinking back into a deep slumber.

She felt tired and drained when she woke mid-morning to the sound of the phone ringing. The caller didn't leave a message. She dragged herself downstairs to make a pot of green tea. It was tempting to cancel Wednesday's clients as well, but she desperately needed the income to pay the bills, let alone to have any hope of negotiating with the bank over the mortgage arrears. And it would be good for her to work. It would help to take her mind off her difficulties. Her fitness for counselling was a different question which she pushed aside. Her monthly appointment with her supervisor loomed in two weeks. Louise was a shrewd woman who would see through any attempt Julia might make to minimise her distress.

Julia sighed as she watched the flower unfurl inside the glass teapot. How had her life become so complicated? She went across to the carrier bags containing her mother's diaries, thinking how straightforward her mother's life had been when she was Julia's age. She had been married, with Julia grown up and James a teenager. At the time she had also been financially secure, thanks to money from the solicitors' practice where Leonard had been partner, and a substantial inheritance from his parents who had both died when Julia was very small.

Sipping her green tea, Julia realised that this was a superficial picture. Who knew what heartache she had endured following Leonard's death, facing the prospect of raising Julia alone until she met James's father, Nicholas? It was a grief Emily had kept hidden from her. She remembered once weeping for her father in the night. Emily had come into her bedroom and cradled her on the bed. 'Shh, sweetheart,' she had whispered as the sobs shook Julia's thin body. 'Shh.' But when Julia had found it impossible to stop crying, she had said, almost sternly, 'Hush, now. Daddy wouldn't have wanted you to be so upset.'

Julia had stopped crying almost instantly. Afterwards whenever grief threatened to overwhelm her, she suppressed it in her mother's presence. It was something she had discussed with a therapist during her counselling training, recognising that her mother's words had led her to believe that she would disappoint her father if she gave vent to her tears. To the eight-year-old Julia, her dead father was as omnipresent as God. It was the therapist who had pointed out that her mother had struggled to deal with her small daughter's distress, and hadn't given the little girl the permission to express her grief.

It was all a long time ago. But memories of her childhood had been surfacing more frequently in the weeks since her mother's death, a natural reaction to the loss of a parent. She wondered if her mother had kept diaries when she was younger, if she had expressed her grief at Leonard's loss in them. Presumably they would turn up at the cottage if she had.

She took the diaries she had found in the desk drawer out of the plastic bags and laid them on the table. In her haste to leave her mother's cottage as the snow fell on Saturday, she hadn't realised how many there were. She counted out twenty-four. She opened one dating back to 1990. The entries were more detailed, going beyond the bare facts of her mother's days. There were records of news which friends and family had shared with Emily, and the odd acidic comment which made Julia smile. These typically related to her neighbour Edith and sister Ada. Julia had always known that each tried her mother's patience, but had never appreciated how much. One more extended entry read,

Edith knocked at the door barely five minutes after James left with his new girlfriend, asking if I would like her to fetch me today's Evening

Post *from the shop. She knew perfectly well I had got one just before James arrived, as she was out in the garden when I came back. 'Why Edith!' I exclaimed, 'I hope the heat isn't troubling you too much. Surely you remember I'd just got one when I saw you earlier.' She didn't look in the least embarrassed. 'It must be the heat addling my brain. How were your visitors?' Her eyes glinted in the way they do when she scents gossip. 'Wasn't that a different young lady with your son? He must be getting quite a reputation for himself, mustn't he?' I wanted to tell her to mind her own business. One of these days perhaps I will. No, I know I won't really. She's a kind soul even if her inquisitiveness can irritate me beyond measure. And guarding my tongue has been second nature to me for so many years it would be hard to break the habit now.*

Julia paused over those words in the final sentence, *'Guarding my tongue has been second nature to me for so many years. . .'* Her mother had been the soul of discretion. Was there a hint here of some secret, just as Linda had suggested? Or was she reading too much into the words?

She flicked forward. The name 'William Prescott' leaped from an entry dated 12th of October.

Ada phoned today. I had the usual sinking feeling when I heard her voice. 'I know you don't usually buy The Echo, *do you?' she asked without any greeting, continuing without giving me chance to reply. 'So I don't suppose you'll have seen the Family Announcements, will you?' I told her I hadn't.*

She waited a moment, and then said, 'William Prescott died. I thought you would like to know.'

'Oh.' I said. My heart began to thud so hard I wondered foolishly if Ada could hear it down the phone.

'Don't you want to know when the funeral is? I was sure you would want to go.'

'Really?' I injected as much coldness into my voice as I could in response to her sly tone. 'Why? I haven't seen William Prescott for years.' And my mind turned to the last time I saw him. Julia came in from playing in the snow. If it hadn't been for her looking on, I would probably have struck the man.

'But he was such a great friend of Leonard's, wasn't he?' Ada pressed. 'I thought you would want to pay your respects.'

Some friend! If it hadn't been for William Prescott interfering, Julia might have had her father for longer. I was well-aware of Leonard's war injuries, that his life would be shortened because of them. But had it not been for that man, I'm certain he would have lived longer. William Prescott robbed Julia of some precious years with her father. Her grief made her grow up before her time. I have never forgiven him. And the memory of his hand creeping up my skirt that day still makes my skin crawl. Of course I never told Ada about him propositioning me a few weeks before Leonard died, but she guessed something. For once she turned up just at the right time, dropping in unexpectedly when he was there. He sprang back before I hit him, and left immediately. Left, as I found out afterwards, to go straight to Leonard's office.

'Emily?' Ada's voice interrupted my memories of the hypocrite.

I heard her note of triumph. She knew she had rattled me. For once I retaliated. 'Why don't you go to the funeral, Ada?' I asked. 'After all, you were very fond of Leonard, weren't you?'

I smiled to myself as the line went dead.

But then the old dread returned. What if, after all this time, as we grow old, she should share my secret?

I wonder sometimes why she has kept silent. I understood when Mother was alive, but she has been dead twenty years now. And Ada grows more like her, more bitter by the day.

Julia stared at the faded black ink of her mother's handwriting on the yellowing page. *My secret.* Whatever it was, William Prescott had known it and had shared it with her father. And her mother blamed her father's friend for precipitating his death. Worse, reading between the lines, it seemed Prescott had made his disclosure to Leonard after Emily refused his advances.

Shuddering, Julia went out into the hall, once again picking up her parents' wedding photograph from the bookcase which had stood in her grandfather's study. She thought again how stiff they looked, especially her mother. She would expect her father to be upright in his naval uniform, but for the first time it struck her there was a tension about her mother's lips parted in the shy smile, the fixed gaze back at the camera, the raised chin. Or was she being influenced by what she had just read, and by Linda's dark hints?

Linda. As the phone rang beneath her, making her start so that she nearly dropped the photograph, she was certain it was her newly-discovered relative. But it was Clare's voice on the other end of the line. Julia sighed in relief.

'Julia? I thought you might be at the office. I was going to leave a message.'

'No, I'm here. I've come down with a bad cold.' On cue, Julia sneezed.

'I can hear you have. Is there anything I can get you, or. . . ?'

Although she would have to brave the freezing weather to go to the corner shop later for food, Julia answered, 'No, I'm OK thanks.' She paused. 'Never mind me. How are you?'

'You know then?' Clare's voice was small. 'You've seen James?'

'Yes. He came round drunk early on Sunday morning. I'm so sorry, Clare.'

There was a strangled sob. 'I don't know what to do. He told me it's over with this girl, but how can I be sure? He says he wants us to try again. What would you do?'

Julia didn't answer immediately, twisting the phone cord with her free hand. If Clare were her client, she would encourage her to find her own answer to the question. But Clare was her sister-in-law, her friend, seeking advice. And what position was she in to advise after Greg's betrayal, knowing full well she would have taken him back if he had apologised and regretted his affair?

'I don't know,' she said honestly. 'I don't know what I'd do. I'm not really the best person to ask, am I?'

'Oh, I'm sorry, I didn't mean. . .'

'It doesn't matter,' Julia said quickly. 'But if you'd like to meet up for a chat – that is, I'm guessing you're not going to Aunt Ada's 8oth now, are you?'

'Actually we are,' said Clare. 'James doesn't want Aunt Ada to know anything yet, not till we've decided what we're doing. And I agree with him. You know how vicious she can be, and how she gossips.'

Julia sighed. 'Yes. I know.'

'I would like to meet for a chat though,' Clare went on. 'I hope, whatever happens. . .' another stifled sob, 'we can still be friends, Julia.'

'Of course. We are friends, good friends, and frankly I'm disgusted with my brother.'

Clare hiccoughed. 'Thanks, Julia. That means a lot. You've been such a rock during all the IVF.' She began to cry in earnest, and barely managed to get out the words, 'See you on Saturday then,' before terminating the call.

Julia felt tears welling up herself as she replaced the handset. Poor Clare. She'd been through such a lot, desperate for a baby, putting her body through those rounds of invasive treatment, disappointed each time, and now James was putting her through this. *Bastard*. Just like Greg.

Her eyes fell again on her parents' wedding photograph. She hugged it suddenly to her chest. Her mother had chosen a good man in Leonard, of that she was certain. But what was the secret her mother had kept from her father, which Emily believed had hastened his death when he learned it from William Prescott? And again, that question which had occurred to her before, *Do I really want to know?* Might the past be best left buried with her parents?

– CHAPTER 11 –

Julia's limbs felt weak as she hauled herself out of bed at 7.30 a.m. on Wednesday. Rain, driven by the wind, hammered against the windows. It was barely light, a dismal January day which matched her mood. At least the rain would shift what was left of the weekend snow.

The main roads to her office were clear, but the pavements were still slippery with compacted grey ice. She stepped carefully from the car into the former playground of the old school. The red-brick building looked more forlorn than ever on the wet winter's day. Water streamed from a broken down pipe to the left of the entrance. More water dripped steadily from a blocked gutter directly above the door, pounding rhythmically on Julia's umbrella as she struggled to extract her key from the front pocket of her black shoulder bag.

'Here. Let me.' Julia jumped as Pete reached round her and put his key in the lock. She hadn't been aware of him following her across the icy yard. 'After you.'

'Thanks.' She pressed the light switch in the lobby. One of the two fluorescent strip lights above them flickered briefly and died.

'So how are you?' The reflexologist put his weight against the door to close it, fighting a gust of wind.

'OK thanks. Bit of a cold, that's all.' She kept her back to him as she opened her mailbox. It was empty.

'I wondered where you were. Hoped you were all right after Saturday.' When she didn't reply, Pete rushed on, 'Did you get my message about the offices? They're up by the shopping centre on the outer circle road. Better location than here. Good rent too.' He moved to her side to check his box, close enough for her to scent his aloe vera soap. She stepped back.

'Right. I'll think about it.' She turned down the corridor which led to their offices.

'I've booked a viewing with the agent later today. Are you free around five?'

'I don't know. I said I'll think about it.' She walked more quickly. The doors to the old classrooms rattled in the draught.

'All right. Let me know. We've not got long before the landlord chucks us out!'

Julia chewed the inside of her lower lip as she unlocked the door into her office. She regretted her curtness, especially after Pete had been so kind on Saturday. She turned, intending to go back and apologise, but the front door banged shut again and she heard him greeting his first client.

The room was colder than ever. She shivered, sneezing as she turned on the fire. She was tempted to leave the blind drawn against the dark winter's day. But she knew from experience that clients liked a view. It was hardly the most scenic – a rutted playground, parked cars and a row of terraced houses across the quiet street, but it was somewhere to focus if eye contact in the counselling session became uncomfortable.

The damp patch over the window recess had expanded. It seemed to be spreading before her eyes, an ugly brown fungus. She sighed as the intercom buzzed and Grace announced herself. The office was hardly the bright welcoming space recommended in her training.

Julia was again struck by the younger woman's slimness as Grace unbuttoned her grey and white checked coat. If anything, she looked even thinner than last week. She seated herself on the edge of the chair as she had in her first session. Today she was wearing a short black corduroy skirt and a powder blue polo neck jumper. She adjusted her plait over her right shoulder with her characteristic gesture. She was one of those fortunate women who would look immaculate whatever the weather, thought Julia, tucking a stray coil of her brunette bob behind her ear, still feeling windswept from the brief walk across the yard from her car. Grace studied her oval nails, avoiding eye contact.

'So you told me last week about your family, how you felt distanced from your late father after he re-married, the difficult relationship with your step-mother, and your fear of being "tainted" because of your mother's mental illness,' recapped Julia. 'That was a lot to share in the first session. I wonder how you've been since?'

'Not good.' Her client ran the forefinger of her right hand along the ridge of each nail on her left.

A squall of wind lashed the rain against the window. Grace didn't look up.

'I know it can be difficult to disclose so much at once. Some clients regret it afterwards.'

'I didn't mind that.' Grace glanced at Julia, twiddling the edge of her plait. 'It just wasn't a good week anyway.'

'Not a good week for other reasons?'

'Exactly. But I don't want to talk about that today.' The younger woman bit her lip before continuing in a low voice. 'I feel ashamed of myself.'

'Ashamed?'

'Yes. I really don't want to talk about it yet. I don't know what you'll think of me.' She brushed a tear from the corner of her right eye.

'OK. I can see it's painful for you. But I'm not here to judge, Grace.' Julia paused. Grace wiped away a few more tears. 'Perhaps you're judging yourself?'

Her client shrugged. 'That's how I was brought up, I suppose. Frances has very clear ideas of acceptable behaviour, of "the Christian way" as she calls it. Father wasn't so vocal, but I could always sense his disapproval.'

'Ah. You mentioned your step-mother was a born again Christian, and your father converted when he met her?'

'Yes. Our lives centred on the church once Father met Frances. We went to two services on Sundays. Soon after they married they hosted a Bible study and a Prayer Group two evenings a week.' She paused. 'There always seemed to be people coming and going at the house. Frances made it clear she wanted me out of the way and would send me off to my room.'

'Very different to the life you'd lived before with your father?'

Grace nodded, tracing a circle with the toe of her boot on the threadbare grey carpet. 'One of the things I missed most was my bedtime story with Father. That stopped when they married. *She* said I was too old for that, a big girl who should put herself to bed.' Grace's voice wobbled. 'But I was only eight, just eight years old. I used to cry myself to sleep.' Her voice broke.

Julia slid the box of tissues across the side table which stood between them. There was a lump in her throat. She knew that she wasn't just sensing the loneliness of the child Grace. She was recalling how she used to cry herself to sleep after her father died when she had been the same age. 'Classic transference,' her supervisor would say, and Julia knew she would warn her against the danger of projecting her own feelings on to her client.

Grace's sobs subsided. She sniffed noisily, extracting another tissue.

'Sorry,' she whispered.

'There's nothing to apologise for,' Julia said gently.

'It was so long ago, I feel like I should have got over it by now. But somehow, with Father dying, it's brought it all up again.' She paused. 'I dream of him a lot. In my dreams I feel like I did towards him when I was a little girl. Not like I did after he and Frances married.'

'So it's as though you're missing the father from your early childhood?'

'Yes.' Grace sucked the end of her plait, a childish gesture which wasn't lost on Julia. 'It's like I'm trying to get him back,' she said slowly. 'How I think he really was. My Daddy.' The childish name gave rise to a fresh bout of weeping. Julia found herself wiping away tears, grateful Grace was too absorbed in her own grief to notice.

'And you felt he changed when he met Frances?'

'Yes. I was with him when he met her. It was a Saturday afternoon in spring. Daddy had taken me to the park. One of those days you always remember, you know?'

'Yes.' Julia did know: the day her father died, the day she knew she was in love with Greg, overshadowed now by the day he left, the day her mother told her of her illness, the day her mother died. . . days etched in the memory. She shivered, reflecting how, for her, the negative personal landmarks outweighed the good. At least Grace was young enough to have the expectation of some happy days – perhaps a wedding, maybe the birth of a child. . . She closed her eyes, telling herself to focus on her client.

Grace was speaking quickly now, re-living the day when her father and step-mother met. 'We'd just started walking home when it began to pour down. I was only wearing a light jacket. Daddy didn't have a raincoat or umbrella. We dived into a café in an ugly grey building, not much bigger than the other houses on the estate. It turned out to be the Evangelical Fellowship Church. It was quiet, there was no one else in besides us. This woman came bustling up, flashing her big white teeth at us in a wide smile. Her smile reminded me of the wolf in *Little Red Riding Hood*.' She shuddered. 'Daddy ordered tea and orange juice. She brought me the juice and some paper and crayons whilst she was waiting for the kettle to boil. "You can make a lovely picture for your mummy," she said. I blurted out, "I don't have a mummy," to save Daddy having to explain. "I'm so sorry, so very sorry. You poor little thing," she said. She patted my shoulder, and I jerked away from her, knocking over the orange juice. I hated it when people pitied me for not having a mother, especially with Daddy there, because his face would close down, and he'd be quiet for hours after. I knew he didn't want to talk about her. And somehow,' Grace paused, chewing on her plait again, 'somehow Frances overdid the sympathy.'

Julia was struck by Grace's reference to 'not having a mother.' Was that how her father had edited out his wife after she had set fire to the family home when Grace was a baby? Her client had said in the first session that they had moved away from the area to make a fresh start and changed their names. It would have been difficult for her mother to trace them when she was eventually discharged from psychiatric care even if she had wanted to. Had Grace ever considered trying to trace her mother? There were many avenues her client might wish to explore, but at this early stage of their counselling relationship, Julia followed her client's lead as Grace recalled her first impressions of her step-mother. 'So it seemed to you that Frances's sympathy wasn't genuine?'

'No.' The younger woman gave her a grateful glance for understanding. 'There was a kind of brightness about her as she mopped up the juice. She got me a fresh glass and gave me a dry piece of paper to draw on. She kept going on about it not being a problem when Daddy apologised for my clumsiness. She said, "No, I was clumsy to assume. . . I'm so embarrassed. . . It must be so difficult for you, bringing up a little girl on your own." When Daddy didn't answer straightaway, I realised that maybe he did sometimes find it a struggle. I'd never thought about it before. He said after a minute, "We manage pretty well, don't we, Gracie?" But that pause told me a lot. And then Frances was off in full flow again, saying what a beautiful name I had. She asked if I knew the hymn "Amazing Grace." It meant so much to her, she said, because it summed up how God loves us so much. I didn't really understand what she was talking about, I'd never heard anything like that in the Catholic church we sometimes attended. But Daddy seemed to be listening carefully, taking it all in. I've heard her say things like that many times over the years, managing to bring God into the conversation whenever she can. She calls it "witnessing."' Grace's lip curled, and Julia found herself mirroring the gesture.

Grace rushed on, 'She invited us to the church service the next day. I thought Daddy would refuse, being Catholic. But we went along on the Sunday morning. Frances made a bee-line for us as soon as we arrived. She was wearing a flowery dress, low cut at the front, and more make up than on the Saturday. Sunday best I suppose, but looking back I wonder if it was because she was hoping Daddy might turn up. Someone joked at their tenth anniversary party – held at church of course – that Frances's sugges- tion that I should draw a picture "for my mummy" in the café was a line she used with all men turning up alone with children, to find out if they were single. I felt sick when I heard that.' Grace swallowed, as though forcing back bile. 'Looking back, I suppose she was worrying she would never marry, being in her mid-thirties. And the church taught that members had to marry Christians. So when Father came along. . .'

Grace paused, looked unseeingly towards the window. Rain was still falling heavily. Up the corridor a door slammed and Pete shouted a cheery 'See you mate.' Grace gave no sign of having heard, lost in her childhood mem- ory. Julia waited silently, knowing it was important for her client to continue her story in her own way.

After a moment the younger woman gave herself a little shake. 'Anyway, Frances complimented me on my dress and stroked my hair. I remember struggling not to jerk away like I had when I spilled the juice the day before. When the service began, she sat down next to me, with Daddy on my other side. It was very different to anything I'd experienced before. There was a worship band with guitars and a drum. It was informal and noisy compared to St Jude's. Frances made a show of helping me find the hymn numbers in my book, though I didn't need any help. Once I snatched the book away and Daddy said sharply, "Grace! Don't be so ungrateful!" And Frances said, "Oh, it's nothing, don't worry about it," with this hurt expression on her face. Daddy told me to apologise. I mumbled I was sorry, and she smiled. I saw a lot of that smile. It always appeared when she'd managed to get Daddy on her side against me. I'm sorry if that sounds childish.' She broke off and looked over at Julia.

'But you *were* a child,' Julia said softly.

There was silence in the room, broken only by the moan of the wind and the rain hammering against the window.

'Yes,' said Grace finally, 'I was just a little girl, wasn't I?' She frowned as she examined her nails. 'Perhaps,' she continued hesitantly, 'perhaps it's like I've lost Daddy twice; as a little girl, and again as an adult?' She didn't wait for Julia to respond. 'Thank you,' she said, with a small shy smile, 'that really helps.' She glanced at her watch, suddenly conscious that the session must be nearly over. 'Could we leave it there for today? I've got a tutorial at 11.30.'

Julia smiled back. 'Of course.' This was when she found her job most rewarding, when clients reached new understandings through having space to talk. She hoped this would be a breakthrough for Grace, even as she sensed there was much more for this troubled and vulnerable young woman to work out.

– CHAPTER 12 –

The rest of the day passed quickly for Julia. She saw three more clients and was typing up session notes when she heard a knock on her office door. Pete poked his shaven head round. 'Coming then?' he asked, jangling his keys.

'Where?'

'Cold affected your memory as well?' Pete's grin faded when Julia didn't return it. 'Sorry.' He rubbed the stubble on his cheek. 'To the offices I told you about.'

'Oh.' Julia recalled rebuffing him earlier. The prospect of spending time alone in the draughty old school on a cold wet January evening wasn't inviting. The paperwork would wait. 'OK. Can you give me a few minutes?'

'Sure, great! I'll drive, then bring you back to pick your car up. See you outside in five.' The door slammed behind him. Julia had the impression he didn't want to give her the opportunity to change her mind. She switched off her laptop and locked her notes in the filing cabinet, hoping Pete wasn't assuming that she had made a definite decision to share premises with him when their tenancies at the school expired.

She approached the subject as she climbed into his mud-spattered blue Fiesta. 'It's good you're being so pro-active about this. I still haven't given it much thought.'

He didn't answer immediately, concentrating on pulling out into the rush hour traffic. The wipers swished a mixture of sleet and rain across the screen.

'One of us has to be,' he said.

Julia frowned at the collective pronoun. 'But I haven't made up my mind yet.'

'No, I know. You've got a lot on your plate. Makes sense though, doesn't it? Pete indicated to overtake a bus slowing to a stop outside an estate agent. A couple, arms linked under a golf umbrella, was browsing the properties in the lit window.

Julia pushed away the thought that she needed to start looking at houses as well as business premises. 'Careful!' She held her breath as Pete accelerated past the bus. The driver of an approaching car honked, flashing his headlamps.

'Sorry. Cut that a bit fine.'

'Do you always drive like this?'

He grinned. 'Didn't think you'd be lecturing me about my driving after Saturday.'

She didn't answer. Pete turned on to the dual carriageway which wound up the hill towards the main routes out of the city. 'Sorry. Can't have been easy, sorting through your mum's things. Did you find anything in those diaries?'

Julia hesitated. 'Not much.' She wasn't sure if she wanted to tell Pete about her mother's reference to a secret, though it would be good to talk it over with someone. She was missing having James to confide in since their row on Sunday morning.

The gears crunched as Pete moved down into second on the steep incline. 'Amazing building,' he said, nodding in the direction of the floodlit cathedral which loomed above on their left. The bells, muffled by the traffic, rang the three quarters.

Hearing them, Julia suddenly recalled them chiming midnight the previous Wednesday. Linda's words echoed in her head again: *'Now isn't the time to explain about our family. I don't want to upset you, to shock you, not with everything else you're dealing with.'* To her relief she hadn't heard from Linda since the phone call on Saturday. She wasn't sure she could cope with the older woman's dark hints at the moment. Julia shivered, then sneezed again. She took a tissue from her coat pocket and blew her nose.

'Takes a while for the heater to take off the chill.' Pete leaned across to turn it up to full blast, his hand brushing her knee.

'I'm warm enough. It's just. . .' She hesitated again. Maybe it would put things into perspective if she told Pete about Linda and her hint of a family secret.

'Just what?' Pete glanced at her as he yanked on the handbrake. The traffic had ground to a halt in the ascent to the traffic lights. Julia's legs jerked involuntarily. 'Bit jumpy, aren't you?'

She took a deep breath. 'It's probably nothing to worry about.' She turned the heater down, struggling to make herself heard above its whir. 'Just a woman who turned up at Mother's funeral claiming to be a long-lost relative.'

'Really? Who is she?'

'She claims to be a distant cousin. An artist. I went to her exhibition last week.'

'Cool. What kind of art?'

'Paintings. I don't know anything about art, but she

seems to be good. There were quite a lot of people there, including the local press.' Julia's shoulders stiffened inside her black trench coat as she remembered Linda pulling her in for the photo.

'So what's the problem?' Pete released the handbrake as the traffic in front resumed the ascent. They crawled a hundred yards before stopping again.

'I don't know. Maybe I'm reading too much into it, maybe things are getting to me more than they should. . .' Julia broke off, unused to so much self-disclosure. It was surprisingly easy to talk to Pete in the cocoon of the car.

'Give yourself a break, Julia. You've just lost your mum.'

She was touched by the genuine concern in Pete's eyes as he turned towards her. 'I suppose so. Maybe that's why I find her, Linda, so. . . overpowering.'

'Overpowering?' The car swayed in a gust of wind. Pete turned up the wipers as the rain began to fall harder.

'Yes. I found myself going along with her to an Italian after the exhibition, and then she hinted – it sounds far-fetched – that there's some kind of family secret.' Glancing up at the bulk of the cathedral as they crept forward the distance of two lamp posts, Julia shivered again.

'That's all, no details?'

'No. She said it wasn't the right time to tell me, that she didn't want to worry me with it after everything I've been through recently.'

'Meaning your mum's death?'

'Yes.' Julia hesitated. 'And my separation. Mum had told her about that too.'

'She seems to know a lot about you.'

'Yes. I've found that unsettling.' Julia was still shivering, though the car was now warm enough for Pete to turn down the heater. 'And I found out from Mum's neighbour that she'd been visiting since last summer.'

'You found out from your mum's neighbour? You mean your mum hadn't told you about her?' Pete released the handbrake and moved forward a short distance before braking again.

'No. It's strange, isn't it? All I can think is that Mother thought it was too insignificant to bother me. From what Linda said, I think she first visited in summer, around the time Greg and I split, just before Mother's heart condition was diagnosed. She must have visited quite a lot – there were four pictures of Mother's cottage at the "exhibition." 'The Open Door,' she called the series.'

'Could it have just been that she was inspired to paint your mum? Artists use a lot of different subjects, don't they?'

'Maybe.'

'You think there's more to it?'

'I just don't know why Mother didn't mention her. Aren't you putting the handbrake on?' Pete was riding the clutch on the incline and Julia found herself air-braking.

'Back seat driver, aren't you?' It was still light enough for Julia to see him grin as he pulled on the handbrake. 'Like you say, your mum might not have wanted to worry you about this woman when you had so much going on.'

'Mmm.'

'But you're not convinced?'

Pete was more perceptive than Julia had appreciated. It encouraged her to continue unravelling the enigma of her newly-discovered relative. 'No. The other thing is that Edith – Mother's neighbour – told me Linda had been back to the cottage since Mother died. So Mother must have given her a key. But why would she go back there?'

'Maybe she left something behind? I'm going to see if this is quicker. We're running late.' Pete turned left up the road winding towards the cathedral. Five low chimes of the bell penetrated the rain hammering on the car.

'She might have left something,' Julia conceded. 'But why didn't she mention it to me, ask me to get it for her? Why hasn't she told me she has a key?'

'That *is* weird. What are you going to do about it?' The traffic lights under the Norman archway changed to red and he pulled up.

'I don't know.' Julia twisted a button on her coat. 'I don't want her going back to the cottage. I mean, I don't know anything about the woman except that she's an artist. And you hear so many things about people befriending lonely old people and hoping to benefit. . . Linda doesn't seem that kind of person, but who knows?' Her voice rose as she vented the thoughts which had been troubling her since Saturday afternoon. 'She's got no right, has she, to go disturbing Mother, then poking around in her home after she's gone? I don't know who she thinks she is. She was even crying about losing Mother last week!' Julia swallowed hard, reaching again for her tissue.

Pete hesitated before turning towards her. 'I know she was your mother, Jules, but it's possible this artist woman had grown fond of her during her visits. You're right, though, she might be after something. Damn,' he muttered, stalling the car after a honk from the van behind drew his attention back to the traffic. He switched the engine back on, indicating to turn right towards the ring road.

Julia waited until he completed the turn. 'You don't think I'm being melodramatic, then?'

'No. Course not. Melodrama is never something I'd associate with you. Cool Jules is how I think of you.'

'"Cool Jules?"'

'Yes. Sorry, I know you don't like me calling you "Jules."'

'That doesn't matter.'

'Wow. Progress.'

Julia couldn't see Pete's expression as he manoeuvred round a bus, with greater care this time. But she registered the amusement in his voice and found herself smiling. Something had changed in her attitude towards him since he had helped her after the skid. And there had been that moment in the kitchen, when he had begun to massage her hand. . . Her cheeks grew warm at the thought. They would never be more than friends, she reminded herself. He was involved in some complicated relationship with someone. Besides, they had worked alongside one another all these years without there being any hint of any chemistry between them. Why was she bothered then that he had described her as 'cool'? It wasn't as bad as being described as 'smug' by James, was it? But even so. . . She kept her voice level. 'You say you find me "cool"?'

'Yeah. That's how you are, isn't it? Always in control. Measured. Never seen you rattled before Saturday. Blimey, real stair rods, isn't it?' He turned the wipers up to full speed as Julia digested his assessment.

There was a pause before Pete continued, 'Not surprised you weren't yourself on Saturday, though, with this weird artist woman on top of everything else. What does your brother make of it?'

Julia hesitated. 'I've not had chance to talk to him about it yet.' It was tempting to confide in him about the row with James, but she felt that would be disloyal.

'Oh?' Pete glanced across at her. When it was obvious Julia wasn't going to add anything, he went on, 'And you've checked nothing's missing at your mum's place? Jewellery, valuables, cash?'

'There was nothing except the cash in her purse. I took that home the day she went into hospital. She didn't have any jewellery or valuables left. No thanks to Nicholas.'

'Nicholas?'

'My step-father, James's father. Mother's second husband. He died ten years ago.' She sighed.

'Not good with money?'

'No. A lovely man though.' Julia smiled. She'd always been very fond of Nicholas. When her mother introduced them he'd produced a fluffy pink rabbit, more suitable for a baby than a ten-year-old. She'd realised that he was more nervous about their first meeting than she was. It had endeared him to her instantly.

'Nicholas made some bad investments and ended up in debt. Mother had to sell her few pieces of jewellery to bail him out. There wasn't much. Just necklaces and earrings my father had bought her for anniversaries and birthdays.' Julia's voice wavered and she found herself blinking back the tears which were never far away.

'Sounds like your dad was an old-fashioned romantic.' Pete turned off the heater, his hand catching her knee again.

She swallowed. 'Yes, I suppose he was.'

'Nicholas sounds a bit like your ex, doesn't he? What

is it with the women in your family that you pair up with financial losers?'

It was a moment before she trusted herself to speak. 'I beg your pardon?'

'Sorry. I shouldn't have said that.' Pete drummed his hand on the steering wheel. The final set of lights before their destination changed back to red.

'No. You shouldn't. Nicholas didn't know what he was doing, not like –' Julia broke off. She'd tried so hard not to criticise Greg since the split.

Pete jumped in. 'But Greg knew, didn't he?' When Julia didn't reply, he went on, 'Come on. Admit it, Jules, the man's a two-timing bastard who's left you high and dry. You were taken in by him hook, line and sinker. You'll feel a hell of a lot better if you admit what he was. *Finally.*' He turned into the car park in front of a small shopping precinct.

Julia's chest tightened. She felt a flush spread upwards from her neck. 'How dare you?' she said. 'How dare you make judgements about my choice of partner? And who do you think you are to give me advice?'

'No need for the high horse! He left you for another woman who he's knocked up. You're in danger of losing your house because he didn't pay the mortgage. Do I really need to spell it out?' Pete shook his head in disbelief. 'This'll be the one.' He swung the Fiesta into a space in front of a unit with a 'To Let' sign hanging above it. The lights were on inside, outlining a figure behind the glass door, presumably the agent.

Julia stared ahead through the windscreen. The heavy rain was already beginning to obscure the neon-lit shops.

She sensed Pete turn towards her but remained motionless. Blood pounded in her ears.

'Looks OK, doesn't it? Bright and welcoming on a foul night, makes a better first impression than the dismal old school!'

She took a deep breath, knowing as she opened her mouth that she was being irrational. But even so. . .

'After what you have said there is no way I will be going into business with you.' She opened the passenger door. 'I will leave you to view the premises and make my own way back to the office by bus.'

She climbed out of the car. A squall of wind blew the door against her left leg as she reached back in to pick up her laptop and bag from the footwell in front of the passenger seat. She clenched her teeth against the pain, keeping her face averted from Pete.

'Don't be daft, Jules.' His voice, faintly amused, was also gentle. Despite her resolution she paused in gathering her belongings. 'I was out of order. Sorry. But I'm trying to help. Honestly. Come on, have a look round. We've not got long before the landlord's notice expires.' Sensing her hesitate, he pressed on, 'And don't go back on the bus on a filthy night like this. It's not going to help you get over your cold.'

She sighed. Her financial circumstances alone meant she should go ahead and view the vacant premises, at least contemplate Pete's suggestion of them sharing. She replaced the laptop and bag in the car. 'All right then. But don't criticise Greg any more, OK?'

'Deal.' Pete jumped out of the car and joined her on the pavement outside the vacant unit. 'I just can't stand seeing a good woman like you being treated badly. You need to take care of yourself, duck.' He placed a hand briefly round her shoulders before passing her to open the door. Julia smiled at the local term of endearment, registering her disappointment that his touch had been so brief.

'Get a grip!' she told herself as the agent, a dark slim young woman in impossibly high red and white striped heels, stepped forward to greet them. She barely glanced at Julia, bestowing her wide smile on Pete.

Julia could see immediately that the premises were unsuitable. There was insufficient floor space to divide into two offices and a reception area. Pete voiced her opinion as he took in the dimensions of the unit. 'Far too small,' he said. 'Is that why the dimensions weren't included in the ad?'

The agent's smile faded. 'I'm not responsible for that. My colleague at the office drew up the particulars.'

Pete shrugged. 'Whatever. But the ad said the premises could be divided into 2–3 offices. No way.' He swept his arm around the unit. 'Maybe you could tell your colleague to provide accurate information and save folk making wild goose chases.'

'I'm sorry you feel you had a wasted journey. We have your details on file and will contact you if larger business premises come on to the market.' The agent's smile was back in place as she opened the door.

The rain was falling even more heavily as they made a dash to the car. 'Typical hard-faced lying agent,' said Pete as he turned the key in the ignition. His usual jaunty air had deserted him.

'There'll be other premises,' said Julia.

'We've not got much time, have we?' He slid the gear lever into reverse. 'I'd hoped these would fit the bill. Good location too.'

'I know. But like I said earlier, I'm not sure what I want to do.'

Pete drove in silence for a few moments as they turned back out on to the ring road. It was less busy heading back towards the city centre.

'Look,' he said finally, 'I don't want to push you, and I know you've got a lot on your plate, but surely it would be easier for us to find premises together instead of going our separate ways.' He paused, drawing up at traffic lights. Looking straight ahead through the spattered windscreen, he added, 'And we get on well enough, you and me, don't we?'

Julia glanced at him. His voice was light, but she sensed he was uncertain in a way she didn't usually associate with him.

'Of course,' she said. 'I'm sure it would be fine. I'm just not very decisive at the moment. Everything seems a bit much.' She massaged her temples and sneezed. 'Mother, the house, the premises, this woman Linda.' She sighed. 'Even going to my aunt's eightieth on Saturday seems like more than I can cope with.'

Pete turned down the street towards the old school. 'Your aunt's eightieth?'

'Yes. She's not the nicest woman. I could do without it to be honest.'

'Are you going with your brother and sister-in-law?' Pete pulled in behind Julia's Mondeo.

'Not exactly.'

'Oh?' He glanced at her and switched off the engine.

133

Julia kept quiet, again resisting the temptation to tell him about the row with James and his affair. She reached for the door handle.

'Well, if you need some company, a bit of support, I'm free Saturday.'

'Really?' Julia's heart lightened as she opened the door. 'What about – your friend?'

In the light cast by the street lamp above the car she saw Pete chew his lip, as if pondering his reply.

'That's not a problem,' he said after a moment.

'Thanks, Pete. That would be great.' She climbed out of the car and picked up her laptop and bag.

'No worries,' he said. 'And I'll keep looking at the ads, see if any other offices turn up and let you know. No pressure. How's that?'

'That sounds good. Thank you.' She smiled at him as he turned the engine back on. He grinned back.

'No worries,' he repeated.

Driving up the street behind him before they parted at the junction, Julia was surprised to realise she was sorry their journey had come to an end. It had been good to have someone to talk to. Even if it was only Pete.

− CHAPTER 13 −

'So your aunt didn't think of changing the venue after you had your mum's reception here?' asked Pete.

'Aunt Ada's not known for her tact.' Julia gasped as Pete narrowly missed the brick gatepost as he swung his Fiesta into the car park of The Wingate.

Hearing her, he grinned as he pulled into a parking space. 'Hey, I never hit anything you know.' He switched off the engine. 'But surely it must have crossed her mind it wasn't the most sensitive idea to insist on holding it here?'

Julia opened the door and climbed out of the car. 'Apparently not.' She tugged at the skirt of her red woollen dress, conscious it had ridden up her thigh. 'In fact she told my sister-in-law at the funeral that it was very inconsiderate of us to hold the reception here since she'd had her eightieth booked since November.'

Clare had reported this when she phoned Julia the day before. Julia had been relieved to hear her sounding more composed than she had on Monday, and they had arranged to meet for coffee the following week.

'Charming.' Pete locked the car and steered her across the wet car park under his umbrella. She sniffed his sage aftershave appreciatively.

'Thanks for coming,' she said as he opened the pub door for her. 'You must have had better things to do on a Saturday afternoon.'

'Than come to a cantankerous old woman's eightieth? Never!'

She smiled back as she passed into the lounge bar. It was so much easier being in Pete's company than turning up on her own. She wondered again about the complicated relationship he was involved in. Perhaps she would find out more during the course of the afternoon.

'Can I help you?' The girl behind the bar, an extremely slim blonde with large blue eyes in a pale face, reminded Julia of someone. Grace. She hoped her new client was having a good week. She'd worked through a lot in their first two sessions.

'We're here for Mrs Maltby's lunch.'

'Follow me, please.' The girl led the way down three steps behind the bar into the dining area where Emily's reception had been held. Julia noticed her legs were thin as twigs under her black mini-skirt.

'There you are, Julia. And who's this?' Aunt Ada was seated to the left of the steps in her wheelchair, wearing the same black dress she had worn at Emily's funeral. Julia recognised the carer from the funeral too. She had a disconcerting sense of déjà vu and was grateful again for Pete's presence.

The old woman plunged on before she had the chance of introducing Pete. 'I wasn't aware you were bringing an extra. Most inconsiderate, not to confirm numbers.'

Julia sighed, placing her gift on a table with the others. 'The invitation said "To Julia and guest", Aunt Ada.'

'Did it?' Aunt Ada narrowed her eyes. 'I didn't expect

you to find anyone to bring. Not after the last one left. What was his name, Gary? Ian? So who did you say this was?' She turned her head slowly towards Pete, flicking her grey eyes over him.

'I didn't,' said Julia tightly. 'This is Pete. A colleague.'

She saw a flicker of something like disappointment pass over Pete's face before his habitual insouciant smile returned. Perhaps she should have described him as a friend. They had moved beyond colleagues, she realised, over the last week or so.

'Mrs Maltby,' he said. 'What a pleasure to meet you.'

Aunt Ada looked at him sharply. Julia stifled a giggle.

'Humph,' the old woman sniffed. 'Well, it's good of you to accompany Julia, I suppose. It can be very difficult to be unmarried at her age.'

'Don't you think it can be equally difficult to be married?' Pete asked the question innocently enough. Aunt Ada drew her shrivelled body up in her wheelchair as far as her osteoperosis would allow. Her lips settled into the thin line Julia had known since childhood.

'What's she been telling you?' she asked. She turned to Julia. 'Have you no sense of dignity, discussing my life with virtual strangers?'

'I haven't said a word,' said Julia. 'And Pete is not a "virtual stranger." We've had neighbouring offices for nearly five years.'

'Hmm. Well, just you mind what you go telling him. And you, young man,' she turned again to Pete whose mouth was twitching, 'you should be more respectful of the institution of marriage.'

'I've got nothing against marriage,' said Pete. 'My mum and dad were happily married for thirty-eight years. But from what you've said, I'm guessing not everyone's so lucky, are they?'

Ada drew in her breath with a bronchial rattle. 'That's none of your business,' she said. 'Are you married yourself?'

'No.' Pete paused and looked unusually serious. 'But I'd consider it if I met the right woman.'

'And how old are you?'

'Aunt Ada!'

Pete lay a hand on Julia's arm. Julia saw her aunt glance at it. She felt reassured by the warm pressure. 'It doesn't matter, Jules,' he said. 'Fifty-one.' He grimaced. 'Unlucky in love, you could say.'

'I'd say if you haven't married by then, you never will,' said the old woman. She paused, and then looked at Julia with a spiteful gleam in her eye. 'Of course Julia's mother was on her second marriage at that age.'

'Because Daddy had died of his war injuries!' Julia exclaimed, stung by the snide remark. 'And she was lucky enough to meet another man who made her happy.'

'Oh, yes. Always popular with the men, was Emily.' Ada looked down her beaky nose.

Julia stared at her aunt. She took in the creased face with the papery lines around the mouth and eyes, the neck shrunken into her shoulders above the curved spine, the worn hands with the protruding veins and swollen fingers. Ada looked more reptilian than ever. *Why did you outlive Mother?*

'Mother was happily married twice,' she said.

Ada raised her head slowly. Her narrow lidded eyes held Julia's. 'Happily for her or for her husbands?'

Beside her Julia sensed Pete stiffen. Her own breath

was coming faster. The blood was pounding in her ears again.

'Happily for all of them,' she said as firmly as she could, though her voice sounded hollow to her own ears.

'Mm.' The old woman smiled thinly. She lowered her head, suddenly disinterested in the conversation. 'Wheel me to the table, will you? It's nearly time to eat. I've no idea where that girl's gone. Call her a carer. Always wandering off.'

'No wonder,' Pete muttered in Julia's ear as she pushed the wheelchair across to the centre of the long table where some people were already seated.

Julia smiled wanly. Ada's barbed comments had made her think again of William Prescott's visit forty-one years ago, her mother's anger towards him in her diary, Linda's hints at a family secret. She hadn't heard from Linda since the art exhibition. Someone had rung her phone a few times without leaving a message and Julia had wondered if it were her, or a nervous client.

'Here's that brother of yours. About time too!' Ada's voice recalled Julia to the present as she attempted to steer the wheelchair into a gap between Ada's niece by marriage and an elderly woman she didn't recognise.

Julia didn't turn round. To an onlooker it would seem she was concentrating on positioning the wheelchair. She wanted to compose herself before facing James. They hadn't been in contact since their row the previous Sunday.

'Here. Let me.' Pete's right hand brushed hers briefly on the handle of the wheelchair. He pushed it into the space.

'Thanks.' Julia smiled at him.

'No problem.' He smiled back, stepping away from the

table. She noticed again how the smile emphasised the crinkles around his eyes. He turned his head and leaned towards her, his stubble tickling her cheek as he whispered, 'Now if there's no place settings, shall we sit as far away from the vicious old bat as possible?'

She stifled a giggle, suddenly relaxed. 'Let's,' she agreed. She was still avoiding looking towards the doorway, not wanting to catch the eye of James or Clare.

They sat down opposite one another at the end of the table. Julia nodded to a white-haired couple sitting two chairs along. She recognised them as Ada's neighbours. They nodded back, before continuing their conversation with two old ladies sitting the other side of them. Snippets filtered down the table above the soft classical music, the clink of glasses and the hum of other voices:

'I've been on the waiting list for my new hip since November,' said the stouter of the two old ladies.

'It makes you wonder what we've been paying our taxes for all these years,' rejoined Ada's male neighbour.

Pete and Julia smiled at one another again. 'Spare me old age,' he said. 'Red or white?'

'Red thanks.' He filled her glass before pouring himself some water from the crystal jug. Out of the corner of her eye Julia watched James and Clare take seats down the other end of the table. She settled back in her chair and took a sip of red wine.

Pete glanced round. 'So what's the story with you and your brother?' He sipped his water.

She pushed a strand of hair behind her ear and toyed with the stem of her wine glass. 'What do you mean?' she asked, not meeting his eye.

'That you haven't looked in his direction since he

arrived, and that he's sitting as far away from us as possible.'

Julia sighed. 'It's complicated,' she said.

'Complicated?'

She looked across at him. 'I don't really want to talk about it,' she said. 'Family. You know.'

Again she detected a flicker of disappointment pass over his face. Pete had a very open face, she realised. Open and honest. Realising he was watching her watching him she quickly took another gulp of wine.

'Good wine?'

'Yes. But I'd better not drink too much before the food.'

'You just relax this afternoon, Jules. That's why I offered to drive, give you a chance to chill.'

'Thank you, that's really kind.' She smiled across at him again. He smiled back, his blue eyes warm. She was the first to break the eye contact.

'Anyway,' she said, aiming for a light tone, 'are you going to tell me about your mystery woman?'

He hesitated, looking towards the doorway where the last guests were coming in. 'Not right now,' he said. 'Maybe later. Blimey, I thought my mother was the only person who wore one of those old-fashioned black coats and hat these days!'

Julia followed his gaze and saw Edith stepping carefully down the steps. She laid her present for Ada among the others. Taking off her ancient black coat and hat, she passed them to a waiter, a gangly young man with acne.

'That's Edith,' she said. 'Mother's neighbour. She goes to church with Aunt Ada.' Her heart sank. The adjoining seats were the only ones vacant. It would be impossible to relax quietly now over the meal with Pete.

141

Edith scanned the room with her beady eyes, waving at Julia when she spotted her. After going across to greet Ada, she came down the table.

'May I?' Without waiting for a reply, she perched on the cushioned chair next to Pete, her brown eyes darting between the two of them like a bright sparrow's. 'I'm so glad to see you have company, dear,' she said. 'My friend Madge was supposed to be coming with me, but she had a stroke on Thursday. From what her daughter said when I rang this morning, I don't think she's going to recover.'

'I'm sorry,' said Julia, though it struck her Edith had delivered the news with a certain relish. The old woman's next words confirmed the impression.

'Thank you. But at my age it's very much a case of survival of the fittest, you know.'

Pete spluttered over his glass of water. He dabbed at his mouth with his white linen napkin. Edith seemed not to notice.

'I look through the Family Announcements in *The Herald* every week to see who I know among the deaths. They bring back memories, you know, people you haven't thought about or clapped eyes on for years.'

Julia shivered, remembering her mother's diary entry of Ada's call when she found William Prescott's name among the obituaries.

'I'm sorry, dear,' said Edith. 'I shouldn't be saying all this so soon after your mother. . . But I am pleased you've found someone.' She smiled, revealing uneven yellowing teeth. 'Thank you,' she said as the waiter set down a bowl of tomato soup in front of her. A sprig of basil floated on the top.

Pete swirled the water in his tumbler and glanced at Julia.

'Oh no,' she said hastily, 'it's nothing like that! Pete and I just rent offices together. We're colleagues. . . friends,' she amended, recalling her glimpse of Pete's disappointment when she had introduced him as a colleague to Aunt Ada. 'Tomato and basil, my favourite.'

'Well,' said Edith comfortably, 'you never know, do you? Anyway, I wanted to tell you that that woman phoned me this morning.' She sipped delicately at her soup.

'"That woman?"' Julia echoed, hand poised over her napkin. But she knew who Edith meant.

'The artist. She sounded upset, said that she'd been trying to get hold of you but hadn't been able to. I told her I'd be seeing you here this afternoon and could pass on a message.'

So Linda had been the caller who hadn't left messages on the answerphone. Julia finally unfolded her napkin. 'Did she say why she wanted to speak to me?'

The old lady shook her white head regretfully. 'No. She said it was a personal matter. I told her I'd let you know she'd been trying to get in touch when I saw you this afternoon.'

'Thank you.' Julia frowned as she sipped her wine. She wondered what Linda wanted. She hadn't yet phoned the art gallery where Linda's exhibition had been held to see if they had contact details for the artist. This wasn't so much because she hadn't had time. It was more that she was far from sure she wanted to hear any more from Linda about a family secret. 'Did she give you a contact number?' she asked.

'No. I was going to ask, but she rang off. Very worked

up, she sounded.' Edith broke off a piece of her white roll and dipped it in her soup. 'Not being nosy or anything, but I've been thinking it's strange that she only met your mother and hasn't bothered with Ada. She's her cousin too, isn't she?'

'I suppose so. Unless she was satisfied enough with meeting Mum. It's not like a close relationship, is it, second cousins?'

'Mmm. Unless,' Edith lowered her voice and leaned across the table towards Julia, 'unless this Linda person isn't who she says she is.'

'What do you mean?' asked Julia.

Her tone was sharper than she intended, and the old lady's hand jerked, spilling a spoonful of soup on to the white tablecloth. Pete dabbed his napkin in his water and unsuccessfully tried to mop up the orange stain.

'Well, you do hear of these people befriending the lonely elderly, don't you?' said Edith. 'Working their way into their affections?'

'But Mother wasn't lonely!' said Julia, though she knew with a pang this wasn't true. How often had she dropped off her mother's shopping without having time for a cup of tea? If only she could have those last few months back. . . She took a long draught of wine, aware that she was getting a little tipsy.

'Of course you and James visited,' said Edith, 'but time does hang heavy when you're old, you know. You young people are so busy with your own lives. And I hope you don't mind me saying so, but your mother was quite retiring, wasn't she?'

'Yes,' admitted Julia. Emily had always seemed content with immediate family members and a few close friends.

Unlike Ada, she didn't attend church. Nor had she involved herself in village events in the way Julia knew her father would have done had he lived into old age. Leonard had been a pillar of the community even as a young man. 'But why would Linda target Mother?' she asked.

'And why try to befriend Julia now?' interposed Pete, who had been quietly eating his soup during their exchange.

'That *is* strange,' Edith agreed.

'Have you told Aunt Ada about her?' asked Julia.

'No. I thought your mother would have done. But from our chat this morning, I don't think she did. Very odd, don't you think?'

Whatever Julia thought was lost. 'Julia! There you are!' To her astonishment, Linda stood in the doorway, teetering in her high-heeled purple boots. Silence spread throughout the dining room as people stopped speaking at the sound of her raised voice.

Linda swayed down the three steps into the dining area. She wasn't wearing a coat. Rain dripped from her short geometrically patterned orange and turquoise dress on to the crimson carpet. Her long curly hair lay tangled about her shoulders like seaweed. Mascara had run down her cheeks and her heavily made up eyes looked bruised from lack of sleep. 'Julia!' she called again. 'I'm so pleased to find you!'

Julia felt a deep flush rise to her cheeks as all eyes turned to her. She didn't move. The wine had gone to her head. She was afraid she would stagger if she rose and went over to Linda. And actually she wanted to pretend she didn't know the bedraggled woman who was wending her way towards her, obviously drunk.

'Whoever is this?' rapped out Ada as her guests continued to stare between Linda and Julia. 'And who let her in? This is a private party!' She turned to the acne riddled waiter. 'You, boy, don't just stand there gawping! Go and fetch the manager!' Then she glared down the table towards her niece. 'Julia, is she one of your cases?'

'"One of Julia's cases?"' Linda threw her head back and laughed wildly. She staggered towards the table. 'Let me guess. You must be Ada.' She leaned across the table towards the old woman in the wheelchair, picking up a bottle of red wine. Ada stared at her.

'Do you think she's dangerous?' squawked Edith. No one moved or responded, frozen by the unexpected visitor.

Linda's hand was shaking as she raised the wine bottle to her magenta lips. 'Happy birthday, Ada!' She tipped her head back, and took a long draught, then tottered to the top of the table. There she waved the bottle around the room of mesmerised guests. 'And good health to you all!' she slurred.

'Who are you?' said Ada, an unusual quaver in her voice. 'What do you want?'

Linda laughed raucously. '"What do I want?" she asks. "Who am I?"' She stumbled the last few steps towards the old woman, then bent down so her face was level. Ada shrank back in her wheelchair. 'Have a good look. I'm sure you can work it out.'

Ada stared back at her and began to tremble. Julia had never seen her aunt afraid and felt an unexpected jolt of sympathy for her. The old lady's fear broke the spell which had mesmerised the guests. Pete rose to his feet, as did James at the other end of the table.

'I think you should leave.' James spoke calmly but firmly as he drew alongside Linda. He laid a hand on her arm. The other guests murmured assent. 'I don't know who you are, but you shouldn't be troubling my aunt, a defenceless old lady.'

'Defenceless you call her, do you?' Linda threw her head back with a cackle of laughter, shaking off James's hand. She looked around the table. 'You don't know the half of it, do they Ada?'

'I don't know what you mean,' Ada croaked wheezily.

'Now look,' began James again, but Linda suddenly gripped her head with both hands and closed her eyes. 'My head! Oh!' She swayed forward, tripping over one of the wheels of Ada's wheelchair. She fell diagonally across the table, knocking over glasses, bowls and cutlery.

One of the guests screamed, others gasped and one old lady began to cry. Those sitting near Ada and the sprawled figure of Linda began to move away from the table, feet crunching in the broken glass and shards of pottery.

'Police! Ambulance!' shouted Edith as the manager finally appeared. He ran down the stairs as he took in the mayhem, nearly tripping over the bottom step.

Linda was lying so still that for a moment Julia wondered if she were dead. It was Pete who had the presence of mind to lift her up out of the mess of glass and crockery. She moaned as he pulled her to her feet, then leaned heavily on him as if she were incapable of supporting her own weight. He guided her to the chair by the table where Ada's presents were massed. Linda's hazel eyes were glassy and unfocused. She began to cry.

Sobered by the disturbance, Julia moved towards Ada.

James had wheeled her chair away from the table. Clare was leaning over her, murmuring soothingly.

'Aunt Ada,' said Julia, taking a mottled hand, 'are you all right?'

All colour had drained from the old woman's face. She was staring at the weeping Linda. She opened her mouth to speak but no words came.

'It's all right, Auntie,' said James. 'We'll make sure she doesn't come near you again. She's clearly mad, whoever she is.' He looked accusingly at Julia. 'How come she knows you, Julia? Is she one of your clients?'

'No, she isn't,' Julia tried to keep her voice level for the sake of the sick woman. 'It's the woman who came to Mother's funeral.' She found her aunt's pulse. It was faint and irregular. 'Call an ambulance, would you? You'll be OK, Aunt Ada,' she said with a conviction she didn't feel.

Ada looked up at her. She raised the index finger of her right hand in the direction of the chair where Linda had been sitting and opened her mouth again. Julia turned, but the chair was empty. There was no sign of the woman. She leaned over Ada.

'It's *her*,' whispered the old woman. She stared up at Julia, her face contorted. She struggled to breathe, her hand grasping Julia's wrist in a painful grip. 'I never told her. . .' she gasped out.

'Never told who what, Aunt Ada?' Julia bent over her aunt, held by the tormented grey eyes.

Again the old woman gasped for air. 'He was. . .' a rattling breath, '. . . alive.' She slumped sideways in her wheelchair.

– CHAPTER 14 –

'Clare and I will follow Aunt Ada to the hospital,' said James, as the paramedics carried the old lady through the hotel door on a stretcher. Ada hadn't regained consciousness in the fifteen minutes it had taken for the ambulance to arrive. 'You look like you're over the limit, Julia. I assume your. . . friend is driving you?'

'Yes, Pete is driving me,' she said coolly. 'I'm not in the habit of drinking and driving.'

James glared at her, knowing the barb was directed at him following his drunken arrival at her cottage the previous Sunday morning.

Clare intervened quickly. 'I'll call you later, Julia, shall I? Let you know how she is?'

'Thanks,' said Julia. She turned on her heel and went back to the lounge bar where Pete and Edith were sitting in brown leather tub chairs by a round table. 'I knew when I first clapped eyes on her there was something not right about her,' the old lady was saying. 'Befriending Julia's mother like that, without Julia knowing anything about her. How do we know she wasn't threatening her too?'

Julia sank into the next chair, suddenly overwhelmed by weariness. 'We don't,' she said. 'But why would she have painted Mum if she was threatening her? She'd taken a lot of care over those paintings. And she seemed genuinely sorry she'd died too.' She remembered how Linda's tears had irritated her at Giuseppe's. 'I can't believe she would have any reason to threaten Mother. But then I can't imagine Aunt Ada. . .'

'From what I saw of Aunt Ada, she wasn't exactly pleasant,' cut in Pete. 'Sorry, but first impressions and all that.' He glanced at Julia, who looked in turn at Edith.

'Don't worry about offending me, duck,' said the old lady. 'I've known Ada nearly sixty years, and she's never been an easy person, not even as a young woman. Bitter she became, after her husband left. And you know,' she turned to Julia, 'I always thought she resented him dying within the year. She said once it would have spared her the shame if he'd died when they were still together.'

'Nice.' Pete looked at Julia. 'So that's what she was on about earlier, asking what you'd told me about her?'

'I suppose so.' Julia shook her head. 'Imagine being so concerned with appearances that you'd prefer your husband dead rather than be separated.' But then, she reminded herself, there was a theory that it was easier to move on with your life if a partner was lost through death rather than separation. It was a theory she had found borne out several times during her counselling practice. Was the same true for her? Would she have coped better with Greg's death than his unfaithfulness? She sighed and laced her fingers pensively over her mouth.

'Don't worry,' Edith leaned over and patted her knee. 'I'm sure it'll be all right.'

'What?' Julia looked up. 'Oh, you mean Ada.'

Pete was watching her. She had an uncomfortable sense he knew something of what she was thinking. Colour rose to her cheeks as she remembered how defensive she had been about Greg with him.

Edith raised a pencilled eyebrow. 'Of course. Who else?'

Julia's flush deepened. She was grateful when Pete took over, maybe registering her confusion, 'This woman, Linda, was very hostile. Ada was seriously rattled, wasn't she? She looked like she'd seen a ghost.'

Julia shivered. She pictured again Ada's trembling forefinger, her hoarse whisper, 'It's *her*.' Pete was right. 'I just don't know what to think. And who knows where Linda went? Do you think she'll be all right?' The woman had looked so disorientated and distressed before she disappeared, almost as if she couldn't remember how she'd come to be there. She had clearly been very drunk.

'I wouldn't spare any sympathy for her,' said Edith briskly. 'She didn't want the police after her, that's why she disappeared so fast. Disgraceful. Turning up here and threatening an innocent old lady, causing chaos and upset.'

Not wanting to upset Edith, Julia refrained from pointing out that 'innocent' wasn't a word she would apply to her aunt. She rubbed her temples, trying to make sense of it all.

'You look done in, Jules,' said Pete. 'Ready to go? I've offered Mrs Bradley a lift and loaded some of Ada's presents into the car. There's just a few left.'

'That's very thoughtful. Thanks.' Julia had forgotten about the presents.

'No worries.' Pete went down to the dining area to collect the rest of the gifts.

Edith patted Julia's knee again. 'He's a good one,' she said. 'You try and keep him.'

'But he's just. . .' Julia sighed. 'Anyway, I think he's attached.' She regretted the words as soon as they were out. She should have made clear that Pete wasn't her type. Edith would think she was interested now.

'Not married, is he?' said Edith.

'No, but. . .'

'Well then!'

Pete emerged through the doorway laden with the remaining presents. Julia rose and relieved him of a few. She wondered if Ada would ever open them and shivered again. She was a spiteful old woman, bitter, as Emily had written in her diary, but it had been a shock to see her so frightened by Linda.

Julia climbed into the back of the two-door Fiesta, knowing the old woman would find this awkward with her hip replacement. She could barely hear Edith's chatter above the noise of the heater which Pete had put on to dispel the condensation. It was still raining hard, and Pete drove carefully along the Burton road where water was backing up above the drains.

She was convinced now that there was a secret in her family's past, something Ada and Linda knew, something related to her mother. More than ever, she shied away from knowing the secret herself. Linda's hints and her animosity towards Ada, her own childhood memory of Emily's anger towards William Prescott, Emily's diary entry recording how she believed William Prescott had told Leonard something which hastened his death, all these pointed to the secret being disturbing. In her mind's eye she saw again her parents' wedding photograph, her mother's stiff pose. It might be cowardly and childish, but she wanted to preserve her memory of her parents' happy marriage, a memory which she had clung to throughout the years since her father's premature death.

Pete slowed down as they approached Scampton Parish Church where cars were parked on both sides of the road. A rotund man in a grey morning suit held a large black umbrella above a plump bride making an unseemly dash for the church door. Two teenage bridesmaids in burgundy were struggling to match her pace and keep the train of her ivory dress out of the mud.

Edith turned round from the passenger seat, smiling at Julia with her uneven yellow teeth. Julia leaned forward to hear her better above the noise of the heater and windscreen wipers. 'Just like my wedding day! Robert had three days' leave from the Army that weekend, and oh, it did rain. I told you your grandfather married us, didn't I, Julia?'

'Yes.' A thought struck Julia. 'Was that the same year Mother got married?'

'I think that was two years later, just after the end of the war, wasn't it? I got married in 1943. I didn't know her and Ada so well then, with them being that bit older and me coming from the next village. I could have got married there, but Robert's mother was keen on us having our wedding here, and she was quite ill by then, poor lady. I didn't mind, and neither did my parents, as we could see it meant a lot to her. Ada was at my wedding though, she was very involved in the parish. I seem to remember Emily was away somewhere, helping out some family on her mother's side or something.'

'Oh? I've never heard about that.'

'Well, it was a long time before you were born, of course. Sad you didn't know your grandfather. Such a lovely man. Very understanding and caring. Maybe I shouldn't say, but I think he would have been sad your mum stopped going to church. A good vicar, he was, always had time for you and practised what he preached. Not always dashing about like they seem to be these days. Do you know, Reverend Smith. . .'

Julia sat back again and let Edith's complaint about Reverend Smith's pastoral shortcomings wash over her. Although she had moved to the nearby village of Ingham many years ago, Edith had continued to attend the church at Scampton. Ada had worshipped there all her life. She wondered where Emily had gone back in 1943. Might the family she had been helping be connected with Linda? It was possible, thought Julia, looking out of the rear side window at the darkening grey sky. Rain continued to fall over the sodden fields which stretched away towards the cooling towers of the two power stations across the River Trent. Linda had said they were related through Emily's mother. She determined to find out if she heard from the woman again. Or would Linda be too embarrassed to make contact when she sobered up?

'What do you think, Jules?' Pete's question broke into her thoughts. She turned forward to find him looking at her in the rear view mirror as he took the left fork for Ingham.

'About what?' she asked.

'Have you been asleep back there? I said you looked knackered!' He grinned, his teeth as white and even as Edith's were yellow and crooked. 'Just wondered if you had a key for your mum's house on you, if you want to go in while I'm here and take a look around in case that mad artist woman's been back.'

'She's not been back when I've been in,' said Edith quickly. 'I've been keeping an eye out.'

'I bet you have Mrs B.' Pete took his left hand off the steering wheel to pat the old lady's knee. 'Better than Neighbourhood Watch, you'll be.'

'Do you think so?' Edith drew herself upright in the passenger seat. I know some people might think I'm nosy, but I just see it as doing my bit. I promised Julia, didn't I, duck?' She turned round to Julia.

'You did, Edith, and I'm very grateful. And I do have a key in my bag, so if you're not in a hurry, Pete. . .'

'No problem.' Pete turned left down the hill as Edith directed.

He parked alongside the row of cottages. Edith looked disappointed when they refused a cup of tea, but cheered up when Julia assured her she would let her know if anything valuable had been taken by 'that mad artist woman.'

The heavy white wooden door refused to budge when Julia unlocked it.

'Here. Let me. The wood's swollen in the rain.' Pete moved forward and put his shoulder to the door. It yielded slightly on his first thrust, then opened on the second. He stepped back to allow Julia in first, brushing briefly against her.

'Nice place. Cosy.' Pete glanced round the compact beamed sitting room as Julia flicked on the light to dissipate the gloom.

She shivered. 'Not on an afternoon like this.'

Pete bent to switch on the fire. 'No harm putting this on whilst we're here. You OK, Jules?'

She brushed away a tear. 'Sorry. It's just I still expect. . . Mother. . .'

'Hey.' He crossed the room and put his arms round her. She cried softly against his leather jacket for a few moments, then broke away.

'I'm sorry,' she said, not looking at him. 'I think it's the wine, and Linda, and then coming here. Maybe not a good idea.'

'Stop giving yourself such a hard time,' he said gently. 'Isn't that what you'd tell one of your clients?'

She half-smiled. 'Probably.'

'There you go. Now,' he assumed a more business-like tone, 'we don't know what your long-lost relative was looking for. You said your mum didn't have any jewellery or valuables, so it doesn't sound like that was what she was after. Where've you cleared so far?'

'Hardly anywhere. Just the desk last week. That's where I found the diaries. There was nothing else in there apart from stationery and old bills.'

'Right.' He glanced round the sitting room again and went over to the bookcase. 'So the only other storage area down here is this? She had some old books, didn't she?' He began to pull out the hardbacks from the top shelf, flicking through them. Julia went across and started to go through the paperback novels on the lower shelves.

'Yes. She got rid of a lot when she moved here after Nicholas died. Some of those books, the local history ones, were my grandfather's. You know, the vicar who Edith was talking about.'

'Cool.'

'What is?'

'Having a vicar as a grandfather.'

'You think so?' Julia looked up at him. 'I wouldn't have you marked down as religious.'

'No? But you don't know me that well, do you?' He gave her a long, unexpectedly serious look.

'No. I don't suppose I do,' she said quietly. She turned back to the novels. How often had she thought, even today, of Pete as 'just a colleague,' someone she rented business premises with?

'Anyway, what about you? Do you believe in God?' Pete coughed as a cloud of dust rose from the book in his hand.

'Not really,' said Julia. She rocked back on her heels, thinking. 'I suppose I fell out with Him when my father died. I was only eight. Mother didn't go to church very often after that. And then religion can cause so many problems, can't it? Not just wars, which people so often say but so many personal hang-ups.' A picture of Grace floated before her for the second time that afternoon. The young woman's step-mother sounded ardently evangelical and Julia was convinced her influence had contributed to Grace's fragile mental state.

'I think there's a difference between religion and personal faith though,' said Pete. He tapped the dusty book he was leafing through. 'I've always admired this lot.'

'Who?'

'The Pilgrim Fathers. Leaving behind everything they knew. All in pursuit of religious tolerance and freedom to worship according to their conscience.'

'But look what that led to! What about the Salem witch trials?' Julia stood up and flexed her foot. 'Ouch. Pins and needles.'

'Human error.' Pete replaced the book. 'Always gets in the way some time. But I don't think that's a reason to give up on God.'

'Mmm.' Julia started on the middle shelf, a

miscellaneous collection of poetry, biographies and local history which seemed to be even more jammed together than the other books. 'I think we'll have to agree to differ. I just think there's too much evidence for the case against God. Too many bad things, too much suffering.'

'What about all that's good in the world?' Pete started at the other end of the shelf. 'Creativity, and beauty, and. . .'

Julia glanced at him as he hesitated. 'And. . . ?'

'And love?' His voice was low and his face averted. Julia was suddenly aware of their physical proximity, of something indefinable in the air between them.

'I don't know.' Her voice sounded falsely bright. 'It's all a mystery to me. I don't think there's anything. . . What's this?'

'I've got one too!' Pete pulled out a black notebook from behind a volume of Tennyson. It matched the one Julia had found inside a book about Lincolnshire airfields.

'More of Mother's diaries,' said Julia, 'but much earlier than those I found last week,' she added, surveying the faded black script on the yellowing pages. '1942.'

'And 1941,' said Pete. 'Wow. I'll leave it for you to read, Jules.'

'Thanks,' She smiled at him, grateful for his sensitivity. 'Look, here's another.'

'And another! That's why this shelf looks so jammed. Your mum kept these old diaries here.'

'All this time. I had no idea.' She shook her head wonderingly as they extracted the rest of the books, uncovering four more diaries which they placed on the desk.

A squall of rain lashed against the window. 'We should go,' she said. 'And we still don't know what Linda was looking for.' She turned the pages of one of the diaries as Pete replaced the books on the middle shelf. It contained entries dating back to 1940.

'No. But those diaries will be interesting. Life of a vicar's daughter during the war.'

'I don't know. There are a few mentions of planes overhead and Scampton airfield, but mostly Mother seemed to write about family, church and the village.' Julia leafed through the diaries. The one from 1940 was the earliest. She spread them across the desk in date order, then frowned.

'Pete, can you check that shelf again? I think we've missed one. I've got one for 1940, one for 1941, two for 1942 going into early 1943 and then one for early 1944. Maybe she gave up after '44, the entries are much shorter, just facts about what she did each day, like the diaries she kept recently. But there might have been another from spring 1943 to the end of the year.'

Pete pulled out the books again. 'Nothing.'

'Perhaps she didn't bother then. Or maybe it's lost.'

Pete stretched his arms above his shaved head. 'Or maybe that's what Linda was looking for when she came back that day. Maybe she took it.'

'But why? It doesn't make sense. Let's go.' Julia switched off the electric fire. The top bar sparked, making her jump. 'I need to get that checked,' she said, shoving the diaries into a plastic bag she had left on the desk the previous week.

'You look like you can't get out of here fast enough!' said Pete as he pulled the front door firmly shut.

'I don't know. It's just something. . .' Julia locked the door, waving to Edith who was apparently tidying her porch.

'Something not right?' Pete looked at her over the roof of the Fiesta.

'No. Oh, I'm probably being silly.' Julia shook herself as she climbed into the car. 'It's been a long day. And I've kept you too long too.'

Pete paused in the action of turning the key in the ignition. 'You can keep me any time you like, Jules,' he said softly. He leaned over and kissed her, a gentle lingering kiss. For a moment she kissed him back, then pulled away.

'What are you doing?' she demanded. Without looking at her, he switched on the engine and turned the car to climb back up the hill from the village. 'You told me you were involved with someone!'

'No, I didn't,' he said. 'Sorry. I shouldn't have done that.'

'No, you bloody well shouldn't, and yes, you did tell me you were involved with someone!' she shouted. She leaned her head back against the head rest and closed her eyes.

He didn't reply as he made the turning on to the road leading back towards Scampton. Then he pulled into an opening by a farm gate and switched off the engine.

Julia's eyes snapped open. 'What are you doing? Can you please just take me home?'

Pete turned away from her, looking out of the driver's window into the rainy twilight. 'I know this isn't the right time,' he said, 'but you were the woman I was talking about last week. You, Jules – Julia – you are the reason I split up with Xanthe. She knew there was someone else. Only of course there wasn't, because you were still with Greg back then.'

He turned to her. She caught her breath when she saw the naked longing and vulnerability in his eyes.

'It's you I want to be with, Jules.' His voice was husky. 'I'd really like to give it a go. I think we could be good together, you and I, don't you?'

She swallowed. 'No,' she said. 'No. I'm sorry, but no. I just can't. . . there's too much. . .'

He looked at the condensation rising on the windscreen and switched the engine back on. 'OK. Forget I said anything.' He laughed, but Julia wasn't deceived. 'Timing was never my thing,' he said.

They drove back to Lincoln in silence, too fast for Julia's liking, splashing through puddles created by the rain and the backed up drains.

'Thank you,' she said, as he drew up outside her house. The words sounded so inadequate. 'I really appreciate all your help this afternoon.' She grimaced. *Too patronising.*

'No probs,' he said. He didn't look at her as she opened the passenger door. 'By the way, I'm taking some leave next week, so I won't see you at the office.'

'OK.' She suspected the decision had been made in the ten minutes it had taken to drive home. She felt a curious mixture of relief and disappointment. She would rattle around in the old school without him, but life was complicated enough without the awkwardness which they would both feel following his declaration. 'See you soon.'

'Yeah. See you soon.' With a screech of tyres he drove off.

– CHAPTER 15 –

'It helped me last week, realising I need to grieve for the father I lost as a little girl.' Grace settled back into her chair at the start of her third counselling session the following Wednesday.

Julia nodded encouragingly, noting that it was the first time that her client had taken the initiative in their meetings.

'I've wondered if that's why I've been dreaming about him as he was when I was a child too. He's younger in my dreams. When I wake up, I feel safe and secure, in a way I haven't since I was small.' She smiled wistfully before her cornflower eyes clouded over. 'Then I remember that he's gone and I feel so sad, so lost.' She paused, twisting her strawberry blonde plait between her fingers. 'It's like Frances took him away from me all those years ago.' She sighed. 'And I know this might be strange, but I blame God too.'

Julia raised her finely shaped dark eyebrows. 'God too?'

'Yes. Daddy got so involved with the church when he met Frances. He'd talk about how he'd met Jesus, how God had sent Frances into our lives, how we had the chance of a new start with her.'

'And how did you feel?'

Grace shrugged. 'I didn't understand.'

'You didn't understand?'

'No.' Grace placed the forefinger of her right hand on her lip, staring into the distance like a child working out the answer to a tricky question. 'I didn't understand what meeting Jesus meant. And I didn't understand what he meant by a new start. I thought,' her voice quavered, 'I thought we were happy as we were. Just me and Daddy.'

She lowered her head into her hands, dashing tears away. Julia resisted a sudden urge to go across and place an arm around her slender shoulders.

The younger woman looked up again, 'Sorry.'

'There's no need to apologise, Grace. Remember, this is a safe space.'

'Yes. Thank you. I do feel safe with you, you know, like I could tell you anything. Almost like. . .'

'Yes?'

'Like you're the mother I never had.' She glanced at Julia shyly. 'Is that OK?'

Julia took a deep breath. She was taken aback by the inner warm glow she felt at Grace's words. But she was well-aware that client dependency was something all counsellors had to guard against. Grace identifying her as a mother figure suggested she was becoming overly dependent.

'I'm sorry. Should I not have said. . . ?' Grace chewed her lip.

'It's all right.' Julia hastened to be clear. 'Obviously you know I'm not your mother, but it's good that you feel able to talk to me so openly.' She hesitated, wanting to move the session onto safer ground. 'Tell me more about how you felt when your father met Frances and found God.'

'I felt lonely. Lonely and confused.' The younger woman hugged herself, looking towards the rain spattered window. 'Suddenly Daddy was never there. He found babysitters for me – teenage daughters of women who worked in his office. One of them, Tracy, would send me off to bed as soon as possible so her boyfriend could come round – I'd creep out on to the landing when I heard her opening the front door, hoping that maybe Daddy had come home early, even that he might have left Frances. No such luck.' Her full lips twisted into a wry smile. 'One day I mentioned Tracy's boyfriend coming round to Daddy. Frances was there. I remember her sharp intake of breath, her shocked expression. She said something about "not wanting to create temptation for these young people, especially with your child to consider." Of course I didn't know what she was talking about. But Tracy didn't babysit for me again. It was soon after that Daddy and Frances got married. When I was older I wondered if my mentioning Tracy's boyfriend coming round led to them getting married so quickly.'

'Oh?'

'Yes. You remember me telling you last week how Frances had this line at the church café for the children of any men who turned up on their own – "Draw a nice picture for Mummy" to suss out if the men were single or not?'

Julia nodded.

'I think she was desperate not to be on her own, and also that she wanted a baby. But the church took the traditional line that sex should only take place within

164

marriage. That's the teaching I grew up with – it makes me feel guilty if, you know. . .' Her voice trailed off.

Julia waited, wondering if Grace's reference to being 'ashamed' the previous week concerned a relationship.

But her client resumed her childhood story. 'There was no question of Daddy living with Frances if they weren't married. So within a year she had what she wanted, a husband and a baby. I was the unwanted extra. For Daddy as well. That's how it seemed to me anyway.' Her voice broke, and the tears flowed.

This time Julia gave into the impulse to go over to her client. She knelt by her side, cradling her head against her, not caring about the dampness spreading over her grey cashmere sweater.

It was Grace who broke away when she had recovered her composure. Julia registered a pang of disappointment as she returned to her chair. She wondered uneasily how much of her interaction with her client she would be sharing with her supervisor the following Monday. She'd always tried to be as open as possible with Louise, but she sensed that this particular client relationship was becoming dangerously close.

'I'm sorry.' Grace giggled unexpectedly. 'Your jumper looks like you've been breastfeeding!'

The comment pierced Julia for a reason she didn't want to analyse. She took a deep breath, trying to recover her professional poise. 'Please don't apologise. You're telling me about feelings of rejection, Grace. To sense your father withdrawing from you must have been very painful after you had been so close.'

'Yes.' The younger woman nodded slowly several times, as if this were a new realisation for her. 'Daddy immersed himself totally in Frances and Suzanne. It was as though I didn't exist. That's why I feel he couldn't have cared about me so much after all, could he?'

Julia hesitated. It was recommended that clients should work out their own answers to their questions. But looking into Grace's beseeching wide blue eyes, glimpsing again the vulnerable child desperate to understand, she framed a response. 'We can't work out what was going on for your father. We'll never know. It sounds like he cared for you very much, looking after you so well when your mother. . .' She paused, veering away from mentioning the fire, the image of the burning house, the sound of the screaming infant, so eerily similar to her nightmare. 'When your mother left,' she said finally. 'I wonder if Frances and his newfound faith offered him stability after the trauma? She sounds like quite a powerful woman.'

'Hmm. You could say that.' Grace sighed. 'You remember I told you my PhD is a psychohistorical study of the relationship between Mary and Elizabeth, and I've wondered if my fascination with them is because of my background?'

'Yes.'

'I see Frances in the role of Anne Boleyn, Elizabeth's mother. The difference is,' Grace laughed mirthlessly, 'Frances lives on. And at least my father was nothing like Henry VIII.' She hesitated, glancing at Julia and then away again. When she spoke again her voice was so low that Julia had to lean forward in her seat to hear her. 'I used to hope something terrible would happen to Frances, that she would die in an accident. And Suzanne with her. Especially after Frances made sure I knew what my mother had done.'

What a cow, thought Julia. The intensity of her reaction towards Frances shocked her. But what kind of woman would tell a little girl her mother had nearly killed her in a fire? She bit her lip, struggling to keep her tone neutral. 'So you didn't know your mother had set fire to the house until Frances told you?'

Grace shook her head. 'She didn't tell me directly. She was too clever for that. She knew my father had kept it from me. I suppose he thought he was protecting me. He just said my mother had left us, that it was better not to talk about it. So I didn't. I was old enough to understand he found it painful. But to hear Frances talking about it with her friend, Elaine. . .' Grace gulped back fresh tears before going on, 'We were in Sunday School, colouring in pictures about the ten lepers who Jesus healed. I remember thinking I knew exactly how the lepers must have felt. Unclean, ignored. That's how Frances treated me. Father too, thanks to her.'

She tugged her plait, looking across at Julia with haunted eyes. 'Frances and my father had been married about a year. Suzanne was a tiny baby. Elaine complimented me on my colouring and Frances said, "I believe her mother was artistic – I do hope she's not going to turn out like her!" She clapped her hand to her mouth when I looked up. "I'm so sorry, Grace, I shouldn't have said that," she said, but I've never forgotten the malicious gleam in her eye.'

The younger woman paused, staring out of the window at the rain swept playground, her eyes unfocused. 'I turned back to my colouring, pretending not to listen. Frances was speaking in a stage whisper. I knew she wanted me to hear. "The woman was mad," she said. "She set fire to the house with Grace in her arms. And you know, with Grace being so quiet and withdrawn, always reading, not wanting to play with other children, I do worry about her."'

'Elaine made some admiring comment about Frances marrying my father when he came with "baggage." Frances said in the pious voice I had come to hate, no longer bothering to lower it, "I feel it's what God wanted me to do, to offer a home to a broken man and his poor child. And look how Philip has grown in the Lord! And now we've been blessed with a child of our own."'

She looked back at Julia, her eyes swimming with fresh tears. 'So that's how I found out that my mother had nearly killed us both.'

Julia passed over the tissues silently. She wanted to say that Frances sounded a little mad too, but it was hardly professional. What chance had this poor girl had with a mentally unstable mother, a weak father, and a manipulative step-mother who sounded like the worst kind of Bible-basher? She suppressed an impulse to cross over to her client and hug her again, wary after Grace's earlier identification of her as a mother figure. 'I am so sorry, Grace,' she said, her voice unsteady. 'So very sorry. I'm wondering how you felt when Frances said this?'

Grace blew her nose. 'I felt sick,' she said bluntly. 'That's when I began to wish Frances and Suzanne dead.'

There was a long silence. The postgraduate student raised her chin, looked straight at Julia. 'Now you see what a terrible person I am. Probably insane like my mother.'

'Who sees you as a terrible person, Grace?' Julia asked gently.

'It's obvious, isn't it? I've just told you I wanted Frances and Suzanne dead! You know,' she plunged on, 'Mary had the chance to have Elizabeth executed in 1554. There was a plot to prevent Mary marrying Philip of Spain, have her put to death, and then crown Elizabeth as a Protestant queen. The Wyatt rebellion. If I'd been Mary, I know I'd have taken the chance to get rid of Elizabeth, given how I feel towards Suzanne. I tell you, I'm as mad as my mother!' She tossed her plait over her shoulder, still staring fiercely at Julia as if daring the counsellor to contradict her.

The older woman suppressed a shudder. She knew it was vital not to seem judgemental. But there was a darkness in Grace's blue eyes which chilled her. The set lines of the younger woman's face made her seem almost ugly for a moment. Julia glanced down, picking at some lint on her black trousers.

'You're telling me that you relate closely to your research subject?' She knew she was ducking the issue by focusing on the academic.

'Yes.' Grace's features relaxed. She spoke for a few moments about her research, her eyes bright with enthusiasm.

Julia let her talk. She knew she should draw her client back to explore her feelings towards her step-mother and half-sister, and her belief that she had inherited her mother's mental illness. She knew too that her supervisor would probe her reluctance to enter the dark place Grace had unveiled. Her client's preoccupation with discussing her research was clearly an avoidance tactic which Julia should challenge.

Lost in her thoughts, it took a moment for Julia to register that Grace had stopped speaking. Her client was looking at her nervously, fiddling with her plait again. Julia realised she was waiting for a response. She bit her lip. 'I'm so sorry,' she said. 'I didn't catch that last bit. The rain.' She gestured towards the window, where a timely gust of wind lashed the rain against the glass.

Grace pulled her plait in front of her face, studying it for split ends. 'It doesn't matter,' she muttered.

'Yes, it does. Whatever you tell me, Grace, is really important.' Julia held her breath. Had she missed something vital?

Her client glanced at her. 'I just said I miss him so much,' she whispered. She looked away again.

'I know,' said Julia. Self-disclosure had been discouraged in her person-centred training, but Grace's story had touched her deeply. She had been thinking more about her own father since James's outburst that Saturday night. 'My father died when I was eight. What you experienced, that withdrawal of your father, the rejection you felt, is a terrible loss.'

Grace frowned and a flush spread over her high cheekbones. 'I wasn't talking about my father,' she said, a new edge to her voice. 'You weren't listening, were you?'

Julia swallowed, clenching her fists in her lap. Never in the eight years since she had started training had she allowed herself to be so preoccupied in the presence of a client. 'I'm so sorry, Grace. I was distracted. You're right, I missed that. Please do tell me again, we've still got a few minutes.'

'Your brochure promised attentive listening.' Grace stood up and began to button her coat, not looking at her counsellor.

'I know. I do apologise. It's unlike me, I'm afraid I. . .'

Grace withdrew the cash for the session from a magenta purse. Her fingers trembled as she zipped it up.

'It doesn't matter,' she said. 'I don't want to talk any more today anyway.'

'Grace, I. . .'

'Don't worry, I realise you must get tired of hearing people talking about their problems all the time,' Grace's voice was cold. She threw the money on to the table beside the tissue box. 'It's just a job for you, isn't it? I suppose you see me as just another sad person needing fixing.' She moved across to the door, pausing with her back to Julia. 'Forget what I said about feeling like you were my mother,' she added, in a strangled voice. 'Does it make you feel good about yourself, thinking you're sorted in comparison with the rest of us?'

'No. Of course not.' Julia rose. 'Please don't go like this, Grace, I can't apologise enough.'

To her horror, Julia felt tears rising. She blinked them away. Grace yanked the door handle.

'Don't expect me back next week,' she flung over her shoulder. The door slammed behind her.

Julia paced the office, dashing away tears, miserably aware of failing the fragile young woman. She wondered too how she was going to explain her inattention to her supervisor, pushing away the thought that at this moment in time it was irresponsible of her to be working.

– CHAPTER 16 –

'So she's tried to get in touch with James too?' Julia emptied a sachet of brown sugar into her black americano.

'Yes. We think so.' Clare took a sip of green tea. She nodded towards Julia's large white cup. 'Not like you to drink coffee. And a *grande* at that.'

'I need the caffeine.' Julia sipped the steaming brown liquid. 'I wondered if she would try and contact James,' she resumed. 'But he wasn't around when she went to the uni?'

'No. He went AWOL for a couple of days early last week, said he had 'flu or something, when we – you know. . .' She bit her lip. 'Anyway, when he went in on Thursday the secretary said this woman had been in asking for him. "Very colourful, rather agitated" was how the secretary described her. James didn't think anything of it at the time. He'd forgotten her from the funeral, but when he saw her on Saturday he guessed it was her. Sounds like she's definitely trying to get to know us, doesn't it?'

'It does.' Julia looked out of the window, misted with condensation on the wet February morning. Would Linda have told James more than she had told her about the family secret she had alluded to?

'Poor Aunt Ada,' Clare went on. 'I wonder if she will regain consciousness? It's been six days, and with every day that passes, they say the chances become less likely. And if she does come round, who knows what damage the stroke has done?'

'It's awful.' Julia stirred her coffee around with the wooden stirrer. 'Did you get the impression Linda had a grudge against her?'

'Aunt Ada?'

'Yes.'

'Oh, I don't know.' Clare wrinkled her snub nose. 'The woman was drunk. You said you thought she was strange at Emily's funeral. She might just be around to cause trouble. Or maybe she's mentally ill?'

Julia pondered, tapping the stirrer against the white saucer. 'Maybe,' she said. 'But I thought she had something personal against Aunt Ada. From what I can gather, I don't think she had anything against Mother.'

'But it's odd Emily never mentioned her to you and James, isn't it?' Clare folded a brown paper napkin into four squares. 'I've wondered if maybe she had some kind of hold over your mother?'

'Oh, surely not!' Julia's tone was sharper than she had intended.

Clare raised a plucked blonde eyebrow. She opened her mouth to say something then closed it again.

'What?' asked Julia. 'What were you going to say?'

Clare toyed with the napkin again, avoiding eye contact. 'Well, it must have crossed your mind that Emily's illness began around the same time Linda arrived on the scene?'

Julia frowned, flicking a cake crumb from the square table. The same suspicion had played in her mind ever since the snowy Saturday afternoon at her mother's

173

cottage, planted there by Edith. But she was in no doubt about Linda's grief, remembering her irritation as the tears slid down Linda's cheeks at Giuseppe's.

'I don't think so. She seemed genuinely upset about Mother's death.'

Clare changed tack. 'But if as you say she had some grudge against Ada, what could that be?' She leaned forward across the table. 'And if Ada dies, I can't help thinking this woman is morally responsible. She gave her such a terrible shock. Don't you agree?'

'I don't know what to think.' Julia recalled the unexpected sympathy she had felt for her difficult aunt, crumpled in her wheelchair.

'I know Aunt Ada's not exactly anyone's favourite relative, but she is family, isn't she?'

Julia grimaced. 'But that's what Linda claims too, isn't it? That she's family?'

'Only some distant cousin though. Maybe she's just lonely. She doesn't have any children, does she?'

'She's never mentioned any, but I don't really know much about her to be honest. And that still doesn't explain her hostility towards Ada.' Julia remembered Ada's gasping words. She shuddered, picturing the old woman's contorted face.

'What is it?' said Clare.

'Just Ada's last words. Before they took her in the ambulance, I mean. Didn't you hear what she said?'

'No.'

'She said, "I never told her he was alive." I don't know if she understood what she was saying, or if she felt guilty about something.'

'Something to do with Linda?'

'Well, I suppose so. Anyway,' Julia looked across at her sister-in-law, 'we're not here to worry about Linda.' *Although she's certainly been worrying me*, she thought, *along with everything else.* It had taken all her resolve to meet Clare as arranged this Friday morning. She had woken with a headache after another broken night's sleep. But Clare was a friend as well as a sister-in-law, and with no clients booked in for the day, she felt she should manage the eleven o'clock coffee. 'How are you and James really?'

Clare sighed. She looked calm enough, but Julia noted the pallor beneath her carefully applied make up, how she was scrunching up the napkin. 'Not great. James says he's given up this student, and I believe him. But I can't help wondering, have there been others? Will there be others? Can I ever trust him again?' Her voice wobbled and a tear slid down her face. She brushed it away impatiently.

Julia remained silent, waiting for Clare to compose herself. After a moment her sister-in-law continued, 'What I'm really struggling with is that this affair might have been going on whilst we had our last round of IVF. I mean, how could he do that?' She looked over at Julia, her almond eyes haunted.

'Do you think it had been going on so long?' countered Julia. She calculated that it was nearly three months since their last unsuccessful course of fertility treatment.

'He hasn't said so.' Clare twisted her wedding ring round. 'But he hasn't said not, either.'

'Have you asked him?'

Clare nodded. 'He was angry. Asked me why I wanted to know, when he'd already admitted the affair.' She smiled wryly. 'Not that he had much choice, after the woman rang home that Saturday and I confronted him when he came back.'

'Did she say something on the phone that made you suspect?'

'She didn't need to.' Clare's raspberry lips settled into a thin line. 'She spoke as soon as I picked up the phone without giving me chance to say hello. "James," she said, "please can you come. I'm sorry about last night. I really need to see you. Today."'

'What an awful way for you to find out! What did you say?'

'Nothing. I stood there for what felt like ages but was probably just a minute or two. In shock, I suppose. Then she said, "James? James?" Her voice was frightened, she'd probably realised it wasn't James on the other end of the phone. Then she hung up.'

Julia groaned, shaking her head. 'You poor thing.' She hesitated, picking up the stirrer again. She tapped it against the white saucer. 'But, and I know this doesn't exonerate James in any way, he did say when he came round on Sunday morning that he had gone round to finish with her that afternoon.'

Clare shrugged. 'Yes. That's what he told me too. But I'm not sure it makes it any better, does it? Like you say, it doesn't exonerate him for having the affair in the first place.' She raised her cup to her lips again.

'No.' Julia hesitated, thinking of what else James had told her, about the strain of the IVF. 'There's something else James told me,' she said carefully, 'and again I don't think for a moment it excuses his affair at all. But he was trying to give some kind of reason.'

'Really? What's that?' Clare stared at her.

Julia took another sip of coffee. She regretted raising the topic, thinking that it might cause her sister-in-law more pain. 'He said what a strain he'd found the IVF,' she said flatly.

Clare slammed her cup down on her saucer. Tea splashed across the table. '*He* found it a strain!'

The couple at the adjoining table glanced across as Julia grabbed a napkin and stemmed the flow of green liquid trickling towards her. Clare bit her lip, before continuing in a low but still furious voice, 'He should try being the woman in the process! Injecting yourself, taking all the drugs, wondering how many eggs are going to be ready, if you're damaging your body in the long run – have you seen the stats for increased risk of ovarian cancer? OK, they're not high, but they're still there. Honestly, Julia, you have no idea what I've been through! Month by month veering between hope and disappointment, then two cycles of this invasive treatment. All for nothing!'

'I know. I'm so sorry. Like I said, I'm not trying to defend James, but. . .'

'But nothing!' snapped Clare. 'It sounds as though you were!' She eyeballed her sister-in-law. 'You've never wanted a child, have you? And even with your precious empathy as a counsellor, you can't begin to know what it feels like to want one so desperately.'

Suddenly Julia found it difficult to breathe. She seemed to see her sister-in-law's flushed face and flashing eyes from a distance. Her blood was thrumming in her ears. She had a peculiar sense of dissociation, as if she were outside herself, looking on. Suddenly a voice she hardly recognised as her own screeched, 'Of course I wanted a child! You stupid self-obsessed cow, I do know what it feels like!'

Then she was weeping noisily, her breath coming in juddering gasps. She was aware of other customers turning to stare at them. The colour had drained away beneath Clare's blusher. One of the staff wearing the uniform red polo shirt and black skirt hurried across. She pointed at the name badge pinned to her ample bosom by way of introduction: 'Shirley. Assistant Manager.' Still in her strange detached state, Julia heard the woman say politely but firmly, 'Excuse me, ladies, could you calm down or leave please? You're disturbing the other customers.'

Scrambling to her feet, Julia snapped, 'Don't worry, I was just going.' Without looking back at Clare, she grabbed her black leather bag from under the table and dashed towards the door.

A woman was struggling to manoeuvre a red buggy inside the coffee shop. In her haste to leave, Julia pushed past, bumping her leg against the pushchair. She didn't stop to apologise, even when the mother called, 'Hey! Watch where you're going! He was asleep!' The infant began to scream.

Outside she realised her legs were shaking. Not wanting Clare to catch up with her, she turned left into a small precinct, leaning against the window of a discount store to catch her breath.

That was when she saw them, coming out of the baby store diagonally opposite. The man was laden down with bags. As they emerged from the shop he reached his hand round the woman's heavily pregnant belly. Even above the piped tinny music, Julia could tune into the deep well-bred voice she knew so well. 'Hey, little girl, did you know you're already costing us a fortune?'

Without a moment's thought she covered the few yards

between them. They both saw her at the same time, and she saw Lisa's questioning frown change into alarm. Instinctively Greg stepped forward, shielding his partner. Julia struck him across the face with the flat of her palm. 'It should have been me!' she screamed. 'It should have been my baby!'

He stared at her as the red handprint spread across his cheek. 'You mad bitch,' he hissed. 'What the hell do you think you're doing?'

She hit him again, this time across the mouth. 'And that's my money you've spent! Money you owe me for the mortgage!' She made a lunge at the carrier bags, with some mad idea of taking them back into the shop and demanding a refund, but he held on to them tightly and swung them out of reach.

'Greg, are you all right? Shall I call the police?' Lisa was crying. Her hands cradled her bulging stomach.

Julia was appalled to see the fear in the younger woman's eyes. Her fury evaporated as suddenly as it had risen.

'Greg,' she said, her voice little more than a whisper. 'Greg, I'm sorry, I –'

'You're crazy,' he said. He raised his hand to his mouth and looked in disbelief at the blood on his fingertips. 'You've lost it, Julia.' He bent towards her, his face close to hers. His dark eyes bored into hers so coldly that she shivered. 'Go away. Stay away, Julia. I never want to see you again. If you come anywhere near me, or Lisa again, I'll call the police. It's over. Got that?'

She nodded dumbly. He put his arm round Lisa's shoulders. 'Come on, darling,' he said. 'Let me get you home. We're done here.'

Neither of them looked back as they exited the precinct. After a few moments Julia followed. Disorientated, she wandered around the car park, unable to remember where she had parked the Mondeo. When she eventually found it, she was soaked through from the relentless rain. She drove home in a daze, remembering nothing of the journey when she drew up outside her cottage. Her head was throbbing and she felt chilled to the bone.

There was a white envelope waiting for her on the doormat, bearing the mortgage company's details on the rear flap. She flicked on the kettle before opening it. As she expected, it was a further letter warning of pending possession proceedings if the mortgage arrears plus interest and costs weren't paid within the next fourteen days. She tossed it into the recycling bin and made a mug of strong tea, scooping in two teaspoonfuls of sugar. In the sitting room she sank down into her armchair, staring into space as she replayed the morning's events.

She'd never lost her self-control so completely as she had done in the last hour, first with Clare, then with Greg. She hadn't known that she was capable of turning into that screaming, violent creature. Nor had she realised until that moment of clarity with Clare in the café how much she had wanted a child.

She had no idea how long she sat and wept, grieving for the child she would never have. She folded her arms across her body, tucking her knees under her, rocking back and forth in the armchair. Eventually she grew calmer, her sobs less frequent. When the phone rang, it made her start. She didn't move from her chair, listening for the answerphone. There was a long pause as the caller didn't respond immediately to her invitation for them to leave a message.

Then she heard her sister-in-law's hesitant voice. 'Julia. It's me, Clare. I hope you're OK. I'm sorry. I had no idea.' There was another pause as if she were trying to think what else to say. Then she hung up.

Julia closed her eyes, resting her head against the back of her chair. It was good of Clare to phone. She wasn't sure she would have done if roles were reversed. She needed to apologise. But not now. Later.

When the phone rang again though, she dragged herself out of the chair and went out to the hall, thinking it would be Clare ringing back. She picked up the receiver, glancing at herself in the mirror above her grandfather's bookcase. Her face was pale, her hazel eyes swollen and circled by dark shadows. The crow's feet at the corners seemed to have deepened. Grey roots were coming through her highlighted brunette bob. With a jolt, she realised how she had aged in the few weeks since her mother's death.

The caller hesitated. 'Julia?'

'Yes?'

'It's me. Grace.'

'Oh. Grace. Hello.' *Another damaged relationship. This one a client.* Julia picked up a pen from the bookcase, tapping it against the walnut wood.

'I really need to see you. Can you fit me in early next week?' Grace's voice, always soft, sounded more childish than ever.

Julia hesitated. She was due to see her supervisor Louise on Monday afternoon, and she didn't need Louise to tell her that she was in no fit condition to be counselling at present.

'Please, Julia.' A stifled sob. 'I'm sorry about what I said on Wednesday. It wasn't fair. I understand you must get distracted sometimes. Honestly, you've helped me so much. I really need your help again now.'

Julia's heart rose. Warmth spread through her. 'Of course, Grace,' she said. 'How about ten o'clock on Monday morning?'

'Yes. That would be fine.'

'Good. I look forward to seeing you then.'

'Thank you. Thank you so much. Bye.'

'Bye for now.' Julia replaced the handset in the cradle. Someone, her client, a young woman who had said she was like a mother to her, needed her. She felt a new sense of energy and purpose. She pushed aside the thought of what Louise would say about her motives for agreeing to see Grace in her current state.

– CHAPTER 17 –

There was no sign of Pete in the old school the following Monday. Julia had avoided thinking about him since his ill-judged kiss after Ada's party. As her footsteps echoed down the poorly-lit corridor she was surprised how much she missed his presence. Apart from holidays, he had always been around during the past five years. Other tenants had come and gone and he had been the one constant.

Julia sighed as she entered her office, mechanically switching on the fire and opening the blind. She fingered the broken slat. No need to worry about that with just a few weeks to go before the tenancy expired. Would Pete still want to share premises with her now? It was, as he had said, an obvious solution, even if she had been non-committal about the idea.

She looked out across the former playground. Rain slanted down on to the rutted concrete where deep puddles had formed. She could hear a steady drip from the broken gutter above the neighbouring disused classroom. She wouldn't miss this place, even if the thought of searching for alternative premises added to her general feeling of fatigue. She yawned as she took her notes from her filing cabinet, wishing she'd picked up a coffee on the way in. She'd overslept after another poor night, broken by dreams she couldn't remember. She'd done little at the weekend apart from catching up with some household chores and paying a short visit to Aunt Ada, still unconscious in hospital after her stroke. Her mind had wandered when she had tried to read or watch TV, and she had been unable to summon up the energy to go out for a walk, even though she knew the exercise would be beneficial. It had been a rush to get in for her appointment with Grace.

Her client came into view beneath a striped red and yellow umbrella. She hesitated a moment inside the gateway, looking back towards the terraced street where a bus thundered past. Julia wondered if she was having second thoughts about the session. She felt strangely bereft at the thought her client might turn back the way she had come. Her heart lifted as Grace turned towards the building and crossed the yard.

A few minutes later she was perched on the edge of her chair looking down at the worn grey carpet. Her posture took Julia back to the start of their initial session. Today the counsellor knew she must take the initiative.

'Grace, let me apologise again about my lack of attention last week. I'm so pleased you contacted me to arrange to come back today.'

'Really?' Her client looked at her directly for the first time since entering the room. There were dark shadows under her eyes. Apparently Julia wasn't the only one suffering from lack of sleep.

'Really.' Julia smiled at her, and was rewarded with a wan smile in return. 'As a person-centred counsellor, I take my responsibility to offer all my clients my full attention when they are here very seriously, whatever is going on for me. I failed you in that last week, and I am so sorry.'

Grace nodded. She dropped her eyes, crossing and uncrossing her long legs in their skinny jeans.

Julia waited a moment. 'Is that OK, Grace?'

Grace turned her head towards the window, pulling her heavy plait forward. 'Yes, I accept your apology. It's just. . . How does it work for you?' She fixed her startling blue eyes on Julia. 'Am I just another client, just another case?'

Julia took a moment, sensing how important her response was if she were to regain her client's fragile trust. 'I hope I don't treat any of my clients as "just another", and certainly not as "cases."' She shook her head in distaste, remembering Aunt Ada's condescending, 'Is she one of your cases, Julia?' when Linda had staggered into the dining room nine days ago. 'I try, as much as I can, to respond to each client as an individual to be treasured.'

'I see.' Grace bit her lip, twisting her slender hands in her lap. 'So you feel the same way towards each client, then?' She darted a quick glance towards Julia.

There was a beat. Julia knew what the professional answer was, but the appeal in her client's eyes led her to respond more personally. 'Honestly, no,' she said. 'There are always some people we feel closer to than others, aren't there?'

Grace nodded and moved back a little in her chair. Julia hoped her client wouldn't push her any further, recalling how at the start of the previous session Grace had identified her as being like the mother she had never had. As Julia had done then, she steered the session on to safer ground.

'So I'm wondering what led you to phone on Friday? You sounded as though it were quite urgent.'

The younger woman tapped her unvarnished oval fingernails against the wooden arm of her armchair. She nodded and took a deep breath. 'I'm pregnant.' She burst into tears.

Julia swallowed and closed her eyes. The ugly scenes with Clare and Greg three days earlier swam before her. She imagined she could sense the gaping emptiness in her womb which had led to that bout of inconsolable weeping when she reached home. Now here was her client clearly distressed to find herself pregnant. *Life is so unfair.* She took a deep breath as Grace groped blindly for a tissue from the box which lay on the side table between them. Julia automatically reached across and handed her one, grateful that the other woman was too distracted to notice anything unusual in her response.

When her client was calmer, Julia said, 'So you've found out you're pregnant, and I'm guessing from your reaction it wasn't planned?'

Grace shook her head.

'And there couldn't be a mistake?'

'There's no mistake.' Grace sighed. 'I went to see my GP after I did the pregnancy test. My cycle is erratic. I hadn't thought about how late I was. He thinks I'm around eleven or twelve weeks. I'll know more when I've seen the midwife. It's a disaster.'

'A disaster?'

Grace nodded, her plait bouncing against her right shoulder. 'It's not the right time,' she said, 'not with where I'm up to with my research.' She hid her head in her hands. 'But that's not the worst thing. Oh, I'm not sure I can even tell you!' She was overcome by a fresh storm of tears. Julia silently handed her a couple more tissues.

After a few minutes Grace's sobs subsided. 'I'm sorry,' she whispered, looking at Julia with red-rimmed eyes.

'It's fine,' said Julia gently. 'Would you like to tell me why you see your pregnancy as a disaster?'

Grace inhaled. 'I don't know who the father is,' she said flatly.

'Ah.'

'I feel so terrible! I've never been involved with more than one man at a time. I broke up with my long term boy-friend when I got involved with the man I was telling you about last week, when you weren't. . . .' She waved her hand dismissively. 'Anyway, that doesn't matter. But it was around the same time, and because I can't be absolutely sure about dates, I don't know which man is the father. What am I going to do?' She gazed wide-eyed at Julia, like a bewildered small girl.

Julia chose her words carefully. 'Are you asking me what you're going to do about your pregnancy, Grace, or about how to deal with not knowing who the father is?'

'I've got no choice about the pregnancy,' said Grace. 'I have to go through with it. I know that.'

'You have to go through with it?'

Grace nodded. 'Absolutely. I might not have retained the evangelical beliefs of my upbringing, but I couldn't live with myself if I had a termination.'

'So you don't think you have a choice?'

'No, definitely not!' Grace's usually soft voice was so sharp that Julia jumped. 'It's a life, isn't it?'

Julia had counselled clients who had had abortions and felt guilty afterwards, and others who had chosen abortion and been certain it was the right decision. She had always been careful to remain neutral, to help her clients towards choices which were right for them. Weary, facing Grace's challenging gaze and newly aware of her grief at her childless state, she found herself answering simply, 'Yes. It's a life.'

'So I will have the baby. But I'm so scared about bringing it – I mean, him or her – up alone.'

'You don't think the father would want to be involved?'

Grace studied the end of her plait a moment. 'I don't want anything to do with the man I broke up with,' she said bluntly, 'and the other man made it clear he doesn't want anything more to do with me.' She began to cry again.

'Ah.' Julia realised this must be the man Grace had said she missed so much, the man Julia had wrongly assumed to be her father when she had been distracted by her own thoughts the previous session. Trying to avoid any possibility that Grace would think she was encouraging her to disclose her pregnancy to either man, she framed an unfinished question. 'But if either man knew he were the father. . . ?'

'You mean by a DNA test?' Grace leaned forward and held her head in her hands. 'Like I said, I never want to see the man I finished with again.' She lowered her hands. Julia instinctively moved back in her seat, recoiling from the anger in the bright blue eyes. 'He was a two-timing bastard,' she spat out.

Julia waited a moment, an image of Greg flashing through her mind. 'Is that something you want to explore further?'

'No.' Grace shuddered. 'I've wasted more than enough time on him. But then,' she brushed away a tear from the corner of her eye, 'that's what the wife of the other man would say, isn't it? What was I thinking, letting myself get involved with a married man?' She gazed across at Julia. The counsellor was grateful that the younger woman didn't wait for an answer given her own recent experience. 'I'm so ashamed. I knew he was married. It all happened so fast. I know I was on the rebound from Mark. I wasn't thinking straight. I was angry, and felt rejected.' She began to cry again, 'And he's so intelligent, and good-looking, I was so flattered. . .' She tailed off, breaking down again.

'Oh, Grace,' said Julia softly, 'I am so sorry.'

She moved across and put her arm round the younger woman's slim shoulders. After a while Grace's sobs subsided and she relaxed against Julia who didn't try to disengage herself. She told herself she was waiting for Grace to move away, that she didn't want her client to feel any further sense of rejection, but somewhere in the recesses of her mind she knew she was relishing the feeling of being needed. Fostering client dependency, Louise would say, but Julia pushed the thought of her upcoming supervision appointment from her mind.

Finally Grace pulled away, still sniffing. 'Thank you.' She half-smiled. 'I knew you would listen and not judge.' She paused, fixing Julia with her wide child-like gaze. 'Like I said last week, I do see you as the mother I never had.'

Julia swallowed, a lump in her throat.

'And that's the other thing,' Grace went on, apparently oblivious to her counsellor's reaction, 'how ever am I going to tell Frances?' Her delicate face suddenly contorted. 'I can already hear her talking about what Father would have said, how disappointed he would have been at my sinfulness.'

Julia blinked at the word 'sinfulness,' but Grace didn't notice. 'Even worse, she's bound to drag up my mother's mental illness.' She screwed up her eyes as if in pain.

'Oh?'

'Yes. You remember I told you about how my mother set fire to the house when I was a baby, holding me in her arms?'

'Of course,' said Julia. It would be impossible to forget, especially after the coincidence of her nightmare on the evening of her mother's funeral.

'And I told you they thought that she had been suffering from postpartum psychosis. You know, where the mother develops mental health problems after childbirth?'

Julia nodded. One of her early clients had experienced the condition.

'Frances has pointed out many times that there's a high risk that I will develop it too. It's genetic, you see.' Grace began to cry again. 'She's always made clear she thinks it would be better for me not to have children because of the risk. And you remember she implied that my withdrawn behaviour when I was growing up was due to mental health problems?'

'Yes. I remember.' Julia passed her client another tissue.

'That's why I'm so scared about being pregnant,' sniffed Grace, 'and the birth. What if I end up sick like my mother? I feel so isolated, so alone. You've no idea.'

But I do, thought Julia, rising from her chair impulsively. *I have never felt so alone as I do now.* She covered the short distance between them and knelt beside her client, opening her arms. Grace rested her head against her counsellor's powder blue roll neck sweater and Julia stroked her strawberry blonde hair, soothing her like a small child. 'You poor girl,' she said softly.

After a few moments Grace moved away slightly, keeping her hand on Julia's arm. Her blue eyes shone with a new idea. 'I wonder, when the time comes, when I have the baby, could you be my birth partner?'

Julia stiffened. Grace immediately released her hold on her arm, standing so suddenly that Julia would have toppled over from her kneeling position if she hadn't grabbed hold of the chair arm. Her client didn't look at her as she pulled on her coat.

'Of course you can't. What was I thinking?' Grace threw some crumpled notes from her coat pocket on to the side table. 'It would breach your precious professional boundaries, wouldn't it?'

'Grace. . .'

Bang. The door had already slammed behind her client.

Through the rain-spattered window Julia watched Grace move swiftly across the slushy playground, nearly tripping in her high-heeled black boots. In her haste she didn't even bother to put up her umbrella.

Without thinking how unprofessional it was to go after a client, Julia dashed out of the office and down the corridor. Opening the front door, she was nearly knocked backwards by a gust of wind. Grace had come to a halt a few yards short of the gateway, her head turned towards a figure walking up the street.

The person turned in at the gateway, battling with a black umbrella which had turned inside out, not seeing Grace who remained rooted to the spot. He was wearing a navy parka, like the one James had. Half-sliding on a patch of ice on the front step, Julia saw that it *was* James who emerged from beneath the umbrella. She sighed. She didn't want him to see her chasing after a disgruntled client. She stepped back into the doorway, ducking away from the dripping downspout.

James halted in front of Grace. He reached out his free arm towards her, then let it fall and opened his mouth to speak. Julia couldn't hear him above the rain, but lip read the word, 'Grace.' But whatever he had to say, Grace didn't want to hear it. She drew herself up to her full height and stalked past him as if he hadn't spoken, turning left up the street without looking back.

'No!' gasped Julia to herself. She sagged against the doorpost, covering her face with her hands. She was certain from the exchange that Grace was the student her half-brother had been sleeping with. He could be the father of her child. Could things get any worse?

Lowering her hands, Julia saw that James was still staring after Grace. He pushed his left hand through his hair, a characteristic gesture of indecision. Julia suspected he was considering following her. Then he turned towards the old school and saw Julia watching him. He raised his chin as he approached her. The defiant gesture confirmed what she had already guessed.

She turned away, going back inside as a squall of wind drove the rain harder across the playground. Let James assume she was seeking refuge from the weather.

Back in the dimly-lit foyer, she thought quickly. Both professionally and personally, she couldn't divulge Grace's pregnancy to James. The baby might not be his. Grace's ex could be the father. And if James were the father, what effect would that have on his fragile chance of saving his marriage? How on earth would Clare react if she discovered that James had fathered a child during his affair, conducted, Clare believed, during their fertility treatment? And that was quite possible, Julia realised, quickly calculating the dates. Grace thought she was eleven or twelve weeks pregnant, and it was almost three months since her brother and sister-in-law's last IVF cycle.

Julia felt dizzy. It didn't help to think that if only she had questioned Grace more closely about her PhD supervisors in that first counselling session, she would have found out that one of them was James. Then she wouldn't have taken on Grace because of the potential conflict of interest. But they had had such an immediate rapport, she and Grace, and that didn't happen with all clients. The truth was, she hadn't wanted to find any reason not to work with the younger woman. And she'd needed the money, even before she'd discovered how Greg had defaulted on the mortgage. A wave of nausea swept over her as she recognised how badly she had misjudged the situation.

James came in, turning to shake his umbrella. He closed the door against the rain and turned to her, not quite meeting her eye. 'Hell of a day,' he said.

'Awful.'

There was a pause.

James looked around the lobby, taking in the peeling paint, the failed fluorescent strip lights. 'This place looks worse than ever,' he said finally.

Julia shrugged. 'We won't be here much longer,' she said. 'The landlord's served notice.'

'Who's we?' asked James. 'You and that bloke you brought to Aunt Ada's lunch?'

'Yes. Pete.' She was taken aback by a pang of sadness saying Pete's name.

'What does he do?'

'He's a reflexologist.'

'Mmm. Didn't look your type.' James looked at her fully for the first time. 'Didn't I notice an earring?'

Julia shrugged. 'Maybe. Anyway, we're not together.'

James half-smiled and raised an eyebrow. 'If you're not now, you will be if you give him half a chance.'

She stared at him.

He laughed. 'Oh, come on, Julia! He couldn't keep his eyes off you!'

Julia spun round and went over to check her mailbox, keeping her back to her half-brother. Had Pete been that obvious? How could she have missed the signs? Too late now. She'd put him off drawing back from his kiss in the car. But she'd made the right decision, hadn't she? Her behaviour recently meant that the last thing she needed now was a new relationship. So why did she replay that kiss and the touch of his hand on her wrist at her cottage?

She slammed the door of the empty mailbox with a clang and turned back to James who was still grinning. 'Why are you here, James? I've got supervision in half an hour. I assume you're not here to discuss my personal life.'

His smile disappeared immediately as his full lower lip jutted out, reminding her of the small sulky boy who always wanted his own way. 'Don't worry. I won't keep you,' he said. 'It was Clare who asked me to call in. She thought you were upset by something she said at the café. Didn't tell me what. And I thought, after last Sunday morning. . .' He paused.

He'd always found it difficult to apologise. Julia felt a

momentary compunction. But it quickly dissolved when he went on, 'But I can see you're your usual collected self. So I'll tell her there's no need to worry, shall I?'

'Yes,' she said coldly.

'Then I'll see you around.' He turned towards the door and retrieved his umbrella. 'One other thing,' he said, his back to her, 'that woman who was leaving, is she one of your clients?'

Julia wasn't taken in by his casual tone. 'That's right,' she said. She couldn't resist adding, 'You don't know her, do you?'

'No, no, she just reminds me of someone. That's all. See you.'

'Liar,' said Julia, but he didn't hear as the door slammed behind him in another gust of wind. 'Two-timing bastard!' Her words reverberated down the empty corridor.

– CHAPTER 18 –

It was only as she drove south through the city for her appointment with her supervisor that Julia realised the full implications of James's affair with Grace. If he were the father of Grace's child, that would make her the baby's half-aunt. Whoever the baby's father was, she couldn't continue counselling the postgraduate student if she had been involved in a relationship with her half-brother, something Julia strongly suspected from James's behaviour. The affair created a conflict of interest for her. That conflict of interest meant she wouldn't be able to see the baby either.

And she couldn't stop thinking about the agony it would cause Clare, having been through those fruitless IVF sessions, to discover James had fathered a child by another woman. Clare was a close friend as well as her sister-in-law. Then too, just days after having been so cruelly confronted with her own grief about her childlessness, Julia felt that this news of another baby was a further twist of the knife. But she couldn't dwell on that when she had to get through supervision. . .

As expected, her supervisor focused on the conflict of interest as soon as Julia outlined the situation. Usually these sessions ran smoothly. Today, though, Louise's probing questions regarding how Julia was handling her grief following her mother's death left her struggling to retain her self-control. Avoiding her supervisor's keen gaze, Julia was aware that she was being less than honest in withholding information regarding her financial plight, although she had explained about the termination of the tenancy at the old school.

'So tell me how you feel about contacting Client "G" to explain you will be unable to offer further sessions for personal reasons.' Twice Julia had slipped by mentioning Grace by name, but Louise retained the usual anonymity of using the client's initial to preserve confidentiality. Her small pale blue eyes bored into Julia's. The other woman looked down at her hands, noticing her usually well-kept nails needed filing.

'Obviously I see it's necessary.' Julia tried to speak neutrally, though there was a lump in her throat as she remembered how her client had clung to her earlier. 'But I'm concerned that Client "G" will be very upset.'

'And how do *you* feel?'

'Sad,' said Julia flatly

'Sad,' echoed Louise. Something in her tone caused Julia to look across at her. 'I'm wondering if that's all. I'm sensing you've become particularly close to this client.'

'I don't know.' Julia shrugged her slim shoulders.

Louise raised her brown pencilled eyebrows so that they disappeared under her low ginger fringe and waited.

Julia shifted uncomfortably in her armchair. She felt like an errant schoolgirl sent to the headmistress. She had chosen Louise as her supervisor because the other woman had impressed her in an initial trial session with her psychological acuity, challenging Julia to examine more deeply what was going on in her relationships with her clients. Today she wished Louise were less astute.

She knew she should mention Grace's identifying her as a mother figure. But she anticipated Louise would then want to explore how she felt about her client's comment. After the recent self-discovery of her pain over her childlessness, the prospect was more than she could bear. The thought of discussing her newly-discovered grief with Louise set the blood pounding in her ears again. Dizziness overcame her and she closed her eyes, trying to dispel it.

'Are you all right, Julia? Would you like a glass of water?'

'Please.'

Louise heaved her large form out of her armchair and went through to the small galley kitchen adjoining her office. She worked from a converted garage at the back of her house. 'Not far to commute,' she had smiled when they first met. 'And because it's self-contained, I don't feel I'm living at work.'

The familiar sound of running water was comforting, and Julia's dizziness had begun to pass when Louise plodded back in and handed her the glass.

'Thank you.' Julia took a few sips, then looked over at Louise. 'I'm sorry, I'm really tired. I haven't been sleep. . . It's been a difficult morning,' she amended hastily.

But Louise had heard. 'And you haven't been sleeping well,' she said. 'I can see that from the dark shadows under your eyes.'

'A symptom of grief,' said Julia quickly.

'Of course.' Louise allowed a moment to pass. 'And general mental strain.'

Julia paused in the action of raising her glass to her

lips, darting a glance at her supervisor who surveyed her expressionlessly. 'I don't usually give advice, as you know, trusting supervisees to take responsibility for their self-care.' She waited. 'Have you seen your GP lately?'

Julia shook her head. Of course she should have made an appointment. The sensation of blood pounding in her ears was happening frequently, and her insomnia was constant. 'I will do,' she promised, hoping Louise would be satisfied with this.

'Good.' Louise paused. She waited for Julia to raise her gaze from the water swirling in the glass which she twirled in her hand. 'I have to say I'm wondering if you are fit to be counselling at the moment.'

'I'm sure I am.' Julia tried to sound calm, though inwardly her heart was beating fast. She placed the glass carefully on the side table to the left of her armchair.

'You're sure? You know how important it is that you are fully fit for counselling and how, as your supervisor, *I* need to be assured of that. Professional standards, Julia. I don't need to remind you that we're working with very vulnerable people. We might cause them harm if we aren't well enough, physically or mentally.'

'Mmm.' Julia nodded, her eyes on her black ankle boots which badly needed polishing. Usually she was so meticulous. She pushed a strand of hair behind her right ear.

'And I'm guessing your relationship with Client "G" has become complicated. You seemed evasive when I asked if you have become particularly close to her.'

'I think it has become complicated,' Julia conceded quietly. She inhaled and looked across at her supervisor. 'And I'm sorry, Louise, but I feel I can't talk about it today.'

'Ah.' Louise folded her podgy hands across her stomach which spilled over the waistband of her baggy grey trousers. 'I'm grateful for your honesty, but you will understand that it causes me concern that you are unwilling to discuss it. I realise you have the difficult task of explaining you can no longer counsel her, and that will end your sessions. But I'm wondering how you are going to react if a similar issue arises in a relationship with another client?'

'Surely that's unlikely,' countered Julia, 'since each client is an individual, and our relationships with each one vary so much?'

'That's true. But you know as well as I do that if we are troubled by a particular issue, it can impact our effectiveness as practitioners if it isn't dealt with. It can even cause harm to our clients.'

Julia nodded wearily, knowing Louise was right. 'Do no harm' was a mantra of the counselling profession, one she had always sought to maintain. Her throat felt constricted as she realised she'd pushed it to the back of her mind in recent weeks. She had been so desperate to work, both as a distraction from her grief and also to safeguard her income. What choice did she have in view of the financial crisis precipitated by Greg defaulting on the mortgage?

Louise's voice came from a distance, interrupting her thoughts.

'So that's why I must insist that you take some time off.'

'Sorry?' Julia stared at her supervisor open-mouthed.

'You need some time off. I'm sorry if it's come as a shock to you, but it's clear to me you're struggling. And I'm very concerned you seem not to realise that yourself.'

'But I can't afford to!' Julia clapped her hand to her mouth as Louise's small eyes narrowed in her round pink face.

'I'm afraid financial difficulty doesn't change the situation, Julia. If you don't take a break, I will have no choice but to contact Professional Standards.'

'Professional Standards?' gasped Julia. 'But you can't, I might lose my accreditation! It could finish my career!' She wiped a stray tear from her cheeks, and swallowed, striving not to break down in front of Louise.

'I'm sorry, Julia, I really am.' Her supervisor's tone was softer as she leaned across and placed a hand on Julia's knee. 'But you are simply not fit to be counselling at present. You've admitted to insomnia. You look unwell, pale and strained. You're still grieving for your mother. You've made clear there is something troubling you arising from your relationship with Client "G".' She paused. 'And that's not all, is it?'

She removed her hand and settled back in her chair, her eyes still fixed on Julia's face.

'Not all?' echoed Julia. She dropped her eyes and flicked a ball of fluff off her black trousers. What else could Louise know?

'No. I'm afraid I've had a complaint. About an altercation you were involved in last Friday.'

Julia put her head in her hands. 'Greg,' she said. 'It was Greg, wasn't it?' *The bastard. Hadn't he done enough damage?* But when she thought of how she had hit him twice across the face, of Lisa's fear as she placed a hand over her pregnant belly, the colour rushed to her cheeks.

'He could have gone to the police,' pointed out

Louise. 'But I don't think from our conversation he intends to do that.'

Julia sighed with relief. The prospect of him pressing charges had never occurred to her. She kept her head down, pressing her fingertips to her forehead, as Louise continued in her usual measured tone.

'Now we've talked through your separation in previous sessions, and although you were naturally distressed by it, I didn't consider that it was affecting your work. But for you to attack Greg so many months later, to lose that self-control which is one of your strongest characteristics, I suspect that something has provoked or upset you deeply.'

She waited. Julia didn't look up immediately. When she did, she saw Louise was watching her, the small eyes kind, her hands steepled beneath her double chin. Julia's heart was beating quickly and there was a weight in her chest. She took another deep breath. Now that she had to take time off, perhaps it would help to share some of her burden with Louise.

'Lisa is seven months' pregnant,' she said. 'They were shopping for the baby when I saw them.' She reached for her glass of water with a trembling hand and drank deeply. 'He told me when we were first together that he didn't want children.'

'My dear,' said Louise, who had two adult sons herself, 'I am so very sorry.'

Julia nodded. Having begun to speak, it was easy to carry on. 'And my relationship with Grace has got tangled up with all this,' she said. 'She told me she sees me as the mother she never had, and I think I'm in danger. . .' she hesitated, twisting her mother's engagement ring around the third finger of her right hand. 'I'm in danger of viewing her as the daughter I will never have.' She took a deep breath, immediately feeling lighter. She hadn't allowed herself to analyse her relationship with Grace with such honesty before. At the same time the thought of not seeing the younger woman again because of her relationship with her half-brother brought tears to her eyes. She bent to find a tissue in her black shoulder bag.

Louise waited until she had composed herself before she spoke again.

'There's a lot about mothers and daughters here, isn't there?'

'There is.' Julia was struck by the insight. She looked towards the window as a rare burst of sunlight broke through the clouds. It fell on a framed picture resting against the wall below the sill. She'd never noticed it before. She could see that it was a Madonna and child painting, unusually painted in red, orange and yellow. The colours of fire, thought Julia, vaguely recalling that Louise was Catholic.

Her supervisor noticed the direction of her gaze. 'The most famous mother of all,' she said. 'The ideal. As you can see, I've not hung the picture yet.'

'May I take a look?' Julia half-rose from her chair.

'Of course,' Louise waved her hand in invitation.

Julia's heart had begun to bump hard against her rib-cage for a reason she couldn't explain. She gasped as she picked up the painting. 'It's quite disturbing, isn't it?'

'It is,' Louise agreed. 'Certainly not your usual serene Madonna and child. But perhaps a more realistic representation.'

'You think so?'

'I do.'

Julia studied the oil painting. Close up, her impression of fire was proved correct. The background of swirling grey and black suggested smoke. Mary's robe was red, with orange sleeves. She wore a yellow head dress above her dark hair, which tumbled in disarray around her shoulders. Flames leaped around her head. Her mouth was open in a silent scream. Her large black eyes, staring out to the left, were pools of fear. She was looking away from the naked baby she clutched to her breast. The tiny fingers of the infant's right hand scrabbled at a strand of his mother's hair. His face was hidden from view, buried against her. Tongues of fire leaped around the infant's head too, illuminating the small dagger he held in his left hand. It was poised above Mary's heart.

'I think it's very realistic,' Louise continued. 'Think of the anguish Mary suffered as the mother of Christ. It was there from the very beginning. The fire symbolises the pain. Yet it's a symbol of the Holy Spirit too. When the Spirit descended on the waiting disciples on the first Pentecost, tongues of fire settled on each one.'

'And her arms are crossed over Jesus too, maybe representing the crucifixion,' Julia observed. 'But what about the dagger?'

'Ah. The dagger. Do you remember the account of the infant Jesus being presented in the temple in Jerusalem?'

'No. I'm afraid not.'

'It was a rite of purification fulfilling the law of Moses. According to Luke's gospel, a righteous man named Simeon was spared death until he had seen the Messiah. When his parents brought Jesus into the temple, Simeon took him and spoke a blessing over him. The words are preserved in the Nunc Dimittis, if you know that.'

'"Lord, now lettest thou thy servant depart in peace?"'
Childhood memories of attending Evening Prayer on various occasions with her parents before Leonard's death flickered into Julia's mind. She recalled that Simeon's words were included in the liturgy.

'That's the one. Then Simeon blessed the family, warning Mary "a sword will pierce your own soul." That's the reason for the dagger.'

'I see.' Julia looked down again at the painting. 'So it's more realistic than the traditional Madonna and child art, as you say. But still very unsettling. Where did you find it?'

'In a gallery near Walsingham, where the Shrine of Our Lady is. I spent a weekend there recently. Apparently it was painted by a local artist.'

Julia's heart thudded. The painting transported her back to Linda's art exhibition. What was it the man in the green Barbour jacket had said about some of her early paintings? *Those the critics described as a feminist revolt against traditional Madonna and child images.* And his wife had replied, *'Full of blood and suffering, Jesus ripped from Mary's womb. And weren't there some with them in flames? Very controversial.'*

'Julia? Are you all right?'

'Yes.' Julia opened her eyes, searching the base of the painting for the artist's signature. There it was in the bottom right-hand corner, pale grey against the deeper grey and black swirls of smoke. *Linda Thurston.* 'I went to the artist's exhibition recently, that's all. In the gallery on Steep Hill.'

'I'm sorry to have missed it. Now I apologise for rushing you, Julia, but I have another appointment in twenty minutes, so if you don't mind. . .'

'Of course not.' Julia glanced at her delicate gold wrist-watch, a twenty-first birthday present from her mother. 'I'm sorry. I've taken too long.'

'Not at all,' said Louise briskly. 'You needed the time today.'

'Thank you so much.' Julia reached for her bag to extract her payment.

Louise waved the notes aside as she hauled her bulk out of her chair. 'Don't worry about that,' she said. 'Put it towards a few days away.' She paused. 'You've been through a great deal, Julia. Your split with your partner, the loss of your mother, some difficulties with your half-brother. Now there is a new grief, the grief of childlessness. It will take time to heal. I know how difficult it has been for you to speak of these things here, but when you look back, you will see it as the time your healing began. And when you've taken the time out that you need, you'll find you resume counselling with a greater understanding and empathy for the troubled souls you encounter.'

Julia gave a wan smile. 'Troubled souls' was such an archaic expression, but for the first time in her life she recognised herself among them. Her mind was clearer than it had been for months. By the door she turned to give her supervisor a hug. 'You've helped me so much, Louise,' she said.

The other woman smiled and said nothing.

Julia crossed the drive to her Mondeo with a lighter step. She would follow Louise's advice and go away. She would go to Norfolk, to Walsingham. The place of pilgrimage, a place people went hoping for healing. Even if she had no faith herself, it could do no harm. She felt she needed all the help she could get at the moment. And if

Linda were from the area, perhaps she would find out more about the family connection – hadn't Edith said Emily had gone to visit family in Norfolk in 1943?

For all her reservations about uncovering the family secret Linda had alluded to, Julia did want to know more about her newly-discovered artist relative.

– CHAPTER 19 –

Sleep was more elusive than ever during Julia's first night in the sixteenth-century inn close to the Shrine of Our Lady in Walsingham. The lumpy mattress in the narrow single bed didn't help. But it was thoughts of Linda which kept her awake. She'd been more upset than she would have expected when a nurse rang from the hospital just before she left home with the news that Aunt Ada had died in the early hours. Driving south that afternoon, she'd mused how the rain-swept fens seemed to reflect her inner emptiness. Loneliness, even. She'd never thought of herself as lonely. But with her fiftieth birthday just six weeks away, Greg and her mother gone, the current state of hostility with James, life was bleak. The realisation that she was now the oldest surviving member of the family added to her dread of the milestone.

Clare had a point: it was hard not to blame Linda for Ada's death. Her confrontation with the old woman had literally frightened her to death. The more Julia thought about it, the more she was convinced that Linda's animosity towards Ada was connected to the secret Emily had referred to in her diary. The secret which William Prescott had known and divulged to Leonard after Emily rejected his advances. A secret which had shocked Leonard so much that his fragile health had crumbled. No wonder her mother had described Prescott as that 'odious man'! The thoughts whirled round Julia's mind throughout the night, like laundry endlessly spinning in a washing machine.

Giving up the struggle for sleep when the old pipes rattled into life at 6 a.m., Julia reminded herself that she had decided to come to Norfolk to find out more about Linda and the family mystery. With Ada gone, the artist was the only person who could shed light on it. Even as she asked herself again, 'Do I really want to know?' shivering under the shower as the low water pressure reduced the flow to a trickle, she sensed she would not rest until she knew the truth.

After a fortifying full English breakfast, Julia went across to the Shrine of Our Lady. She was surprised by the number of visitors on the wet February day. Looking on as people of all ages and backgrounds queued at the 'Holy Water,' she wished she were less of an agnostic. Pete, she was sure, would relish this place. *Pete. . .* Would he still consider sharing premises with her after she had rejected his mis-timed kiss? Even if his motives hadn't been entirely business related, he had genuinely been trying to help. Watching the pilgrims at the shrine, it occurred to her that if she didn't believe in divine help, she shouldn't be so quick to reject human assistance.

Back at the pub, already busy with lunchtime trade even though it was barely noon, she ate a bowl of carrot and coriander soup with more appetite than she'd had in weeks. Up in her room she steeled herself to call James and Clare to discuss arrangements for Aunt Ada's funeral. James had agreed to contact the undertakers the previous day. She rang their landline, hoping to get Clare.

The possibility that James might be the father of Grace's baby had exacerbated the conflict with her half-brother – the fact that she knew about Grace's pregnancy and couldn't tell him about it because of client confidentiality put her in a very difficult position. The more she thought about it, the more she worried about the effect on Clare if she discovered that the woman with whom James had had an affair was pregnant. She still felt embarrassed by her outburst to Clare in the café, but she had appreciated the effort her sister-in-law had made to phone her after the altercation. Clare at least would understand something of the pain she was experiencing as she confronted her own childlessness.

Thankfully it was Clare who picked up. James was out at the university. The funeral had been set for Tuesday week at Scampton Parish Church, the church where Ada had been a lifelong member, and where her father had been vicar. James had made an appointment with the vicar to go through the arrangements the following Monday. Julia confirmed that she was happy for him to see the vicar alone, if she weren't back from Norfolk.

'So you've not decided when you're coming back? It's not like you not to know exactly what you're doing.' Clare sounded concerned.

'No.' Julia looked down from her bedroom window to the street below, busy with pilgrims coming and going from the shine. Many of them were hidden away under umbrellas, their colours brightening the wet day. 'I'm just giving myself some time.'

'That's a good idea.'

'How are things with you and James?'

'Not great.' Clare paused. 'You know, Julia, with your mother and Ada dying so close together it's made me think about how precious life is. I know they were old, that they'd had their time, but it's made me realise you've really got to get on with what you want, haven't you?'

'Yes.' Julia wasn't sure where Clare was going with this. For some reason she thought of Pete, the pleasant pressure of his hand massage that evening, how she had wanted to respond to his kiss but pulled away a week last Saturday, her mind telling her she wasn't ready for a new relationship. She bit her lip, wondering if she could call him on the pretext of discussing business premises.

'So I think this might be it for me and James,' her sister-in-law continued. 'His affair isn't the only reason. I've been asking myself why I'm staying with him when I so desperately want a child and he's not so bothered. And of course our fertility problems lie with him anyway.'

Julia froze. 'They do?'

'Yes. Perhaps I shouldn't have told you that, he doesn't like people to know. But without the treatment, the chances of him fathering a child are zero.'

'Ah.' So James wasn't the father of Grace's child. Julia exhaled.

'You won't tell him you know, will you?' Clare asked anxiously.

'No. Of course not.'

'Thanks. So I'm thinking, and I hope this doesn't sound selfish, that I might leave James after all, give myself the chance of meeting someone else before it's too late.' She paused. 'Sorry. I don't mean to be insensitive.'

Her sister-in-law rolled a pen along the beech table by the window, registering an inner pang. 'Don't worry about it,' she said after a moment. 'For the record, Clare, not that you need my blessing or anything, but I don't think you're being selfish at all.'

'Thank you,' said Clare quietly. 'That means a lot, you know. Like I said the other day, whatever happens between me and James, I hope we can stay friends.'

'Of course we can.'

'I'd better be going. I've got to be back at the office at two. You take care, Julia.'

'I will. Bye.'

The call ended, Julia went out into the rain. Picking up her car from the pub car park, she drove out of Little Walsingham along a meandering country lane with no destination in mind. For once it wasn't raining, and although the sky was still overcast, Julia's mood lightened. Louise was right, a few days away would help. She felt too that a burden had been lifted with the discovery that James wasn't the father of Grace's child.

Thinking of her supervisor brought Linda's disturbing Madonna and child painting to mind. Louise had said she'd found it in a gallery in the area. On cue she saw a sign for the Great Walsingham Gallery and turned into the courtyard. If this wasn't the place where Louise had found Linda's painting, someone in the gallery might know something about the artist. And even if she had reservations about whether she wanted to uncover the family secret, she would like to find out more about her mysterious relative.

There was only one other customer in the gallery, a white-haired man in a black suit. He was speaking quietly with a woman knitting behind a trestle table in a corner, his back to Julia. The measured tones of a Bach violin concerto on Classic FM filtered through the large airy space. Julia looked around the exhibition of vibrant oil paintings of coastal landscapes. No work by Linda Thurston there.

'Can I help you?'

Julia turned towards the desk. The elderly man was making his way to the door. She saw a flash of white at his throat: a priest. Walsingham was crawling with them.

'I wondered if you had any paintings by an artist who I believe might be local? Linda Thurston?'

She jumped at a crash across the room. A picture lay on the floor, knocked off a shelf by the priest who was stooping to pick it up. Instinctively Julia moved across to help.

'Are you all right, Father?' The woman laid down her knitting with a clatter.

'Yes. Thank you. Very clumsy of me – I almost lost my footing. I don't think there is any damage to the picture.' He inspected the seascape carefully, then turned his attention to Julia.

Julia was trying to place his nasal accent. North American, probably Canadian. Close up, she realised he was older than his upright carriage suggested. Deep lines were etched into his forehead and the corners of his eyes and mouth. His Adam's apple was prominent in the wrinkled skin of his neck. But his piercing blue eyes, scanning her face with a strange intensity, were those of a much younger man.

'You're quite sure? Do you want to sit down for a moment? Maybe I could get you a cup of tea?' Reaching them, the plump woman placed a small freckled hand on the priest's arm, darting a nervous glance at the painting. Her rather moony face cleared when she saw it was unharmed. She took it from the priest and replaced it carefully.

'No. Thank you. I must be on my way.' But he made no move, seeming rooted to the spot. *The shock*, thought Julia.

'It's that join in the floor.' The woman pointed down at the wooden floor with a stubby forefinger. 'I've nearly tripped over that myself before now. Someone's going to have a nasty accident there one day. Lucky it wasn't you, Father.'

'I might say providential,' said the priest, still staring at Julia. She found herself looking away from his penetrating gaze.

'Of course,' said the woman. She giggled like a nervous schoolgirl. 'You would say that. I must tell them again, though. It's time they did something about it, levelled it off.'

'I'm quite all right.' The priest finally tore his eyes from Julia and walked slowly towards the glass door, which was spattered with fresh rain drops. There he turned and looked back at them. 'I'll see you again, I expect.'

'See you soon, Father,' answered the woman, even though his eyes were fixed on Julia. He raised his hand in acknowledgement before disappearing into the drizzle.

'Remarkable man,' said the woman, moving back towards her desk. 'Travelling all that way from Canada at his age. I find London enough these days.' She patted her grey curls complacently and settled back into her chair. She picked up her knitting, a bright creation of red, orange and yellow. *Colours of fire* thought Julia.

She shuddered. She seemed to be seeing fire every-where at the moment, ever since that nightmare on the evening of her mother's funeral, and the strange coinci-dence of Grace telling her how her mother had set fire to the house when she was a baby. Then there was Linda's painting of the Madonna and child engulfed in flames. . .

'So you're interested in Linda Thurston's work?' The woman deftly joined a new ball of flame-coloured wool into her garment.

'Yes.' Julia paused. For some reason she didn't want to acknowledge her relationship with Linda. Whatever that relationship was. 'Someone I know bought one of her paintings nearby recently. It could have been from this gallery.'

'I remember, just a couple of weeks ago.' She glanced at Julia over the rim of her bronze-framed glasses. 'A rather large lady, not that I've got room to talk.' She pat-ted her stomach beneath a shapeless pink sweatshirt and smiled, revealing small even teeth. 'Can't resist cake, that's my problem. Yes, your friend bought one of the Madonna and child pictures.'

'That's right. I wondered if you had any more?'

'Just one left, I think.' The woman laid down her knit-ting again. She pulled out a large box from under the desk and hefted it on to the table. Puffing with the effort, she rooted through it until she found a print. She handed it to Julia. 'Not to the taste of some of the Walsingham pilgrims.'

'No. I've heard they are controversial.' Julia studied the picture.

This time Mary was dressed in traditional blue, her right hand supporting the infant Jesus whose head rested on his mother's shoulder. Smoke and flames billowed around them, but both Mother and child gazed out serenely, apparently oblivious to the lethal danger. Julia caught her breath.

'They certainly were.' The woman resumed her seat and her knitting. 'Of course, the artist was ill at the time she painted them, poor thing. Mentally, that is.'

'Oh?'

'Yes. It was a terrible tragedy for the family.' The woman bent her head to check her pattern. Julia started as the quiet strains of Bach were replaced by Mozart's violent 'Dies Irae.'

Julia waited for her to start the next row before asking, 'What happened?' Her mouth was dry.

The woman glanced up again. 'I don't really like to gossip. But I suppose if you asked any older residents, they'd remember, so I might as well tell you.' The gleam in her eyes made Julia doubt her discretion, as did her stage whisper as she leaned forward. 'She set fire to the house when she was at home alone with her baby.'

Julia had the strangest sensation of time slowing. She closed her eyes, revisiting her nightmare again: the woman at the upstairs window of a house in flames, a baby screaming. Her voice seemed to come from far away. 'What happened to the baby?'

'She survived. A little girl. The husband came back just in time and they were both rescued. She was sectioned, sent away for years. Today they might have been able to treat her better.' She paused as she finished another row. 'Let's see. . . knit three, purl to the end. That's it. Where was I?'

'You said the mother was sectioned, placed in an institution?'

'That's right. She was suffering from that condition some women have after giving birth. It wasn't so well-treated back then. What do they call it, post-natal depression? No, worse than that. . .'

Julia's head pounded. 'Post-natal psychosis?'

'That's it.'

'And the husband and baby? Where did they go?' Julia's voice was little more than a whisper. She was sure she knew the answer.

'They changed their names, and moved north. I heard he re-married after the divorce. She finally came back to the area two years ago. I'm not sure I'd want to, would you? Still, home's home, I suppose. And she's made a good job of restoring the old farmhouse.' She laid down the knitting and reached for a tape measure.

The room was spinning round Julia. She clutched the table for support. Grey curls bent over her knitting, the woman didn't notice.

'The old farmhouse?'

'Yes. Out by North Creake Abbey. Just a few miles up the road. Strange, I always think. It burned down centuries ago, before Henry VIII's dissolution of the monasteries. Makes me wonder if there's something in a place that means history repeats itself. Too much of a coincidence otherwise, isn't it?' Her fingers were suddenly still on her needles as she looked up at Julia, obviously wanting an answer.

'I don't know, I. . .' Julia had had enough of coincidences for one afternoon. Was it coincidence or – what was the word the priest had used? – 'providence' that had brought her to this gallery this afternoon to find out that Linda's baby must surely be Grace? 'Do you remember how long ago this was?'

'Oh, must be over thirty years ago. Let me think. Yes, I was pregnant with my eldest son, and he's thirty-two now. So it must be thirty-three years ago. Do you have children?'

'No.' Julia turned away from the desk. 'Thank you. You've been very helpful.' She nearly ran to the heavy glass door without looking back.

The wind had risen, blowing fresh rain across the courtyard. In the car she checked her road atlas with trembling fingers, heart banging in her chest. She wasn't sure what she would do when she reached Linda's house. Client confidentiality meant she couldn't tell Linda that she knew Grace. She would have to take advice from Louise. But perhaps Linda might volunteer something of her history herself, so she could make sure it tallied with Grace's account. Not that she had any doubts left. The timing, location and details fitted exactly with what her client had told her.

She drove a few miles along a winding lane before turning at a brown heritage signpost for North Creake Abbey. No other cars were parked in the field designated as a car park where she pulled in. The iron gate squeaked as she entered the site, passing a man walking his Labrador. He nodded an acknowledgement. She regretted not bringing her walking boots to Norfolk as the heels of her black ankle boots sank into the grass, sodden from weeks of rain. At least she'd brought her faithful black waterproof. She fastened the press stud of the hood as the rain began to fall more heavily, wishing she'd asked the man if he knew the house where Linda lived. She looked back towards the gate, but the man and dog had disappeared.

The light was beginning to fade as she passed beneath a Norman archway and squelched through the area she guessed had been the nave. Only low walls had survived here, although elsewhere the height of the ruins hinted at how imposing the abbey must have been before the fire. At the top of the former nave she stepped through an opening to the left. There were no buildings visible from here, and she was about to turn away and walk back down the other side of the ruin when something white caught her eye on some sort of ledge in the wall.

Close up, Julia realised the ledge was actually a piscina, the place where the priest would have washed the sacred vessels. She was surprised to see it contained the stub of a white candle together with an assortment of cards. Some of the cards had names and dates on, 'To Mother. Always in my thoughts. Jenny. 27.12.01.' She found herself dashing away tears as she read that. Jenny's mother had died just a few days before Emily. Then another, 'For Jake. Rest with the angels, precious one. 12.2.01–14.7.01.' A kind of shrine, she supposed. It felt intrusive to study the cards, but a morbid curiosity compelled her to look through the rest.

Time slowed for the second time in an hour. The words on one card, penned in a familiar bold sloping hand, leaped out at her. 'To my baby. 34 today. God bless you. L.' *Linda*, thought Julia. *Linda and Grace.*

She shivered suddenly. There was something eerie about the deserted abbey on a darkening wet February afternoon. The makeshift shrine, the card she was sure Linda had penned for Grace, added to her unease. And there was something else too: the uncanny sense that something had led her here. Julia shook herself, showering the cards with raindrops. She was being fanciful. She needed to collect herself, to leave the abbey behind and to find the house where Linda lived.

Making her way back down the opposite side of the ruin, Julia noticed what she hadn't been able to see before: the wall here on the south side was in good condition. Beyond it lay a house. Her heart nearly stopped beating. She leaned against the wall for support, overcome by a dizzying sense of *déjà vu*.

It was the grey farmhouse from the picture at Linda's exhibition, standing in the shadow of a ruined abbey. And it was identical to the house in her nightmare, she realised suddenly. Julia could see the window where the woman had stood engulfed in flames. She hadn't made the connection before. This had to be Linda's house. She had reached her destination.

– CHAPTER 20 –

Julia had no idea how long she stood there in the abbey
grounds, gazing over the garden wall at the house below.
Lights were on downstairs. There was another at the
upstairs window where the woman had stood in her nightmare, flames leaping around her. As she looked, she saw a
figure approach the window. For a heart-stopping moment
she wondered if she was going to see her nightmare re-
enacted. But then the light dimmed, and she realised the
figure had been someone drawing the curtains as dusk
descended. A quotation floated up from the recesses of her
memory as she stared at the house, heedless of the rain
which continued to fall steadily, pondering what had
brought her here. *'There are more things in heaven and
earth. . .'*

The phrase brought to mind the priest she had seen in
the art gallery. He would be someone who understood
more of this than she did. It went beyond the rational,
beyond coincidence. What was his word again? Providence.
That was it. Providence. Or maybe fate. Whatever it
was, she felt she had been led here.

The back door of the house was opening. In the light
which spilled out into the garden, Julia recognised the tall,
erect figure of the elderly priest. It was as if she had

spirited him up. She remained by the wall, strangely unsurprised to see him. He trod purposefully across the neglected lawn and flower beds, shielded from the rain under a large black umbrella. He stopped under a gnarled apple tree and looked up at her.

'I thought it was you,' he said. 'I didn't expect you so soon. But maybe it's for the best. I don't know how much longer. . .' His voice broke, and he passed his hand briefly over his eyes. 'Bring your car round the lane to the house.' He turned away abruptly.

Julia was past asking questions. She went back to the car park in a daze and drove down a narrow lane which forked off to the left, guessing correctly it would bring her to the house. She pulled in behind two other cars on the verge. Walking slowly down the rutted drive, she tried to avoid the puddles in the gloom of the wet February evening. She had nearly reached the front door when a woman opened it, pausing to zip a navy fleece over a blue nurses' uniform.

'I'll be back later, Father!' she called. She glanced at Julia waiting to let her pass in front of the doorstep. 'Your visitor's here.' She picked up a bag and clipboard from the floor beside her, then stepped out. 'Don't wake her,' she said. 'Watch Father too. He needs to rest.'

'I don't. . .' Julia began. But with a wave of her hand over her shoulder the nurse sped off up the drive, late for her next appointment.

Julia stepped into the hall. Water dripped from her waterproof onto the flagged floor. She suddenly realised how cold and wet she was from standing so long by the abbey wall. Evidently the priest, treading noiselessly down the carpeted stairs, thought so as well. 'Let me take your coat,' he said. 'I'll make a cup of tea. The nurse boiled the kettle.'

Obediently Julia handed him her waterproof. He hung it on a coat stand in a corner and disappeared through one of three doorways leading off the hall. She caught a glimpse of herself in the large oval mirror which hung on the wall opposite the front door and raked her hands through her damp hair. She looked a mess, with her usually sleek bob wavy from the rain, the shadows under her eyes more pronounced than ever in her pale face.

She followed the priest into a long low-ceilinged kitchen. Copper pans hung above an Aga next to an oak dresser which housed an assortment of brightly coloured plates and bowls. The wine rack alongside was nearly full. A plump grey and white cat lay asleep on a multi-coloured knitted blanket on a wooden rocking chair in front of the Aga. Julia yawned. The warm comfortable kitchen made her realise how tired she was. She settled into a dining chair at the long oak table.

The priest lifted the kettle from the stove. His large hand was trembling as he poured water into a striped yellow and red teapot.

'Would you like me. . . ?' she asked.

'No, no.' He cut her off. 'Do you take milk? Sugar?'

'Just a little milk, thank you.'

He poured milk from a bottle in the fridge into two mugs which matched the teapot and set the items on an orange tray. His familiarity with the kitchen surprised her. She wondered if Linda were very ill. He seemed to know his way around.

The priest seemed to read her thoughts. 'Linda had surgery to remove a brain tumour a week last Monday,' he said abruptly, stirring the tea in the pot.

'A brain tumour? That's terrible.' Julia bit her lip, wincing as she remembered how quickly they had all, she, James, Clare, Pete, Edith, assumed Linda was drunk when she disrupted Ada's lunch. 'So that's why she behaved so strangely at my aunt's eightieth,' she mused.

'Your aunt?' The priest stopped stirring the tea, his hand hovering shakily above the teapot.

'Yes. Linda turned up unexpectedly at the party. Two days before her surgery, I suppose.'

'Ah. That's where she went then.' The priest resumed stirring the tea.

Julia decided there could be no harm telling him what had happened. 'She said something to my aunt which upset her. In fact she had a stroke. She died yesterday morning.'

The priest didn't respond, but crossed himself.

'Ada looked like she'd seen a ghost. She said something strange too.' Julia shivered, remembering the old woman's struggle to gasp out what had proved to be her final words.

'Oh?' The priest bent his white head over the teapot as he lifted it. His hand was trembling more than ever, but after his earlier refusal of help Julia didn't offer to pour instead.

'Yes. She said, "I never told her he was alive." Then she collapsed.'

The priest set down the teapot with a crash. Tea dribbled from the spout across the table.

'I'm sorry, I should have poured. Let me get a cloth.' Julia went across to the sink and picked up a dish cloth.

The priest didn't object, sitting down opposite her as

she wiped up the tea. She finished pouring and handed him a mug. He laced his long white tapering fingers around it without raising it from the table, looking down into the steaming liquid. The silence stretched between them.

'I'm sorry to hear Linda's so ill,' she said eventually. 'Will she – is it. . . ?'

'That's in God's hands,' he said quietly. 'She will have a course of radiotherapy, if she is strong enough. She should have stayed in hospital, but wanted to leave as soon as possible. Not surprising, given her history.' He chewed on his thumb nail.

Julia drew in her breath, sure that his reference to Linda's aversion to hospitals tied in with the years the artist had spent in psychiatric care as recounted by the woman at the gallery.

Before she could ask him anything more, the priest said abruptly, 'She's sleeping now and shouldn't be disturbed today.' He looked up from his tea, and his startling blue eyes bored into Julia's. 'She's not to be upset.'

'Of course not. I didn't come here to upset her.' Julia's tone was sharper than she intended. But as she spoke she wondered if her words were wholly true. She'd intended to find out more about the fire, make absolutely certain that the baby was Grace. Raking up the memories would inevitably cause Linda distress. But might the reunion of the mother and daughter – a daughter carrying Linda's grandchild – help the sick woman and give her some peace of mind? Or would the shock be too much for her? And what effect would meeting her mother have on Grace? It was possible she might lose her again very soon given the serious nature of Linda's illness. She closed her eyes as the questions tumbled through her mind.

The priest took a few sips of tea and set his mug down. He rested his lined chin on his steepled hands. 'She wanted to see you,' he said eventually. 'There is something she needs to tell you.'

The family secret. Julia looked down at her tea. Her heart beat faster. Her voice seemed to come from a distance. 'She said she knew something about my – our – family.'

'Yes.'

Julia drank. The tea was still too hot and scalded her throat. 'Do you know what it is?'

A shadow passed over his face. 'I do.' He rose suddenly and went over to the window, his back to her. His broad shoulders were tense inside his black jacket.

Julia took more sips of the burning liquid. Priests, she knew, were bound by confidentiality, as were counsellors. Greg had once described her, sneeringly, as 'a kind of secular priest,' dismissive as he was of both religion and therapy. She hadn't liked the expression, but understood what he meant. With the decline of institutionalised religion, people were turning to counsellors instead of clergy as a source of support.

Why did I stay with him so long? The question had run through her mind repeatedly during the last fortnight. His indifference towards her losing her cottage because he hadn't paid the mortgage, his lies about his affair with Lisa, and worst of all, his callousness towards her about his partner's pregnancy, had exploded into her outburst at the shopping centre. Five days later, Julia still shrank inside as she recalled striking him, visualised again Lisa's shock and fear.

She'd known almost immediately that it had been the exposure of grief at her childlessness which had propelled her to attack him. Now, in the quiet kitchen where the only sound was the rain tapping on the window, she tried to imagine how the sick woman upstairs must feel about her tragic experience of motherhood. A misunderstood mental illness had led to her separation from her daughter. She saw in her mind's eye Grace's haunted face as she said in that first meeting, 'I don't know whether she's alive or dead.' Was the fire somehow related to the family secret Linda wanted to tell her?

Thinking about the strange events which had brought her to this house, Julia made a decision: she would take advice from this elderly priest who seemed to know Linda so well. First though she wanted to know more about him. His presence here puzzled her.

'I've been trying to place your accent,' she said. 'Are you from Canada?'

She saw his back stiffen as he took another gulp of tea, still looking out over the dark sodden garden. 'Yes. I'm Canadian.'

'So you've come to Walsingham on some kind of retreat?' she hazarded.

He hesitated. 'Walsingham has always interested me,' he said slowly. 'The shrine, the devotion to Mary.' He paused, then turned to look at her, his eyes scanning her face in that unsettling way. 'I also had family reasons for coming over.'

'Oh?' Julia's prompt usually elicited a further response from her clients, but was met with silence by the priest. He turned back to the sink, downing the rest of his tea before rinsing out his mug under the cold tap. Anxious that he might ask her to leave before she had asked him about the tragedy in Linda's past, Julia plunged on.

'I know that as a priest you can't disclose to me what Linda has told you,' she began, setting her mug down on the table, 'and I don't know how it connects with what Linda wants to tell me about our family. But I think I've found out something which might help her. And I would appreciate your advice, as a priest, about whether I should tell her, especially as she is so ill. It's something which I think might set her mind at rest.'

Julia took a deep breath, pushed a strand of damp hair behind her right ear. 'I probably shouldn't be speaking to you about it. I'm a counsellor myself. Like you, I'm bound by confidentiality. I will need to speak with my supervisor before saying anything to Linda. But I won't if you think it might do more harm than good.'

The priest turned round slowly, his face expressionless. Professionally so, thought Julia, knowing how she sought to maintain a neutral expression with her clients.

He nodded to her to continue.

'It's what you said earlier about providence. I never believed in providence before today. Perhaps I might call it fate. But I seem somehow to have been led here, if that makes sense.'

Again the priest nodded without speaking. And again Julia found herself unnerved by his piercing gaze. But having begun her story, she didn't falter.

'The woman at the gallery told me Linda set fire to this house when she was in here with her baby. She was ill, suffering from post-partum psychosis, which wasn't understood very well at the time, thirty-three years ago. She was taken into psychiatric care, and her husband and daughter moved away and changed their names. Linda has never seen her daughter since. Is that right?'

'Yes,' said the priest quietly. 'That's right.' His blue eyes remained fixed on Julia's. 'Is that all you know?'

'No.' Julia paused. 'I think – I'm certain – I know Linda's daughter. She's one of my clients.'

The priest half-stumbled across the kitchen to his chair and sank down into it. 'Thank God,' he whispered. He covered his eyes with his hands. 'Thank God.'

Julia was surprised by the intensity of his reaction, even though she appreciated that priests could become involved in the lives of the people they encountered. They weren't required, as counsellors were, to retain the same degree of detachment. Not that she had been detached from Grace. She swallowed. She had become too involved with the postgraduate student, overstepping the boundaries. But here was a chance for her to make up for some of her mistakes.

'Do you think it would help Linda to meet her, if her daughter is agreeable? I'm sure she would, but of course I will need to speak to her, after I've checked with my supervisor.'

The priest raised his head. Julia saw there were tears in his eyes. His voice was hoarse. 'It would most definitely help.' He dashed away the tears. 'You must excuse me. The foolishness of a sentimental old man.' For the first time since they had met, he half-smiled.

Julia smiled back, though she realised she was close to tears herself. It was astonishing, little short of a miracle, that she had dreamed of this house, that Grace had come to her for counselling just around the time she had first met Linda at her mother's funeral, that now there was the possibility of reuniting a sick woman with the child she hadn't seen since for over thirty years.

'I'll ring my supervisor as soon as I get back to the inn where I'm staying,' she said. 'Shall I come again tomorrow? Perhaps I could see Linda if she's up to it?'

He didn't answer immediately, reaching across the table for a large bulky brown envelope. He picked it up and held it to his chest for a moment. He swallowed, and Julia realised he was in the grip of some strong emotion.

'This is for you.' He slid the envelope towards her, resting a trembling hand on one end as she placed her hand on the other. He seemed reluctant to let it go. 'Read it this evening. When you get back to where you're staying. You will find out the rest of what Linda wants to tell you in there.' He extended his long fingers so that they covered Julia's briefly. 'I hope that you will be able to come back tomorrow.' His eyes contained a plea which Julia didn't understand.

There was something else she didn't understand too, she realised, as she made her way out to the hall. He took her waterproof from the coat stand and held it open for her to step into.

'How did you know who I was in the gallery?' she asked as he opened the door. The rain had stopped. All was quiet save for the water dripping from the trees. Looking up, she saw a cloud pass across the pale crescent moon, the moving red light of an aeroplane.

On the doorstep she turned back to him, about to repeat her question, thinking he hadn't heard. He leaned forward and placed his hand gently on her cheek. 'You have the same heart-shaped face,' he said in a choked voice.

Julia remembered the photographer's comment at Linda's exhibition: *Hey, there is a family likeness you know, both the same heart-shaped faces, similar upturned noses too.*

'As Linda?' she asked. But the priest had already closed the door behind her.

– CHAPTER 21 –

Julia's mind was spinning with the afternoon's revelations as she drove back to the pub. She showered and changed before ordering poached egg on toast in the bar. Restored by the food and the warmth of the log fire, by the reassuring normality of the busy pub after the strange events of the day, she returned to her room with a large glass of red wine. She'd only recently acquired a mobile phone but was glad of it as she set about making three calls.

Her supervisor confirmed Julia should notify Grace as soon as possible that she had found her mother in view of Linda's fragile health. Louise insisted, though, that any reunion must be proposed by her client without any pressure from Julia. She reminded Julia again that she couldn't continue to counsel Grace. Her connection with Linda created a further conflict of interest in addition to the likely relationship between Grace and James. However distantly, Julia's connection with Linda meant that she and her client were also now related. The knowledge warmed Julia as she rang Grace.

The young woman was naturally overwhelmed at the news that Julia had found her mother. 'It's a miracle!' she sobbed.

Her counsellor had to agree. 'It does seem that way.

But Grace, like I said, she is very seriously ill. She might not recover. You're certain you want to come? If you do, I can ask a friend to drive you if you prefer not to drive yourself.'

Louise had suggested that it would be advisable for someone to drive Grace to Norfolk if she wanted to meet her mother, given the charged emotional situation. This was something which Julia had already considered. Asking either James or Clare was out of the question in view of her half-brother's brief affair with Grace. The only other person she could think of was Pete. It would give her a pretext to speak to him after that awkward moment in his car following Ada's party when she had pulled away from his kiss. And she could mention she had decided to share business premises with him too when their tenancy at the old school expired.

Assured by Grace that she desperately wanted to meet her mother and would appreciate a lift to Norfolk, Julia took a large gulp of the indifferent house red and located Pete in the short list of contacts in her phone.

He answered on the second ring. 'Hello?'

'Hi, Pete. It's me, Julia.'

'Julia. Where are you?'

She wished he didn't sound so cautious, wished that he'd called her 'Jules.' But her personal feelings weren't important at the moment, she reminded herself. She took another swig of wine.

'Near Walsingham. I wondered if you could help me with something.'

'Oh?'

'You remember the woman who gate-crashed Aunt Ada's party?'

'Impossible to forget.'

'She lives round here. She's seriously ill. Cancer.'

'Oh. Sorry. How come you've found her there?'

'A long story. The thing is, she and her daughter were separated years ago in tragic circumstances. By a strange coincidence. . .' She paused. Coincidence hardly covered it, but the priest's word, 'providence,' didn't come naturally to her sceptical mind.

'Yeah?'

'I know her daughter too. She's in Lincoln and she'd like to meet her mother. It's urgent, with her mother being so ill. It's probably not a good idea for her to drive, as it's such an emotional situation. So I wondered. . .'

'No probs.' Pete jumped in. 'I'll bring her. Tomorrow morning, first thing?'

She sighed with relief. 'Thanks, Pete. I really appreciate that. I'll give you her number so you can confirm with her. She's got the address.' Julia read out Grace's number.

'OK.'

There was a pause. Julia took another gulp of wine.

'And Pete?'

'Yes?'

'It'll be good to see you. Bye.'

Julia pressed the button to end the call without giving Pete chance to reply. Her heart was beating like some silly schoolgirl's, and she hadn't even approached the subject of sharing business premises as she had intended. But she was smiling as she replaced her phone on the mahogany chest of drawers. Alongside it lay the brown envelope the priest had given her. She picked it up and turned it over thoughtfully, remembering how the priest had seemed reluctant to hand it over.

Her hands hovered over the seal as she remembered what he had said: '*You will find out the rest of what Linda wants to tell you in there. I hope that you will be able to come back tomorrow.*' She'd been so preoccupied with her plan of reuniting Linda and Grace that she hadn't realised the significance of his words. What Linda had to tell her extended beyond the fire and her separation from her daughter. Was the priest hinting that it might disturb Julia so much she might not want to see Linda again?

With trembling fingers she broke the seal on the envelope and drew out a black leather book. Her heart banged against her ribs as she opened it and recognised her mother's flowing script. It was the missing 1943 diary.

13 May 1943

My life has started today. That is how I feel, even if the words on the page seem dramatic.

It began just like any other day, except that summer has finally come. Early May has been cold and grey. Today the sun was shining. When I flung open the window in my bedroom at half past seven the air was already warm. I put on my blue dress with the white roses. It will be its fourth summer, and it has faded from washing, but it is one of my favourites. Mother glanced askance at it when I sat down to breakfast and Ada cast a critical eye. As always she looked very neat and sensible in her white blouse and green skirt.

Father was already in his study. The scent of lilac wafted in through the open window. He greeted me with his affectionate smile and continued to make notes for Sunday's sermon. I resumed sorting through the local history books which old Mr Smithson has passed on to him since his eyesight failed. No one else in the village is likely to appreciate his collection like Father. I'm sure he would have been a History teacher if he hadn't gone into the Church.

We worked in our usual companionable silence, broken only by Father sounding out an unfamiliar Greek word as he worked through his text. He told us at supper last night that it's the story of the woman caught in adultery in John's gospel. He said he finds it a very difficult passage.

Mother raised an eyebrow, saying she thought it was very straightforward. Ada said, glancing at Mother, 'From what one hears about the goings on at the air base, it sounds like a very relevant text, Father.'

Father replied sharply. 'The Lord was warning against judging, Ada. No one was able to cast a stone at the woman, because none was without sin. We would all do well to remember that.'

I would have liked to ask Father more about the difficulties of the text from John's gospel this morning but very soon Mother came in to announce a visitor. Evidently Father had met a Canadian Air Force officer at evening service and to Mother's obvious irritation he had come to continue their conversation.

The airman entered the room and shook hands with Father. Father is not small, but our broad-shouldered visitor towered above him. Then he turned and noticed me and my heart raced. He truly dazzled, his blonde hair golden, his face shining, his blue grey uniform immaculate. He has the clearest blue eyes I have ever seen. Dust motes danced between us.

I couldn't tear my eyes away from him until recalled by Father, who bade me make some tea for our guest. The airman raised an eyebrow quizzically.

'My apologies.' Father smiled, pushing his half-moon spectacles higher up his nose. 'This is my daughter, Emily. Emily, this is Wing Commander Brooke.'

Wing Commander Brooke nodded his head towards me. He smiled, his teeth white against his tanned skin. Laughter lines are already forming around his mouth, although I suspect he is only in his mid-twenties.

'Delighted to meet you, Miss Goulceby.' He spoke slowly. His smile faded, but he continued to look at me. Under his scrutiny I experienced an unfamiliar sliding in the pit of my stomach. A blush rose to my cheeks, but I held his gaze, unable to look away.

'And you too, Wing Commander Brooke,' I replied.

I left to make the tea as Father and Wing Commander Brooke began to talk about mediaeval churches in the area.

Ada was in the kitchen, angrily rolling pastry. I brewed the tea and watched her. She pounded the pin over the pastry, her back stiff beneath her white blouse, a damp patch visible between her narrow shoulder blades. Our relationship has always been prickly, but since Christmas there has been a new coldness in her attitude towards me. She criticises me more than ever for my unsuitable clothes, my clumsiness, my preference for spending time with Father and his books rather than helping with domestic chores – and resents me for the attention I received from Leonard Wheeldon at the Christmas Fayre.

I placed cups and saucers on the tray with the milk jug and sugar basin. The pastel flowers on the tea set faded long ago, but it is the best we have. And I was determined Wing Commander Brooke should have the best.

Praying that I wouldn't drop the laden tray, I returned to the study, thankful to leave Ada behind. So often I find Father's study a haven within our troubled household. I'm sure that accounts for the amount of time he spends there when not at church or on pastoral visits. He is meticulous in his sermon preparation, but some of my happiest hours are when we browse his collection of local history books together, and I like to think he feels the same.

I set the tray down on the bureau in the hall to open the study door. Hearing the murmur of voices inside, I experienced again the slippery sensation in the pit of my stomach. Somehow the study did not seem so safe to me with Wing Commander Brooke within it. There was something about his steady gaze which unsettled me.

But I was as powerless to leave the room when I returned as a fly caught in a spider's web. The airman looked towards me as I walked in. I had the strangest feeling that with that one glance he knew everything there was to know about me, as though my thoughts and feelings – my soul, Father might say – was laid bare. I flushed again.

The airman stepped forward, his hand brushing mine as he took the tray. My hand twitched involuntarily at the touch. I moved sideways, catching my hip on Father's desk. I drew in my breath at the stab of pain, and was grateful neither man seemed to notice. Wing Commander Brooke set the tray down amidst the books and papers which always clutter Father's desk. He withdrew to his former position by the window. The scent of lilac wafted in on the breeze, stronger than ever.

I busied myself pouring the milk and tea into the cups, my head bowed so that my hair framed my rosy face. The room was silent apart from the steady ticking of the grandmother clock and the low hum of the bees in the lavender outside.

I spooned a teaspoon of sugar into Father's

cup and passed the tea across the desk to him. He smiled in acknowledgement and took a few sips.

I turned towards Wing Commander Brooke. He was surveying me with the same intent gaze. I was suddenly aware of my too tight dress, my uneven fingernails, the damp patches under my arms, the strands of hair moist against my flushed forehead. For the first time I wished I had taken an interest in the magazines my old school friends enjoy reading, with their photographs and advice on fashion and hairstyles.

A bead of perspiration rolled down my back as I took the tea over, fixing my eye on the cup, fearful I might spill it as my hands continued to tremble. I passed it to him, careful to avoid his hand brushing against mine again. Yet at the same time I longed for the touch, wanting to find out if it were possible that there was some invisible current between us.

One glance up at him as I handed over the tea told me there was. His eyes seemed to darken as they held mine. I found it impossible to break the contact. I was rooted to the spot, my hand on one side of the saucer, his on the other, our gazes locked.

At his desk Father replaced his cup on his saucer. The clink of china broke the spell which *seemed to bind me to Wing Commander Brooke. I crossed the room and seated myself in the armchair across the desk from Father.*

Father was speaking and I tried to compose myself and concentrate. He was explaining that the tiny church at Coates by Stow has a rare mediaeval rood loft and screen which he was sure the airman would like to see. Before I knew what was happening Wing Commander Brooke spoke to me, locking his eyes on mine again, asking me to join them for the visit!

Father looked between us, as if considering something, a question hovering as he cleared his throat. After a pause he suggested we all go a week tomorrow. It seems Wing Commander Brooke has a day's leave before six days of flying, but Father and I are committed to the Church Bazaar tomorrow. As Father spoke a shadow crossed Wing Commander Brooke's face.

My heart skipped a beat. News of deaths of the airmen at the base always saddens me, but I have never had a personal interest in them before. I realised, sitting there sipping tea in the sanctuary of Father's study, that I won't experience a moment's peace during future campaigns.

Not until I know that Wing Commander Brooke is safe.

I was awake early this morning. Raising the blackout blinds, I lay some time in bed, like a cat in the sun, thinking about Wing Commander Brooke. Sleep came late last night as I thought of him, his eyes holding mine, his hand touching mine on the tea tray. Ada would frown at my foolishness, day-dreaming about a man with whom I have spent barely half an hour. She was more sour than ever yesterday afternoon when we went to the Village Hall to set up for the bazaar. Nothing I did was right. Mrs Renshaw declared herself delighted with my arrangement of the knitted infant clothes, but then along came Ada complaining that I should have arranged them according to colour instead of size. Mother agreed of course, but I couldn't help smiling to myself when Mrs Booth complained today that she didn't have time to check sizes in the jumble of colour co-ordinated clothes. I stole a glance at Ada, who pretended not to hear. She was looking towards the door as soon as the bazaar opened and I knew she was watching for Leonard Wheeldon. His mother swept into the hall soon after two o'clock, eye-catching in a dress with large pink roses against a black background. Mother, running her hands over her best dress of the last two summers, commented later that Mrs

Wheeldon must have used most of her cloth-ing coupons on the purchase.

Mrs Wheeldon brought over three sets of white hats and bootees for our stall. Ada was serving Mrs Morton at the time. The poor lady has aged considerably since the news came that Ronald died in the Battle of the Java Sea last year.

My sister pushed me aside as I reached out to take the baby clothes and gushingly enquired after Leonard. So far Leonard has survived where Ronald Morton has not.

I avoided looking at Ada while Mrs Wheeldon spoke to me, complimenting me on my pretty dress. She said she would be back with Leonard later after he had rested from his long journey. I could feel Ada's glare burn-ing into my back until Mrs Wheeldon made her exit, greeting people to the right and left as she went. I glanced over at the refreshments table to see if Mother noticed, knowing she would be irritated by the other woman's airs.

Ada went off to powder her nose. When she returned, I saw she had re-applied her new red lipstick. She was unusually lively dur-ing the next hour, speaking and laughing louder than necessary. Observing her fre-quent glances towards the door, I realised she was hoping that when Leonard arrived he *would see her happy and animated. I felt an unexpected sympathy for her, realising her hopes of Leonard run deep. I am sure, though, that her attachment to him is nothing like my instant connection yesterday with Wing Commander Brooke. Leonard and Ada were childhood friends; there is nothing mysterious about Leonard Wheeldon. But I have so much to discover about my Canadian airman. (Already I think of him as 'mine' without knowing anything about him apart from his interest in mediaeval churches)!*

As the church clock rang three, Leonard arrived, smart and upright in his naval uniform, deeply tanned from service. His mother hung off his arm proudly, guiding him round the hall. It was unfortunate that just as they arrived Father was judging the best spring cabbages. I couldn't help comparing Mrs Wheeldon's parading of her son with Mr Entwistle's elevation of his prize cabbages. The old man beamed with pleasure at winning the prize for the eighth consecutive year, whilst his arch-rival Mr Tyson glowered to receive second prize yet again.

I began to giggle, and Ada nudged me sharply as Mrs Wheeldon shepherded Leonard in our direction. She put her hand on my shoulder, telling me to go and make the tea. But

Leonard immediately stepped in and offered to join me.

Ada scowled as I moved away with Leonard alongside me, and Mother scowled too as we approached her refreshment stall. But she favoured Leonard with one of her rare smiles before turning to me to say disapprovingly, 'I hope you haven't abandoned Ada on the stall, Emily.'

I knew what she was thinking and I quickly explained that Ada had sent me for tea. Mother sighed sceptically and turned back to Leonard who was shaking hands with William Prescott. I couldn't help noticing how William's Army uniform seemed to hang off his slight frame. He looked like a schoolboy playing dress up.

Ada glared at me when I returned with the last cup of stewed tea from the pot, but brightened when I told her that Mother was making fresh and Leonard would bring her a cup. The truce was short-lived as Mrs Wheeldon turned to me again and asked me to visit one afternoon for tea, saying her husband has a collection of history books she thought I might be interested in.

I was surprised but pleased she had thought to ask me. Ada stopped in the action of folding a white matinee jacket as Leonard approached the table with a cup of steaming tea.

I was shocked as Ada leaped in. 'We would love to come, wouldn't we, Emily? Thank you so much, Mrs Wheeldon. Tomorrow would be quite convenient.'

Leonard glanced at his mother, his dark brows furrowed. Mrs Wheeldon raised her own eyebrows in return with a half-smile. It occurred to me the invitation had perhaps been intended only for me. But I remained silent, thinking it would be better for Ada to accompany me. I don't want her to harbour any further resentment towards me. I realised yesterday that it began at the Christmas dance when Leonard partnered me. Leonard knows Ada better. Perhaps if they spend some time together, their friendship might develop into something more.

Ada's unusual vivacity drained away when the Wheeldons departed a few minutes later. I offered to finish up on my own when she complained of the heat. Few people remained besides the stallholders, although I noticed William Prescott and his mother were still drinking tea with the Entwistles. Mr Entwistle, usually so quiet and serious, looked very animated, no doubt still revelling in his success with the spring cabbages.

My head was bent over the shillings, half crowns and sixpences when a voice said, 'So *even our church bazaars owe their origins to England?'*

I started, knocking over two piles of coins which scattered across the table and rolled along the floor.

'I apologise. I didn't mean to startle you.' Wing Commander Brooke bent to pick up the half crowns from the floor.

'No – I – it's the heat – I didn't expect to see you here.' I bit my lip, wondering if he would realise my admission meant I had been think-ing about him. Which of course I had.

He stood, placing the money on the table. 'Did you not?' He eyed me steadily, and I mar-velled again at his bright blue eyes.

'No. A church bazaar. I'm sure you must have more interesting ways of spending your days off.'

'Do you think so?' He continued to look at me, sweeping up some coins on the table with his right hand.

I dropped my eyes, unnerved once more by that piercing blue gaze, and made a show of gathering some coins myself. I saw how long his fingers were, the square cut nails, the fine blonde hairs on the backs of his hand. I noticed also a faint residue of paint: blue, red, yellow, all the primary colours.

'As you see, I spend some of my free time painting.'

His comment disconcerted me. He had seen me looking at his hands. The thought I had yesterday, that he could see to my very soul, returned. My hand froze above the pile of shillings.

He too stopped stacking coins. Slowly his hand inched towards mine across the table. He covered my small hand with his large one. Very gently he stroked my thumb. I shivered.

'Life is precious, Miss Goulceby. I fly again tonight.' He paused and his voice was husky when he spoke again. 'I had to see you. You know that, don't you?'

I lifted my gaze to his as he continued to stroke my thumb, with greater pressure. I couldn't speak. My heart was pounding so hard that I thought it must burst out of my chest, that he must hear it.

I can only hope, thinking that he is in one of those planes screeching above the village now, that he saw my answer in my eyes.

He withdrew his hand so suddenly that I jumped again. He had spotted Mother bearing down upon us. I quickly resumed stacking the coins, aware that William Prescott was also edging towards the table.

Mother nodded curtly to the airman, grudgingly thanking him for his help. He went over to speak with Father who was engaged in conversation with Mr Tyson. I saw Father's shoulders relax beneath his black jacket when Wing Commander Brooke approached, and was unaccountably pleased that Father liked him.

William Prescott handed me some coins, remarking that I had seemed startled by the airman. His sly smile widened as I felt a telltale blush spread upwards from my neck and he made some cryptic comment about keeping an eye out for Leonard's interests.

Mother and I collected the coins silently for a few minutes. From the tail of my eye I saw the airman leave the hall. Then Mother spoke. 'Be careful of that young man, Emily. Too many girls find themselves made fools of by handsome men in uniforms. Remember you know nothing about him at all.'

I pretended that I didn't understand, cursing another rush of colour to my cheeks.

I was relieved that Father came towards us at that moment, delighted by his conversation with Wing Commander Brooke. Mother commented that she hoped he had also spoken with Leonard and told Father about our invitation to tea at the Wheeldons.

I kept my belief that Mrs Wheeldon had

only intended to invite me for tea to myself, realising that Mother shared my sister's hope that her friendship with Leonard might develop into something more. But I am quite certain that however long Leonard and Ada have known one another, their bond is nothing compared to the bond I feel from just two meetings with Wing Commander Brooke.

15 May 1943

I have never felt so fearful as I do tonight. The aircraft roared overhead two or three hours ago. The sound has become so familiar over these last three years that it doesn't fill me with dread in the way it did when the war started. Hearing it, I've always prayed for the safe return of the men on board. But tonight the depth of my fear and dread surpasses anything I have known before. What if he does not return?

How can it be such a beautiful spring night and there are men out there intent on wreaking destruction and death in their flying machines?

I torture myself that I might never see those clear blue eyes gazing into mine again, never hear that quiet Canadian voice again, never know his touch again. I can't stop thinking about how his large hand advanced across the table to cover my small one, how I trembled at his touch. I hear him saying, over and over in that altered voice, 'I had to see you. You know that, don't you?'

It does no good for me to remind myself I have only met him twice. Those two meetings have changed my life. I know that even if he doesn't return tonight.

I can't sleep. Writing helps. I need to think about something else, or I shall go mad. I will convince myself he will be killed. He could be dead by now.

Please, God, bring him back. Bring him back to me.

I kept away from Ada as much as possible this morning, unable to share her excitement at the prospect of tea with the Wheeldons. I sought refuge with Father in the study, though I was distracted from my task of sorting through the remainder of Mr Smithson's books. Father was muttering to himself as he completed his sermon on the woman caught in adultery. I was glad his mind was elsewhere so I could day-dream about Wing Commander Brooke.

It was another warm, sunny day. Through the open window I could hear the bees buzzing through the lavender, the scent of lilac in the air. I could imagine it was Thursday again, that any moment Mother would come in announcing our visitor, and there he would be, his short hair golden in the sunlight, turning his searching gaze towards me. . .

I jumped when Father asked if I was all right. He had finished his sermon and noticed I hadn't turned a page of my book. I said I was tired from lack of sleep because of the heat. I was ashamed to lie to Father, but I could hardly tell him that I had lain awake imagining Captain Brooke's hand moving beyond my hand, caressing me, his lips on mine!

Father came round the desk to me and raised my chin so I had to look at him. It was a gesture familiar from childhood whenever he sensed I was anxious. He asked if there was anything troubling me. I said there wasn't. Then he mentioned our visit to the Wheeldons, cupping his chin as he does when he is considering something carefully.

'Emily,' he began, 'you are of an age where matters of the heart will assume a new importance. My hope for you – and indeed Ada – is that one day you will be happily married.'

He paused. I shifted in the armchair, watching a bluebottle fly against the window without finding the opening.

'I don't wish to embarrass you,' he said gently. 'But I would like to offer you some advice, which you may or may not choose to *follow.' He picked up a newspaper from his desk and walked across to the window, batting the insect through the gap. Keeping his back to me, his voice was strangely choked when he spoke again.*

'When you marry,' he said, 'make sure you marry for love. Never marry to fulfil anyone's expectations, or for convenience, or social standing. If you do, if you marry for any reason other than love, you will regret it.' He turned and crossed the room to where I sat. I was surprised by the urgency in his eyes as he placed one hand on my shoulder and tilted my face towards him again with the other. 'Do you understand, Emily?'

'Yes,' I replied. 'I think I do.'

But many questions milled around in my head, buzzing around like the bluebottle he had just set free. Had he any inkling of my feelings for Wing Commander Brooke? Was he giving me his blessing, where Mother had warned me against the airman? Was he concerned I might marry someone who I did not love in the future? Was he – and I found my mind skittering away from the possibility, because it was too painful to contemplate, although in truth I knew the answer – was he telling me that he and Mother were unhappy? Had they married for some other reason than love – to fulfil expectations, for convenience, or social standing, which he rejected as grounds for a happy marriage?

He was watching me closely, as if trying to determine from my expression whether I did understand. With a pang, I noticed suddenly how he has aged in recent months: his slim shoulders have become a little stooped, the wrinkles around his mouth and eyes have deepened, his hair, now completely grey, has receded further from his lined forehead. I realised how this war is taking its toll on him. Although funerals of airmen at the village church are usually conducted by the Padre, Father is always present. Whilst he never discusses his experiences in the trenches during the Great War, I have often contemplated in recent years how terrible it must have been for such a gentle and sensitive man.

I didn't wish to be a cause of anxiety to him. Under his scrutiny, I repeated that I understood. I was relieved to see the strain disappear from his face and his usual kindly smile return.

He sent me off to rest before lunch, the only time he has ever dismissed me. We have never discussed human feelings so openly before and I was still much affected by his choked voice when he advised me to marry only for love.

I hesitated in front of his walnut desk. He had returned to his armchair and was absently twisting the cap on his fountain pen, looking beyond me. I asked him if he were happy.

He pulled the cap off the fountain pen with such force that I jumped and took a step back. There was an anguish in his eyes that I hope never to see again as he asked how he could be happy when so many good men are dying across the world, just as they did less than thirty years ago. He said how terrible it was to look over his congregations on Sunday mornings and see women like Mrs Morton or Mrs Renshaw or Mrs Wright grown old before their time because they have lost their sons. He spoke of the distress he feels when he speaks with a young man like Leonard who he had christened and confirmed, and sees the shadow pass across his face as he thinks of the men he was unable to rescue at Dunkirk, remembering them rather than the many he did help to save.

He paused and I looked down, ashamed at the childishness of my question. I have never heard my father speak with such passion and despair. He continued more quietly, 'Nor am I happy when I meet a fine young man like Wing Commander Brooke, a man who reminds me of myself at that age with his intellect and sensitivity, and wonder, lying awake at night, if he will be in one of the aeroplanes which returns safely to the base, or if he too will be lost.'

I turned quickly and walked over to the window, suddenly dizzy. I placed my hands on the sill and gulped in the lilac scented air. I heard the laughter and shrieks of children in the school playground, the drone of aircraft, the rising roar of an approaching motor cycle. Just as it passed the vicarage gateway, Father spoke again, very softly. 'A question which I am quite sure is also tormenting my youngest daughter.'

My back to my father as the roar of the motorcycle faded to a distant hum, I decided to dissemble. Whether I chose to do so to save myself from embarrassment, or to protect him from anxiety on my account, I could not say. Perhaps it was both. I turned towards him and said, as if I hadn't heard his final words above the din of the motorcycle, 'I am sorry, Father. Of course you can't be happy with this war going on, remembering your own experiences in the Great War. And you were right. I am tired. I should rest before lunch.'

He looked at me steadily for a moment. Then he sighed and glanced down at the papers on his desk. He shuffled them together without looking up at me, and his voice was unusually cool. 'As you wish, Emily.'

I went upstairs to my room and wept. I wept because I was tired. I wept because I was afraid for the Canadian airman, and confused by my tumultuous feelings for him. And I wept for my father, who carries such burdens and such sadness, and who I had disappointed by my evasiveness.

I splashed water on my face when Mother called me down to lunch. Father had left the house on a bereavement visit. Mother was harassed by extra chores. Florrie had not turned up though it was one of her two days working for us. Ada was unusually cheerful, just as she was at the bazaar yesterday, no doubt looking forward to going to tea at the Wheeldons. I was grateful they were too preoccupied to notice my low mood.

I thought of pleading a headache to avoid going, but it was better to be occupied. Otherwise I would be unable to stop thinking about Wing Commander Brooke and the conversation with Father. Besides, Mrs Wheeldon had been kind to remember my interest in local history. I was also unsure what reception Ada would receive if she went alone, since I believed Mrs Wheeldon had only intended to invite me to look through her husband's books.

Ada chattered away as we walked the half mile to the Wheeldons' house. As we turned down the driveway past the immaculate lawns, she pinched my arm, telling me to spend a long time with the books so she and Leonard could 'have a proper conversation.' She made some silly comment about how jealous Hilda and Mary would be if they knew we were invited for tea. I snapped at her, reminding her of the terrible experiences Leonard has been through, still preoccupied by my conversation with Father.

Her expression darkened, but I had no time to apologise as Ethel opened the door to us, looking unusually subdued. I must ask Florrie if everything is all right with her when she is next in as they are such great friends. Ethel, like Florrie, is such a cheerful girl, and I would hate to think anything is troubling her.

Mrs Wheeldon sent me into the study to look at the books with Leonard and shepherded Ada into the sitting room. Ada gave me a black look, but even she must have seen I had no choice other than to follow our hostess's instructions and join Leonard.

Leonard stepped forward from behind the solid oak desk as I entered. I couldn't help comparing Father's study unfavourably with the Wheeldons'. Father's chairs are old-fashioned and his carpet threadbare. Mr Wheeldon's desk was clear except for a pile of books and a blotting pad. Father's is always cluttered. Thinking about how often I have helped him find his reading glasses in the jumble made me smile. Leonard smiled back, no doubt thinking I was smiling because I was glad to see him. For some reason I felt I must make it clear that I was smiling at the contrast with Father's desk.

There was an awkward pause. Remembering what Father had said earlier, about how Leonard thought about those he had been unable to save at Dunkirk more than those he had helped to safety, I asked him if his experiences on board ship were very terrible. He said that he finds the time when nothing is happening dull, with too much time to think. He finds that worse than being engaged in battle. He murmured what a privilege it is to serve for the freedom of our country.

I felt rather in awe of him, thinking how the war has changed the carefree boy we grew up with into this responsible young man.

He changed the subject, remarking how pretty I looked in my dress. I was immediately embarrassed, and pointed at the pile of books, suggesting we should look at them since his mother was delaying tea. I mentioned Ada was with her in the sitting room, giving him the opportunity to go and see her and leave me with the books, but he didn't move. I chattered on about how beautiful the top volume was, bound in its fine red leather. He said it was a book of rambles in the Wolds, and asked if I would like to go there some time. I pretended I hadn't understood the invitation was just for me, mentioning how much Ada enjoys walking. He looked a little irritated. I was relieved that Mrs Wheeldon came in then, followed by Ada who wore a determined expression which I know well.

Mrs Wheeldon said that Ada would also like to look at the books, exchanging a glance with Leonard which I couldn't interpret. I quickly mentioned Leonard's suggestion of a walk in the Wolds, and she was most enthusiastic. I couldn't help noticing that Leonard smiled less warmly than usual, and it worried me that he had wanted me to go with him to the Wolds alone. He seemed withdrawn as we looked through the books and had tea. I was glad when it was time to return home. Now I am so tired, worn out with lack of sleep and all these emotions.

Some planes are returning. Please God, let him have returned.

Awake very early today, but too excited to sleep again. I haven't known this kind of anticipation since my fifth birthday when I was desperate to see if Mother and Father had bought me the doll I was longing for. They had, and I was beside myself. Annabel was my most precious possession until I was nine when one day Ada dropped her on the path and her poor head smashed beyond repair. I wept bitterly, and Father promised me a new doll, but Mother said I was getting too old. I never knew why Ada took her outside, but I still recall her half-smile when Mother told me to calm myself, sending me to my room, and saying I should forgive Ada because it was an accident.

But I remember we had had some silly quarrel earlier that day. I never believed it was an accident.

A long time ago. And now we are both grown up, even if I feel like an excited child this morning.

Father told us at supper yesterday he had seen Wing Commander Brooke at the airbase when he was meeting the Padre. He said the airman was tired after his six days of duty, especially as he had been involved in the mission to destroy the German dams, but that he is very much looking forward to our visit to St Edith's Church today. The village has been agog with news of the mission against the dams. Perhaps it will be a turning point and hurry the end of the war, so that he will be safe.

And Leonard, too. I have been thinking about Leonard since our meeting last week. He returned to duty two days afterwards, so I didn't see him again. I would have liked to wish him luck. I am sure the sense of awkwardness which I felt in his father's study that afternoon arose because I was so tired and upset, fearful for Wing Commander Brooke and troubled by the conversation with Father. Nothing more. I've never felt ill at ease with Leonard before, I know him too well.

I will go down for breakfast early, although I have little appetite. I can only guess how slowly the time will pass until eleven o'clock! I will wear the floral empire dress again.

2 p.m. 21 May 1943

How do I write about this morning? I am a different girl than the one who wrote in here just a few hours ago. Not a girl any more. A woman.

We met Ray – I finally discovered his Christian name today – at the church at eleven o'clock as arranged. I was pleased with this arrangement, as I sensed Mother's unhappiness with our excursion. She looked at me coldly at breakfast and suggested Father shouldn't be taking time off with a funeral tomorrow. She also said that she could do with my help at home, since Florrie hadn't come in again this week. Father replied that he needs a day off before tomorrow's funeral for poor Mrs Renshaw – her sudden death on Monday affected him deeply. Father says that whatever is written on the Death Certificate, she died of a broken heart, following the loss of Michael at Dunkirk.

I was waiting in the garden for Father by half past ten, reading a guide to local churches including St Edith's. It was much too early for the two-minute drive to church, but I wanted to escape Mother's pursed lips and Ada's jealous glances.

When Father came out he looked agitated. He hemmed and hawed, then explained Mrs Green had telephoned to say her mother had taken a turn for the worse overnight. Mrs Green hoped Father could call, and stay until the old lady passed. I was bitterly disappointed, thinking this would mean the end of the outing, even whilst I chided myself for my selfishness when an old lady lay dying.

Then he suggested I could still go with Wing Commander Brooke, who could drive on after we dropped him off at Mrs Green's. He said he suspected Mother wouldn't approve, but he knew how much I had been looking forward to the trip. This time I wasn't embarrassed by his perspicacity. 'Life is precious, Emily,' he said, 'and we appreciate this most deeply in wartime. Wing Commander Brooke has endured some difficult and dangerous missions these past few days, especially over the German dams. The peace and beauty of St Edith's will offer him the refreshment he needs before he flies again.' His grey blue eyes twinkled. 'So will your company.'

My heart was full at his kindness, and at the knowledge that he understood something of my feelings for the airman. (Although I suspect if he knew how I lie awake at night longing for Wing Commander Brooke, he would be horrified.)

The heat had intensified over the past three days and there was no breeze. My heart rose when I saw the airman from the rear seat of the Morris Minor. He was standing at the gate, his broad back to us as he contemplated the church. Hearing our car, he turned. Father leaped out quickly to explain the change of plan. I saw a flicker of doubt cross

Ray's face and my heart sank, thinking that after all he would decline to accompany me alone. He hesitated and then came forward, folding his large frame into the passenger seat. He barely glanced at me, greeting me only with a curt, 'Good morning.'

I spent the journey to Mrs Green's house in a miserable silence, doubting that he had any regard for me at all, despite his words at the bazaar only a week ago. Had I read too much into his words, 'I had to come,' as his hand enveloped mine?

Father took his leave of us at Mrs Green's house and Ray settled behind the steering wheel. Father said he felt sure that Ray would find the atmosphere of the church restorative after the strain of recent days.

That was the only allusion Father made to the war. I determined not to mention it myself. I have regretted my impulsive question to Leonard about his experiences. It was the question of a clumsy girl, and I was resolved not to appear so naïve to the Canadian. From the sideways glance I stole at him as I climbed into the car beside him, I noticed with a pang the shadows under his eyes and a hollowness in his tanned cheeks which I hadn't seen before.

I waited for him to speak as we drove along, acutely aware of his physical proximity.

I jammed myself against the passenger door to keep some distance between us. The sliding sensation in my stomach recurred with a new force now I was alone with him. He stared ahead at the road in front of us, as though he were concentrating carefully, though there was little traffic. Eventually I spoke, pointing out the left turn for Coates.

We turned on to the narrow lane, the banks high with white cow parsley and haw-thorn blossom. Suddenly the silence was bro-ken by the drone of aircraft. I looked up to see three planes climbing higher and higher into the blue sky ahead of us where clouds were beginning to mass. With a gathering roar they turned and dived down together. They seemed to be swooping towards us as we bowled along the road. For one terrifying moment I thought they were going to crash, so low did they come, and so close to one another. I held my breath and sighed with relief as they separated at the last possible moment, then turned and began to climb again.

Sensing my alarm, Captain Brooke glanced at me, smiling, telling me the pilots would be some of the new boys showing off. I smiled back, relieved at the release in the tension between us.

Then he asked me to tell him about Saint Edith, and I explained about the two possible

Saint Ediths to whom the church might have been dedicated: Saint Edith of Wiltshire or Saint Edith of Tamworth. I said that the latter is the favourite candidate since Lincolnshire had trade connections with the West Midlands at the time of her death in the tenth century.

We began to discuss some of the less well-known saints, a subject which he knew far more about than me. He told me he is a Catholic, that his mother had been very devout, bringing him up with the stories of the saints.

The sun disappeared behind a cloud just as I realised I had been so absorbed in our conversation that we had passed the turning for Coates. I felt foolish, but he only smiled and turned the car round in the next gateway.

As we drove down the tree-lined farm track leading to the church which stands next to the imposing red brick farmhouse, he told me his favourite saint was Catherine of Bologna. I said I had never heard of her and he told me she is the patron saint of artists.

I looked instinctively at his hands on the steering wheel, and saw the residue of paint under his square finger nails. He caught my glance as he pulled the car on to the grass verge before the church and told me he had been painting earlier, when he couldn't sleep.

He switched off the engine, still gazing at me. The question was there in my mind, 'Could you not sleep because you were thinking about me just as I couldn't sleep because I was thinking of you?' But of course I didn't ask.

Then he said that Catherine of Bologna is also the saint to petition in order to resist temptations. He cocked his head on one side, considering me. I saw a fresh cut under his chin where he must have nicked it when shaving. He asked if I prayed to resist temptation, using my Christian name for the first time, which made my heart leap. But I was tongue-tied by the question. I felt like I was standing on shifting sand, about to sink. I didn't answer, turning away from his searching eyes and reaching for the door handle. It was slippery beneath my damp palm.

Outside the car all was still beneath the gathering clouds. No breath of air stirred the leaves of the horse chestnut trees which spread a canopy over the low brick wall fronting the church. A bead of sweat trickled down my spine, and my blonde braid hung heavy against my neck. I could hear him walking a few paces behind me, the swish of the grass and the snap of a twig beneath his feet. I was conscious of my hips swaying as I entered the gate into the churchyard, a conviction that his eyes were on me.

I paused in front of the identical grave-stones beside the east wall commemorating the Motley family. I have always been moved by their simplicity, preferring them to the ornate monument to the Maltby family near the south wall. I read the names in my head, trying to distract myself from my acute awareness of this man and the meaning of his question about resisting temptation. He stopped beside me and I was again struck by his bulk next to my slight frame.

'Listen,' he said suddenly.

'I can't hear anything,' I said.

'Exactly. Even the birds are silent. A storm is coming.'

He had barely spoken when the first roll of thunder rumbled in the distance.

'Are you afraid of storms?' he asked.

I shook my head.

'I was never afraid of them either,' he said, 'not until I was caught flying in one for the first time.' He reached suddenly for my hand and I let him take it. 'It was back in Canada, near Vancouver when I was training. The aero-plane was tossed about and I was certain I wouldn't make it back to base. The plane below was struck by lightning and fell to earth.' He *swallowed and stared into the middle distance. 'My friend John was flying it. Every time I have seen lightning since, I see the blazing plane falling to earth.'*

'I am sorry,' I said quietly. I clasped his hand more tightly.

He returned the pressure and we walked hand in hand towards the church door as the thunder rumbled nearer. The first heavy raindrops fell as he raised the heavy latch with his free hand and drew me inside.

I heard his intake of breath as he took in the beauty of the rood screen and loft. I was as ever spellbound by its magnificence, even though I have visited the church many times with Father. In a whisper I pointed out the Virgin Mary's haloed head to him, and the head of St John on the right.

A flash of lightning illuminated the Virgin's halo, and the pressure of his hand on mine increased momentarily. I wondered if he gripped my hand more tightly because the lightning evoked the memory of his friend's fiery descent again. I hoped that if he were tortured by that terrible image in the future, he would remember this moment as well, standing with me in that tiny ancient church, seeing the Virgin's halo lit up.

'"For the place where you are standing is

holy ground,"' he whispered suddenly, turning to me and reaching for my other hand.

'Moses at the burning bush,' I whispered back.

He nodded, staring down at me as another flash of lightning lit up the rood loft above us. He raised his left hand and stroked my cheek. 'It's true you have no fear of storms, isn't it, Emily?'

I shook my head without speaking, gazing back at him because I could not look away. Heavy raindrops lashed against the windows, but I knew he was not talking about the thunderstorm which raged outside.

Then he lifted my braid and kissed my neck, gentle butterfly kisses. I closed my eyes and thought, 'Please don't stop,' and the words were so loud inside my head that I was certain I must have spoken them. Then he lifted his head from my neck and I opened my eyes to meet his. I gasped at what I saw in them, those piercing blue eyes darkened with an intent I had never seen. His hand moved down to cup my breast and I gasped again. Then his lips were on mine as he struggled out of his jacket and dropped it to the stone floor, pulling me down with him, kissing me deeply now.

I thought I would burst as everything in me rushed to meet him. I wanted it never to end.

Later we sat wordlessly in one of the uncomfortable pews with its carved poppy heads. His arm around me, we gazed together at the rood screen and loft. I rested my head against his chest, listening to his heart slow, and to the rain outside. I longed to stay there for ever.

Presently a shaft of sunlight stole through the nave window near the pulpit, illuminating the Virgin's head again. To me it was a blessing.

Together, still silent, we went out into the churchyard. The birds were singing and it seemed I heard them more clearly than I ever had before.

We walked slowly through the wet grass hand in hand. We paused by the Motley gravestones, washed clean by the rain. The overhanging trees dripped upon us. Beyond the gate the cow parsley along the wall gleamed white, and the sun-kissed hawthorn blossom dazzled me.

We lingered by the gate, looking back at the simple stone church. He drew me to him and kissed me, a lingering, more gentle kiss than those he had covered me with before. 'Promise me, whatever happens, you will remember how we have loved one another. Promise me you will know that I love you,' he whispered.

My eyes filled with tears, mingling an inde-scribable happiness and an unsurpassable sor-row. The fear that he might not return from another mission is unbearable now. 'I promise,' I answered, when I was capable of speech.

He drove us back to the village. No further words passed between us. Our bodies had said everything there was to say. Outside the vicarage he reached across and took my hand. His clear blue eyes searched my face and his lips brushed mine one last time.

Then he was gone. The car door slammed behind him. Through my tears I watched him walk away up the village street with his long easy gait. I watched him until he dis-appeared from my view where the road bends up the hill.

I knew he would not look back, and he did not.

4 a.m. 22 May 1943

I passed the rest of yesterday in a daze, spend-ing the afternoon looking through Mr Smithson's books in the study. I suspect I left them more muddled than when I started. I couldn't put him from my mind, and went over every moment we had shared together that morn-ing. I know it will be etched in my memory for ever.

For once I was grateful that Father was out on parish visits and didn't join us for supper. Neither Mother nor Ada asked me about my outing. Ada was clearly bursting to divulge something she had found out from Mrs Wheeldon about Florrie but suggested it wasn't suitable for me to hear. Mother tartly replied that if Father thought it was suitable for me to be 'gallivanting around the countryside with unknown Canadian airmen,' I didn't need to be protected from news about Florrie.

Ada lay down her cutlery on the plate with a clang which startled me in my agitation. I dropped my fork, splashing a mess of carrot, potato and swede across the white tablecloth, incurring Mother's anger. She impatiently asked Ada to tell us whatever news she had of Florrie. With a theatrical sigh, Ada said, 'She is in trouble,' emphasising the last two words. Turning to me, she explained that this was why Ethel had been so subdued when she opened the door to us at the Wheeldons – she had been worrying about the matter since Florrie had confided in her.

Mother tutted and immediately said it would be impossible for us to keep her on, in view of Father's position. I didn't understand and said we should surely help her if she was in trouble. Mother snapped at me that it would be highly unsuitable, and that a vicar couldn't be seen to condone 'immorality.' Still bewildered, I asked what she meant.

Mother was impatient with my naivety and explained that 'in trouble' is a euphemism, that Florrie is expecting a child. She repeated that it would be impossible for us to help her in any way and that we must give her notice immediately. She asked Ada if Mrs Wheeldon had any idea of the identity of the child's father. Ada, mouth downturned, said that she didn't, but that Ethel and Florrie had been out dancing with the GIs a lot.

'Silly girl. A ruined life. And as for the child. . .' Mother sighed and shook her head.

There was a ringing in my ears, and I felt the room swim around me as though I were on a roiling ship. I asked to be excused. A great weariness overcame me. When I reached my room, I went over to the window and lifted the blackout blinds a fraction. I looked out over the peaceful garden, wondering if he would fly tonight.

From the kitchen below, I could hear the murmur of Mother and Ada's voices and knew they would still be discussing poor Florrie's plight. The faint scraping of knives across plates as they prepared to wash up set my teeth on edge.

Without undressing, I climbed under the blankets. The storm had cleared the air, and the night would not be so hot and uncomfortable as the previous few nights. But I felt cold, cold and very tired. I heard Father come in, his measured tread as he crossed the hall to the kitchen. I knew he would be hoping to find me there so that he could ask me about Ray's response to St Edith's Church. The thought of his kindly questions was more than I could bear. There was so much I could not tell him of what had happened that morning.

As I closed my eyes, Mother's harsh words echoed in my mind, 'Silly girl. A ruined life. And as for the child. . .'

I curled up like an infant and hugged myself, trying to shut out her voice. But the words repeated themselves until sleep finally came.

A few moments ago I woke suddenly, sitting bolt upright in bed. My heart is still pounding as I write, though I don't recall any nightmare.

If Mother's cruel words towards Florrie rang in my ears as I fell asleep, it was Ray's words which I heard clearly when I woke, 'Promise me, whatever happens, you will remember how we have loved one another. Promise me you will know that I love you.' And

I said aloud in my silent room as though he were here with me, 'I promise.'

The planes are roaring overhead. They will be on their way back now.

Please, God, let him have returned.

27 May 1943

I knew immediately from Father's face. I was sitting in my usual chair in the study leafing through a book. The rain was pounding against the window. I didn't hear him come in until he was standing in front of me.

If I noticed how he had aged last week, he was an old man today. Stooped, head bowed, moving his forefinger back and forth across his mouth, searching for words.

'No,' I whispered.

'Yes,' he answered. 'I am so deeply sorry. I have been with the Padre at the air base this morning.'

'NO!' I screamed, leaping out of my chair. My book fell to the floor with a crash.

Father started, knocking his leg against the desk, then put his arms around me. Mother ran in from the kitchen. Father sent her back, asking her to make tea, explaining Wing Commander Brooke had been killed.

Once the initial storm of weeping was over, I sank back into the armchair. Father moved round the desk and settled into his own chair. Mother brought in the tea without a word and left immediately. I closed my eyes. Father stirred the tea in the teapot. The clink of teaspoon against china was unbearable in its ordinariness. I placed my hands over my ears and rocked myself like a baby. The tears came again.

When I was calmer, Father pushed the cup towards me, urging me to drink. Obediently I took a few sips. Outside the rain had stopped and the sky was brightening. Seeing it, I had a moment's hope. I asked if there might be a mistake, but he shook his head.

Father didn't want to tell me how it had happened but I insisted. Eventually, smoking his pipe, a habit which he usually restricts to the evening, he told me. He said Ray was on a bombing mission to Dresden. The group was ordered to pass over the city again. As the end plane in the group, Ray's was particularly vulnerable to attack. The pilot of one of the other planes saw it take a hit from enemy fighters and it went down immediately. The pilot saw a fire beneath soon after.

Fire. Ray died in a burning aircraft. Just like his friend John, whom he had told me about during our morning at Coates.

I suddenly remembered how I had woken suddenly a little before four the morning after our outing, how I had heard his voice as clearly as if he had been there with me. 'Promise me, whatever happens, you will remember how we have loved one another. Promise me you will know that I love you.'

I asked if Father knew when it had happened. He told me it was just before four on Saturday morning.

The time I woke and heard his voice. I could not breathe as I gripped the arms of my chair, desperate to hold on to something solid. I saw how the short fair hairs on my arms had risen. My spine tingled. Was it possible that Ray had communicated with me as he left this life? Rationally I rejected the idea. I must have been dreaming, re-living the events of the day. But surely this was more than coincidence?

Six days ago my world burst with colour. Now all is dull and muted, dark and grey like the sky outside, heavy with unshed rain. I want to believe that he spoke to me as his spirit departed. Are such things possible? Perhaps I will ask Father one day.

It wasn't a question I could ask him today. As I looked at him sunk back in his chair pulling on his pipe, his face grey and exhausted, watching me with concern, I was reminded how quickly he too had formed a bond with my Canadian airman.

Then Father said something I could never agree with, that he regretted encouraging our friendship. I was quick to reassure him how glad I was to have met him – I nearly added 'loved him' – but broke off in time.

We sat in silence for a while and I closed my eyes, the better to see and feel those images seared on my memory, infiltrating my very being. I saw him standing in front of the window in that very room, the sun lighting his blonde hair golden. 'My angel,' I thought. His voice, 'I had to come,' as his hand crept across the table and enclosed mine at the bazaar. And then, 'You really are not afraid of storms, are you, Emily?' as he began to caress me in that tiny church where the shaft of sunlight illuminated the Virgin's head. . .

When Father spoke again, I sensed he was weighing his words carefully. He asked if there was anything which had passed between me and Ray which had caused me any concern. I did not hesitate in reassuring him, 'No.' All that had passed between Ray and me had been natural and straightforward. The power of our feelings for one another had been a revelation to me, but that was not something I could discuss with Father.

Relief spread across his face, before he winced suddenly, as if in pain. His right hand flew to his chest. I was alarmed, but he reassured me that it was just indigestion.

From the corner of the room the grandmother clock chimed twelve. The ordinariness of the sound pierced me as the clink of the teaspoon on the saucer had. The peculiar calmness of a few moments earlier evaporated and fresh tears threatened. I swallowed them, not wanting to worry Father further.

Perhaps he sensed my fragile self-control, because he suggested I might like some quiet time in my room, and that he would arrange for Mother to bring up a sandwich for me. I readily agreed and here I have spent the rest of the day, re-living those precious moments with Ray. I have wept. I have by turns cursed God for snatching my beloved away so soon, and then been thankful that we did know and love one another, even for so short a time.

We spent barely five hours together yet I feel I will never live as fully as I did with him. How is that possible?

How can I live without him?

4 October 1943

I hate Mother. HATE her. And Ada too. They are so cold, so judgemental, lacking all understanding.

I thought Father might understand. I

thought he would suggest another plan than this cruel, unnatural one of Mother's. But he turned grey at my news, pressing his hand to his chest for a moment, just as he did on the morning he told me of Ray's death. Even in my agitated state, as I appealed to him tearfully to let me stay at home, I had a fleeting concern for him as he sank into his armchair.

Mother seemed not to notice as she insisted that I must go to Norfolk, saying that if it hadn't been for his encouragement, nothing would have happened.

It was she who guessed, of course. I have spent these months since Ray died going about my daily routine just as I used to, meaningless though it has become. Helping Mother with the endless domestic chores seemed futile, parish meetings useless, social occasions tedious. A month after we received the news of Ray's death Father proposed we should begin work on the local history book I suggested a year ago. But a project which would have given me pleasure before seems as pointless as everything else now. I had even given up on this diary until today. Now I am driven back to it as an outlet for my distress, fury and despair.

The only place I have found some solace is the kitchen garden. I have tended the vegetables assiduously over the summer months. I was out there pulling up some carrots this afternoon when Mother came out. Her eyes were pebbles, grey as the October sky, as she asked me when I last menstruated. I was startled. Since the monthly bleeding started when I was thirteen and she gave me perfunctory instructions about sanitary napkins, we have never discussed the subject. She places the napkins in my underwear drawer each month without comment.

I had been aware that I hadn't bled recently but given the matter little thought. It has been exhausting trying to maintain my usual outward demeanour in the midst of my grief for Ray. When I have considered it, I've wondered if the shock of his death might have caused the cessation.

I told her I couldn't remember, pressing my hand to my side as I felt a twinge which has become familiar lately. She asked if it were weeks or months, and I said again I didn't know, pointing out my cycle has always been irregular.

Feeling the trembling in my lower regions again, I placed my hand there, drawing her gaze. Her voice was ice when she asked if I were aware that I had put on weight recently. I am. I have been surprised how Ray's death has had no effect on my appetite.

Her eyes narrowed into slits. She enunci-
ated her next words slowly. 'Has it occurred to
you that you might not only be eating for yourself, Emily?'

I felt dizzy as the implication of her words
sank in. I leaned on the spade for support,
staring at her open-mouthed.

'I assume the. . . father' – she spat the word –
'would be the Canadian airman, would it?'

I nodded dumbly.

She took a step towards me and raised her
right hand, slapping me across my left cheek.
'You stupid slut!' she hissed.

I bent my head, nursing my stinging cheek.
I was as shocked by her language as by the
blow. She has never struck me before. She
turned away from me, telling me to get out of
her sight so she could think.

Blinded by tears, I ran up here, flinging
myself on the unmade bed, burying my head
in the pillow.

Some moments later, still tearful but a
little calmer, I went across to the window,
looking out over the kitchen garden I had
tended so carefully. The murmur of Mother's
voice on the telephone floated upwards from
the hall.

I felt the fluttering again. Finally I realised what it was: the baby. My baby, Ray's

child, stirring inside me. I laced my hands over my stomach and breathed deeply, looking over the vegetables growing below. They all need lifting soon, before the first frost of autumn.

As my eyes travelled over the produce a sense of wonder overcame me. It came to me that the seed planted by Ray in my womb was just like them, needing care and nurture.

A shaft of sunlight cut through the grey sky, half-blinding me. I shaded my eyes, remembering the sunlight which had illuminated the Madonna in the church after Ray and I came together. Warmth suffused me. For the first time in these dark months I saw a pinprick of hope. For surely this baby was the fruit of love, a gift from God?

I don't know how long I stood there, cradling my stomach. Presently Mother rapped on the door. My heart sank at the sight of her stony face, and my fragile hope ebbed away as suddenly as it had risen. She didn't look at me as she told me to go down with her to Father in the study.

She insisted I should be the one to tell Father about the baby. I trembled to think how he might respond. Then I thought that after the initial shock he, more than anyone else, would understand my revelation that my child is a divine gift. New life after death, the triumph of *love. This, after all, is the message which he preaches from the pulpit week by week.*

But when Father turned grey and sank back into his worn armchair after I told him I was expecting Ray's child, a cold dread seeped through me. Mother's voice, as she relayed the arrangements she had made, was as matter of fact as if she were shopping for groceries. She told me I will go to stay with her cousin Winifred and husband on their farm in Norfolk tomorrow. When I am well enough to travel after the birth, I will return home, leaving the child with them. It seems they always wanted a child but Winifred has never conceived.

I was appalled at the prospect of being parted from my baby, but my screaming and shouting had no effect on Mother who didn't look at me as she urged Father that this was 'the best possible arrangement.' He finally capitulated when she berated him for his irre-sponsibility in leaving Ray and I alone together the day we went to Coates. His head sunk towards his chest, his voice quavery like that of a much older man, he said quietly, 'I think your mother's solution is for the best, Emily.'

'But. . .' My voice shook with fresh tears as I looked at his hunched form.

'There are no "buts", Emily,' Mother inter-posed sharply. She turned towards me,

sensing her victory and sent me upstairs immediately to begin packing. She closed the study door and stood in front of it. I knew she was making sure I didn't return to make a fresh appeal to Father. She said she would arrange for a taxi to take me to the station in the morning, saying Father will be too busy.

As I tearfully pleaded with her, she turned her head away in disgust, speaking of the 'disgrace' if the village found out. She urged me to think of Father, if not myself, saying, 'I know you would not wish to cause him embarrassment, however uncaring you might be about the impact of your downfall on myself and your sister.'

I stared at her as she stood there, ramrod straight, face resolutely turned from me. I hesitated too long before protesting that of course I cared about her and Ada. But it was a lie, and we both knew it. There was nothing more to say so I came up here and started sorting some clothes.

Later I was aware of the front door opening and closing behind Ada, the low hum of her voice and Mother's in the kitchen. I knew better than to expect any sympathy from my sister.

Half an hour later I heard Ada's heavy tread on the staircase. I stiffened as she knocked at the door. She came in without waiting for my response, hauling in the battered brown suitcase which we used to take on our family holidays in the summers before the war.

Her grey eyes flicked across my stomach. Instinctively I cradled it. Two bright red spots flared in her cheeks as she asked how I could be so 'shameless.' I queried what she meant and she asked how else I would describe my conduct.

I looked at her, my plain sister with all her pettiness and prejudices. I was shocked at the wave of dislike which passed through me. 'You wouldn't understand, Ada,' I said contemptuously.

Her flush darkened. 'If you mean I don't understand your immorality, you are quite right.'

'Immorality? Who are you to judge? We were in love!' I protested.

'In love?' She looked at me down her nose.

My hand itched to slap the sneer from her face. Somehow I managed to control myself. My next words were calculated to wound. 'Yes. Truly in love. Not like in your silly simpering way with Leonard Wheeldon.'

She stepped back as if I had struck her after all. There was a pause. Then she hissed, 'You will regret saying that, Emily.'

The door slammed behind her.

I sank onto the bed, gripped by a sudden fear. There is little love lost between Ada and me, but surely she would never deliberately harm me? Then it occurred to me that nothing worse could happen than that I should be separated from my child, as now seems inevitable. Mother was right, of course. Whilst I might not care about my own reputation, I would not want to bring shame on Father.

I did not see him at supper. Mother told me he had dined early as he had a meeting. I suspected she had arranged things this way, wanting to keep us apart before I leave in the morning. Perhaps she is worried that I might persuade him to allow me to bring up the baby here if I have the opportunity, whatever the embarrassment to the family. But witnessing how swiftly he yielded to her suggestion, how frail he seemed at that moment, I don't think he has the strength to stand up to her. And I do see how difficult his position will be, a vicar whose daughter has a child out of wedlock.

Without Ray, I see no alternative than to submit to Mother's plan. But how will I bear carrying this baby and then giving him or her up into the care of virtual strangers? We last visited Winifred and Thomas when I was seven years old. I know nothing of them. And how much love will they give to a child who is not their own? The fluttering sensation in my womb starts again, as if the baby senses my anxiety.

My head is aching. I need to rest, to prepare myself for the journey to Norfolk tomorrow.

I have never felt so alone.

6 October 1943

I cannot think how I will endure the months here until the baby is born. The farmhouse is dark and oppressive with its small windows, low beamed ceilings and sparse furniture. It lies in the shadow of a ruined abbey. I walked there this afternoon when there was a break in the rain which has fallen steadily since I left home yesterday morning. Winifred lent me a voluminous navy mackintosh not only because of the rain but also, she said, to hide 'my condition.' It is hardly perceptible even to me, but I saw no point in arguing.

I did not see Father or Ada before I left home. Needless to say, I had no wish to see my sister, but I longed to take my leave of Father. Mother told me over an early breakfast that he was resting before his morning meeting and that I should not disturb him. She was unmoved by my protests that I must say goodbye to him, saying that my news had come as a great shock to him and he needed to rest. There was something odd in her expression, and picturing how he had sagged at my revelation, how he has aged in these last months, I asked anxiously if he were quite well.

Her hand was trembling as she lifted the earthenware teapot but her voice was crisp as she pointed out that some fathers would not offer their daughters a home in the circumstances. It was only later that I realised she had evaded my question about Father's health.

I could not, I cannot believe that Father condemns me, because he is always so understanding and forgiving. He wanted us to keep Florrie on but gave way in face of Mother's insistence that to do so would suggest he condoned 'immorality' and 'set a poor example to the parish.' I am more sorry than he will ever know that I have caused him so much trouble, and it took all my strength to remain composed and not rush into his room before I left.

Mother stepped back into the hall when I moved forward to kiss her cheek when the taxi arrived. She closed the door without so much as a wave.

In the taxi, overwhelmed with misery and anxiety, I deflected the driver's attempts at conversation. My heart sank when he told me he had another passenger for Lincoln station.

It sank even further when we pulled in along the High Street to pick up William Prescott in his army uniform, evidently returning to service after a few days' leave. I know he is a friend of Leonard's but I have never warmed to him. With his ginger hair and moustache and pointed face he has always put me in mind of a fox. I was in no mood for small talk, but thought that I should make an effort, so he would not suspect anything amiss. So I greeted him politely, asking if he had enjoyed his leave. He said he had, but with a sly smile added that he had missed Leonard.

I smiled non-committally, looking out of the window as a tractor rumbled by. I had scarcely thought about Leonard all summer. I recalled the jibe I had made to Ada, and her threat. No matter how much I reason she won't harm me by disclosing my secret because of the shame to our parents, I am still uneasy.

I didn't like his appraising look, and pulled my coat more tightly around me as he commented how well I looked, and how I seemed to have grown up since the last time he saw me at the church bazaar. My heart beat faster as the memory flooded back: Ray's hand enclosing mine on the table of the children's clothing stall, Mother approaching from one side, William Prescott from the other. I bent my head, making a pretence of checking my handbag. I was glad I hadn't braided my hair which fell forwards to hide my burning cheeks.

He asked where I was going as the driver turned the windscreen wiper on. I told him that I was going to help my mother's sick cousin near Walsingham, the story Mother had concocted.

My heart thumped hard against my rib-cage when he remarked on the coincidence that his grandmother also lives in Walsingham. He wrote down her address for me, urging me to call on her during my visit. I closed my eyes, overtaken by dizziness as the cathedral came into view on our left. He leaned over me, placing a small freckled hand on my knee, asking if I were all right. I moved away, lying that I don't travel well in the back of cars. The baby fluttered and I fought back the impulse to place my hand on my stomach.

Mercifully we drew into the station then. As soon as I was out of the taxi and William had disappeared into the crowd I dropped the paper with his grandmother's address on to the ground.

On the slow train journey through the rain swept fens towards Kings Lynn I thought for the first time about the difficulties of the deception planned by Mother. How is it going to be possible to pass the baby off as Winifred's? As to my own feelings about giving up my baby, Ray's child, the pain is more than I can bear. I try to tell myself that my grief for Ray, which I am quite sure will remain with me throughout my life, would be worsened by the constant reminder that his child would bring. I shut out the voice that says a child would offer some comfort, something of him still left in this world.

I was slow-witted from the shock of discovering my pregnancy, the speed of my despatch from home and the unfortunate meeting with William Prescott. I was no nearer a solution regarding the details of the plan when Thomas collected me at Kings Lynn and drove me to the farm. He was silent throughout the journey, which seemed interminable. I felt as if we travelled for miles along the narrow lanes banked high with hedges through the unrelenting drizzle.

Winifred, though, has thought everything through, as I discovered when she came to my room this morning, waking me from a deep but unrefreshing sleep. She and Thomas barely spoke during supper last night, and I was too exhausted and apprehensive to attempt conversation. I wondered if they regretted their *offer to help me and raise the child as their own. I know now from Winifred that she certainly does not.*

She picked up the rosary beads from the bedside table and began to talk about 'God working in mysterious ways.' She confided how she has prayed fervently for a child throughout her marriage and never given up. Her wide blue eyes gleamed in her broad weather-beaten face. I made a move to get out of bed, but she pushed me back, urging me to rest and saying she would bring me tea.

But she made no move to fetch the tea. I sank back against the pillows as she went on about how Mother's phone call was the answer to her prayers. I froze as she moved the blankets back, uncovering me, looking greedily at my stomach beneath my white nightdress, asking 'Has it quickened yet?'

'Quickened?'

'Have you felt the baby move?'

On cue the child fluttered in my womb. I nodded. 'Can I touch?' Without waiting for my answer, Winifred placed her hand on my stomach. I willed the baby to stay still, but it moved again, and Winifred felt it. Her face broke into another moony smile. 'Praise God!' she said, clasping her hands together and closing her eyes. 'And praise Mary, Mother of God!'

Her reference to Mary reminded me again of the sun illuminating the Madonna in St Edith's church that morning with Ray, the sunbeam in the garden when I realised I was pregnant two long days ago. I had felt blessed then.

Now here I was, sent away from home in disgrace, to have my baby with strangers, to leave him or her with them. I turned my head away on the pillow, trying to hide my bitter tears from Winifred. She misunderstood the source of my sorrow, and placed her large work roughened hand on my shoulder, reassuring me that 'the Lord forgives the penitent.'

But I am not penitent. This child was conceived in love, and I do not believe that love was sin, whatever everyone around me says. And yet – to lose my child after bringing it to birth? Could there be any greater punishment?

Worse followed as she told me she would deliver the baby without any help from a doctor, confident because she and Thomas have delivered 'scores of calves.' She pointed out we wouldn't want a doctor in case 'my sin' were made known around the village. She believes it will be easy enough to pass the baby off as hers. She said she and Thomas live quietly, without many visitors, and laughed about how she wouldn't be the first woman to think she'd reached 'the change of life' only to be proved wrong by the arrival of a child.

Then she said, threading the rosary beads through her plump fingers, that she will be sorry to miss church. 'Still, He is always with us, isn't He, and Mary, the blessed Mother?' Her wide eyes shone and she seemed to look beyond me as she went on, 'And to think I too will soon be a mother!'

Beneath the blankets I clenched my fists. I closed my eyes and she leaned forward, patting my shoulder, apologising for tiring me and urging me to rest again.

And at last she was gone, leaving me alone with my bitter thoughts. After breakfast I returned here, explaining I was still tired after yesterday's journey. Apart from the brief walk around the ruined abbey, deserted on a damp October afternoon, its gloomy atmosphere matching my mood, I have kept to my room most of the day.

I am exhausted, drained, and more miserable than I have ever known. Even writing in here no longer helps. I do not know how I will go on.

– CHAPTER 22 –

'Julia. I'm so glad you came.' Linda extended a bony hand above a colourful patchwork quilt.

Julia paused on the threshold of the spacious bedroom, disoriented to realise she was in the room engulfed in flames in her nightmare. She approached the double bed and took the slender hand. Linda's head had been shaved for surgery. Without her usual vibrant make up, her eyes were sunken pools in her white face, her lips pale. Her pallor was deepened by her blue and green checked pyjamas. Julia suspected she might have passed her on the street without recognising her.

Julia swallowed, still reeling from the revelations in her mother's diary. She had so many questions. But where should she start? The priest, who had shown her in and brought her up to Linda's room without a word, had moved across to the window. He had his back to them, his shoulders rigid in his black jacket.

She began with the obvious. 'How are you feeling?'

Linda managed a wan smile. 'Not so sick today,' she said. 'I slept well. It helped, knowing you were near.' She licked her dry lips. 'Would you pour me some water?'

'Of course.' Julia poured water from the glass jug on

the bedside table into a blue plastic beaker. She passed it to Linda, whose hand was shaking as she raised the cup and took a few sips.

'That's better.' The sick woman handed the beaker back to Julia. 'And how are you, Julia? You've read the diary?' Her brown eyes searched the younger woman's face.

Julia nodded, suddenly unable to speak. She had read the diary through the night, falling into a fitful doze towards dawn. She recalled jumbled dreams of churches, fires and planes. She had woken after barely two hours, too wired to go back to sleep. After a quick shower she'd skipped breakfast and driven straight over.

Linda reached out her hand again, and Julia took it. 'I know it must have been a terrible shock to you. I was waiting for the right time to tell you. I promised Mother I would delay telling you until you were in a better place. She knew how upset you would be when she died, and she'd been so worried about you after Greg left. I took the diary from her cottage a few days after she died. Her neighbour saw me. Did she mention it?'

Julia nodded, a lump in her throat as she realised how Emily had tried to protect her, even when she knew she was dying. And Linda too. But the thought of them discussing her together made her uncomfortable. She had struggled not to withdraw her hand when Linda referred to 'Mother.'

The sick woman continued, 'Then I found out about the tumour, just after my exhibition. That was why I was having those terrible headaches – you remember how I was at Giuseppe's? And not knowing how long I've got, if I will get better. . .' She closed her eyes briefly.

Julia dashed away a tear from the corner of her eye. Linda's grip on her wrist tightened.

'Don't cry on my account, Julia. I found Mother, and Father. . .'

Julia frowned, puzzled about the mention of 'Father' and cringing at the second reference to 'Mother.' But she didn't interrupt.

'. . . and you and James. If only I could see. . .' Linda broke off. Then she too was crying. Julia leaned forward and held her to her, this half-sister she hadn't known existed until a few hours previously.

'You can see her,' she whispered. 'She's coming. Your daughter is coming today, Linda. My friend is driving her.'

Linda gasped as the priest turned from the window and came towards the bed. Julia saw that he too was brushing away tears.

'She agreed to come? Father told me you've found her. It's a miracle, isn't it?' The sick woman's eyes were luminous in her white face.

Julia brushed away a few more tears. 'She's longing to meet you.'

Linda held her other hand out to the priest. 'Did you hear, Father?'

The old man stooped and clasped Linda to him. Julia's heart beat faster. Of course. Not 'Father' the priest. Why hadn't she realised? The Canadian accent, the blue eyes which had captivated Emily so long ago still startling, undimmed by old age.

'You're Ray?' She stared at him. His shoulders were shaking and he made no effort to stop the tears which streamed down his lined face. He nodded, in his turn incapable of speech.

'Why didn't you go back for her? She thought you were dead!' Julia was trying not to shout at the old man, but her voice had risen, and both he and Linda flinched.

He disentangled himself from Linda, held up his hand and took some deep breaths. When he had composed himself, he explained, his voice hoarse: 'I did go back. My plane went down over Dresden. I bailed out just in time, before the fire. . .' He raised his hands to his lined forehead and shuddered. 'I was taken prisoner. As soon as I was released, I made my way back to Scampton.'

He paused and began to pace between the bed and the window. He didn't look at either woman, staring down at the wooden floor beneath his feet, as if the rest of his story were written there.

'I saw Ada in front of the church. She was placing flowers on your grandfather's grave. He had died just a few months after I was there. I offered my condolences. And of course I asked where Emily was.' He broke off again, a muscle twitching in his cheek. 'And Ada told me she was married to Leonard, to your father. She made it clear I should leave and not return. Like a fool, that is what I did.'

Julia didn't understand. 'Like a fool?'

The priest sighed, a long drawn out sigh which conveyed sixty years of regret and sorrow. 'Ada lied,' he said quietly. 'Emily hadn't married Leonard then. They were only engaged. They didn't marry until six months after my visit.'

He fell silent. Linda coughed. Julia automatically passed her the beaker of water. The sick woman's gulps sounded unnaturally loud in the hushed room.

'So that's what Ada's final words meant,' said Julia eventually. 'When she said, "I never told her he was alive."'

She never told Mother you'd come back.' She thought back to what she had read in the diary. 'But she was so jealous of Leonard's interest in Mother. If she had told her you were alive, if you and Mother had married, that would have left Leonard free. Wasn't there a chance he might have married Ada?'

Ray shook his head. 'I doubt that very much. I suspect that Ada wouldn't have married him anyway, knowing she was his second choice after Emily. You can tell from the diary that he already admired Emily, preferred her to Ada, even if Emily didn't want to admit it that summer.'

'Yes. And Ada threatened Mother too, didn't she?' Julia remembered Emily's diary entry about Ada bringing the suitcase to her room for her journey to Norfolk. 'She said Mother would regret taunting her about Leonard when it was obvious Mother was getting back at Ada for her self-righteousness and total lack of empathy for her falling pregnant.'

'"Lack of empathy" is a very modern phrase,' said Ray quietly. 'Maybe there was an element of revenge in Ada's deception. But in fairness to your aunt,' his mouth tightened, and Julia suspected he was struggling to be charitable towards Ada, 'remember that times were very different then. You know from the diary how badly Ada and your maternal grandmother reacted to Emily's pregnancy. My reappearance would inevitably lead to the secret of Linda's birth being discovered. It would be a scandal to people in the village, people whose good opinion mattered so much to your aunt and grandmother. I believe that in those few moments when your aunt saw me approach she calculated it was better for Emily's wedding to Leonard to go ahead. She probably saw it as saving the family's reputation.'

He stopped pacing, and held his head in his trembling hands. 'I was much to blame of course. I should never – but the fear that I might not return – and the connection we had, and she was so beautiful. . .' He sank to his knees beside the bed, burying his head in the patchwork quilt, overcome by shuddering sobs. Linda stroked his white hair as if she were soothing a small child, tears rolling silently down her pale face.

It was a moment before Julia spoke, struggling with a mixture of emotions: pity for this man who had been so tragically deprived of a woman's love, mingled with discomfort that that woman had been her mother, who had gone on to marry another man, her own father. But the truth needed to be spoken.

'My mother loved you,' she said slowly. 'Just as you loved her.'

Silence followed, broken only by the sound of the old man weeping.

After he had recovered, he moved round the foot of the bed to Julia, cupping her chin with his hand so that she was forced to look into his eyes. He bit his lip. His voice shook as he said, 'From what your mother told Linda, you may rest assured that she did love your father. Differently to me, but she did love him.'

'She did, Julia,' Linda affirmed from the bed. 'She told me he proposed to her in a letter he sent from his ship when he was serving in the Pacific. It was the year after I was born. She said what a good man Leonard was, how proud she was to be his wife.'

Julia fished out a tissue from the pocket of her grey wool jacket. Even though she too was now crying, she felt a burden had been lifted. Ever since reading her mother's diary in the early hours she had been tormented by the thought that Emily had been unhappy with her father. The image of her standing so rigid in their wedding photograph, that shy but tense smile hovering around her lips, had mingled with her dreams.

'Thank you,' she whispered. Ray pressed her shoulder again before dragging the room's single armchair towards the bed. He slumped into it. Julia realised how difficult it must be for him to recount these painful memories. But she had more questions.

'What did you do, when Ada told you Mother had married my father?'

'I went straight back to Canada.' He massaged his temples with his long white fingers. 'I was, in every sense of the word, a broken man. In time I entered the seminary and became a priest. I tried to put the war and my memories of your mother behind me, throwing myself into my parish work. Then Linda traced me. Until I heard from her just before Christmas, I had no idea of her existence.' He laid his hand on his daughter's arm. 'My bishop was very understanding and arranged my trip to Walsingham.' His voice faded to a hoarse whisper. 'But I was too late to see Emily one last time.'

Julia went over to the window, looking towards the ruined abbey. Its columns rose unevenly. A milky sun gleamed in the pearl grey sky above. She remembered how unhappy her mother had been that first day here, the despair of her final entry in the 1943 diary: *I am exhausted,*

drained, and more miserable than I have ever known.
Even writing in here no longer helps. I do not know how
I will go on.

She shivered, wondering how Emily had coped until
Linda's birth, what it had been like for Linda growing up
in a staunchly Catholic household. She turned back
towards the bed where her half-sister lay, her life in the
balance in these early days after surgery. Yet she looked
more at peace than Julia had ever seen her since their first
encounter at their mother's funeral.

'So you were born here? Everything went. . .' she bit
her lip, appalled by the callousness of it all, '. . . according
to our grandmother's plan?'

A shadow passed over Linda's sunken face. 'I was born
prematurely,' she said. 'Mother told me last summer that
our grandfather died of a heart attack less than two
months after she came here. It was probably the terrible
news which meant she gave birth early. She told me
she never forgave herself, believing that her pregnancy
was the shock which caused his heart attack.'

'Poor Mother,' murmured Julia, tears rising again.
'And then she left you with Winifred and Thomas?'

Linda nodded.

'Winifred sounded. . . very religious?' Julia framed the
question carefully, out of deference for the priest, thinking of her mother's references to rosary beads and
Winifred's insistence that Emily's plight was some kind of
answer to prayer.

'Yes. She brought me up in the Catholic faith.' Linda
paused, a pained expression on her face.

'Or her version of it!' Ray said with a sudden savagery.

Linda laid a placating hand on his arm. Julia wondered

again at her composure. Perhaps being so ill gave you a different perspective, but Julia was sure she wouldn't be so calm if she'd experienced as much tragedy in her life as Linda had.

The sick woman turned towards Julia, patting the quilt to indicate she should sit down on the bed. 'I didn't know until Winifred died that she wasn't my mother,' she said. 'She kept it secret all those years. Thomas never said anything either. He died when I was fourteen. It was only when she died, here in this room, that she told me. But she didn't tell me anything about my real mother, about Emily. I was twenty-four when Winifred died, and four months pregnant. I married Philip three years earlier, as much as anything to get away from home. I found it oppressive here and I felt very isolated. Winifred wasn't one for company. I'd wanted to go to College to study Art, but she'd pressed me to help her with the farm instead, although it was failing by then. I met Philip at a Catholic gathering for young people in Norwich. We got on well enough. After a few months he asked me to marry him. We lived in Norwich, and moved back here when Winifred died. She left the house to me.'

Julia nodded. She remembered Grace had told her that her father had been Catholic before he was 'born again' when he met her step-mother Frances.

Linda's eyes were unfocused as she stared towards the door. 'It was a terrible shock, finding that the woman I had called "Mother" all my life wasn't my mother after all. It obsessed me for the rest of my pregnancy. I had a difficult birth. Soon after I began hearing voices and hallucinating.' She looked at Julia, who took her hand.

'No one understood,' Linda went on. 'I began to produce these frightening Madonna and child paintings.

Philip was out a lot working, and I found being here alone with a baby very lonely. The story of how the abbey had burned down hundreds of years ago played on my mind. Winifred had spoken a lot in her later years about judgement and hell fire, and I think somehow, it all got tangled up in my mind, so that one day. . .' Her voice trailed off and she raised her hands to her shaved head, rocking back and forth. 'And I lost my baby!' She made a terrible keening sound.

Julia shuddered, thinking of Grace, the vulnerable young woman who had touched her so much with her tragic story. Hopefully she would be here soon. Looking at Linda as she sank back exhausted on to the pillows, Julia feared they might not have long together. But perhaps the restoration of her father and daughter, and the news of a grandchild which Julia had left for Grace to tell, might prove more effective than the radiotherapy?

There was a knock at the front door. Linda's eyes lit up. Ray sprang to his feet and began to pace the floor again.

Julia walked slowly down the stairs and opened the heavy wooden door. Grace stood on the doorstep. A few feet behind her, Pete was bent over the grey and white tabby cat which purred appreciatively as he stroked its ears.

Grace's wide blue eyes – so like her grandfather's, Julia suddenly realised – were shining in expectation. From the dark circles beneath, Julia suspected that the younger woman was as sleep deprived as she was.

Grace tugged at her plait with the familiar uncertain gesture. 'Is she well enough for me to see her?' Her voice sounded more like a little girl's than ever.

'Yes. She's upstairs. With your grandfather.'

'My grandfather?'

Julia didn't trust herself to speak, moving back into the hall. Grace stepped forward and wrapped her slim arms round her. 'I don't know how you've managed it, Aunt Julia,' she whispered, 'but thank you so much.' She slipped past her and up the stairs as Ray's tall figure emerged on the landing.

Aunt Julia. Julia found she was close to tears again. She resolutely shut out thoughts of what Grace must be thinking about her affair with James, after discovering that he was her half-uncle. Time enough for that later. Julia was certain Grace would be totally preoccupied at present with being reunited with her mother and meeting her grandfather.

She walked out towards Pete. 'Thank you so much for bringing her, Pete.'

'It wasn't a problem.' He rose from the cat which wound briefly round his legs before slinking away past the side of the house. Julia detected a slight flush on his cheeks. His eyes didn't quite meet hers. She took a deep breath. If she had learned anything from the startling revelations of the last twenty-four hours, it was that life was just too short.

'I'm sorry,' she began, 'about my reaction in the car that day. I was all over the place.' She held out her hand. 'It wasn't that I'm not interested,' she went on softly. 'I just need a bit of time.'

He took her hand and met her eyes. 'No worries.' He grinned. 'Does that mean I get to call you "Jules" now?'

She smiled back. 'I think so.'

Hand in hand they walked through the garden. Clumps of snowdrops gleamed white in the sunshine. Julia's heart lifted as she gazed at them, so fragile but so resilient. After the long dark winter spring was finally coming.

– ACKNOWLEDGEMENTS –

I had no idea how much work was involved in transforming text into novel. Many thanks to the team at RedDoor Publishing for their enthusiasm, support and advice. In particular I have been very grateful for their patience with my queries about the mysterious process of creating and marketing a book! Thanks to copy editor Laura Gerrard for her eagle eye and to Jason Anscomb for capturing the mood of the story perfectly in his cover design. Thanks too to Angela Montague at Push Creativity for creating my web-site and for opening up the world of social media to a self-confessed technophobe!

I would like to remember my mother who encouraged my love of reading and always said I should write a book. Thanks to Dad for his endless optimism and support of all my endeavours including this.

Finally, thanks to my husband, Neil, for encouraging my 'harmless hobby' and to my daughter, Alice, for putting up with my distraction when writing. I am grateful to you both for keeping me grounded in the real world and for reminding me that there is, in fact, more to life than books.

– BOOK CLUB QUESTIONS –

1. How did you react to Linda at the start of the novel? Did your feelings change as the story progressed?

2. During his row with Julia, James tells her that their mother Emily had once said, 'Julia struggles to understand us mere mortals. It can be difficult living with someone with such high standards.' He also describes her as 'smug.' Do you think there is any justice in these comments about Julia?

3. What do you think about Emily's decision to fall in with her mother's plan and leave her baby to grow up with relatives, without divulging her secret in later life?

4. Linda tells Julia she promised their mother not to tell Julia about the family secret until Julia was in a 'better place.' Do you think Linda made the right decision to withhold the story from Julia once Emily had died?

5. Julia's life unravels during the course of *After the Funeral*, but there is hope for her at the end. What has she learnt? How has she changed?

6. Emily dies before Ray has the opportunity to meet her again. What effect does this have on the revelation of their love affair?

7. Mother/stepmother and daughter relationships are central to the novel. How do these relationships influence and affect Emily, Linda, Julia and Grace?

8. How hopeful are you that Julia and Pete might have a future together?

9. How important are setting including place, weather, season and year to the atmosphere of *After the Funeral*? What impact is created by references to art and spirituality?

10. Loneliness is a theme of the novel. How does loneliness shape the characters?

– ABOUT THE AUTHOR –

Gillian Poucher was born in Bolton. After studying History at undergraduate level, she worked as a Solicitor before training as a church minister. She was ordained into the United Reformed Church in 2006 and completed her PhD in Biblical Studies in 2013. Gillian lives in Lincolnshire with her husband and daughter. *After the Funeral* is her first novel.

gillianpoucherauthor.co.uk

You can follow Gillian at:
🐦 @GillianPoucher
📘 @GillianPoucherAuthor

Find out more about RedDoor Publishing and sign up to our newsletter to hear about our **latest releases, author events,** exciting **competitions** and more at

reddoorpublishing.com

YOU CAN ALSO FOLLOW US:

@RedDoorBooks

RedDoorPublishing

@RedDoorBooks